"Dammit, Ka

Edward's voice b
"Sir, I've got Shu
from Domi."

Brady announced, "Commander, I just tried checking in with Domi but she didn't respond. Do we scrub?"

"Stand by," Kane said flatly. "Everybody, just *stand by*."

The Cadillac lurched as the tires rolled into a rut and Shuma reached out a claw-tipped hand to steady himself. Kane settled the rubber-cushioned stock of the OCIW into the hollow of his shoulder and held his breath. The skin between his shoulder blades seemed to tighten and the short hairs at the back of his neck tingled.

He squeezed the trigger.

Other titles in this series:

James Axler
Outlanders®

GRAILSTONE
GAMBIT

A GOLD EAGLE BOOK FROM
WORLDWIDE®

TORONTO • NEW YORK • LONDON
AMSTERDAM • PARIS • SYDNEY • HAMBURG
STOCKHOLM • ATHENS • TOKYO • MILAN
MADRID • WARSAW • BUDAPEST • AUCKLAND

First edition February 2008

ISBN-13: 978-0-373-63857-4
ISBN-10: 0-373-63857-4

GRAILSTONE GAMBIT

Copyright © 2008 by Worldwide Library.

Special thanks to Mark Ellis for his contribution to
the Outlanders concept, developed for Gold Eagle.

Printed in U.S.A.

So pass I hostel, hall and grange;
By bridge and ford, by park and pale,
All-arm'd I ride, whate'er betide,
Until I find the Holy Grail
                    —Tennyson

The Road to Outlands—
From Secret Government Files to the Future

Almost two hundred years after the global holocaust, Kane, a former Magistrate of Cobaltville, often thought the world had been lucky to survive at all after a nuclear device detonated in the Russian embassy in Washington, D.C. The aftermath—forever known as skydark—reshaped continents and turned civilization into ashes.

Nearly depopulated, America became the Deathlands—poisoned by radiation, home to chaos and mutated life forms. Feudal rule reappeared in the form of baronies, while remote outposts clung to a brutish existence.

What eventually helped shape this wasteland were the redoubts, the secret preholocaust military installations with stores of weapons, and the home of gateways, the locational matter-transfer facilities. Some of the redoubts hid clues that had once fed wild theories of government cover-ups and alien visitations.

Rearmed from redoubt stockpiles, the barons consolidated their power and reclaimed technology for the villes. Their power, supported by some invisible authority, extended beyond their fortified walls to what was now called the Outlands. It was here that the rootstock of humanity survived, living with hellzones and chemical storms, hounded by Magistrates.

In the villes, rigid laws were enforced—to atone for the sins of the past and prepare the way for a better future. That was the barons' public credo and their right-to-rule.

Kane, along with friend and fellow Magistrate Grant, had upheld that claim until a fateful Outlands expedition. A displaced piece of technology…a question to a keeper of the archives…a vague clue about alien masters—and their world shifted radically. Suddenly, Brigid Baptiste, the archivist, faced summary execution, and Grant a quick termination. For

Kane there was forgiveness if he pledged his unquestioning allegiance to Baron Cobalt and his unknown masters and abandoned his friends.

But that allegiance would make him support a mysterious and alien power and deny loyalty and friends. Then what else was there?

Kane had been brought up solely to serve the ville. Brigid's only link with her family was her mother's red-gold hair, green eyes and supple form. Grant's clues to his lineage were his ebony skin and powerful physique. But Domi, she of the white hair, was an Outlander pressed into sexual servitude in Cobaltville. She at least knew her roots and was a reminder to the exiles that the outcasts belonged in the human family.

Parents, friends, community—the very rootedness of humanity was denied. With no continuity, there was no forward momentum to the future. And that was the crux— when Kane began to wonder if there *was* a future.

For Kane, it wouldn't do. So the only way was out— way, way out.

After their escape, they found shelter at the forgotten Cerberus redoubt headed by Lakesh, a scientist, Cobaltville's head archivist, and secret opponent of the barons.

With their past turned into a lie, their future threatened, only one thing was left to give meaning to the outcasts. The hunger for freedom, the will to resist the hostile influences. And perhaps, by opposing, end them.

Prologue

To the measured thunder of drums and the skirl of pipes, the warriors of the grail danced among the Merry Maidens.

The glow of the full Moon struck gray highlights on the stones that stood in a circle on the moor. The dark megaliths loomed like weathered sentinels, standing guard over the passing aeons. Centuries of erosion had carved deep fissures and furrows across their surfaces.

Many times in the dim past, the six- and seven-foot-tall stones had watched humans dance within their embrace, performing their ceremonies to bring rain or increase fertility. This night, the gathering was no common dance ritual.

The circle was full of excited people and more little groups straggled in across the moor. They were not dressed in the homespun linen usual for farmers or fisherfolk—the men wore leather and brass warrior's harnesses, and the moonlight glittered from spearpoints and great broadswords. Peat and faggots had been laid in a shallow trench around the megaliths and they flamed with fish oil, so the ring leaped high with a border of flame.

The beat of the *bodhrains*, the Celtic drums, and the fierce screech of the pipes sped up the heartbeat and sent the blood coursing. The air was heavy with the smell of smoke and home-brewed poteen.

As graceful as cats, the women danced to the wild music. Their skirts slit at the sides, and wearing silver ornaments on their pale limbs, they laughed as they circled the great stone slab in the center of the ring of standing stones. The slab crawled with symbols and glyphs, cup-shaped hollows surrounded by labyrinthine spirals. Radial lines stretched out in all directions.

The people knew the spiral patterns symbolized the maze of life and death, the departure from the womb and the return to it. The women clapped their hands and sang as they went through the wild, twisting convolutions of the dance that mimicked the designs cut into the stone.

A tall woman came forward, her carriage as erect and as straight as a tree. Her simple black robe clung to her supple figure. A scarlet sash girded her narrow waist. The fabric of the robe was so gauzy it concealed nothing, clinging to her breasts and buttocks and thighs like a layer of oil.

The woman's long hair was as blue-black as a raven's wing, intricately woven into round braids on either side of her head, with some strands spilling artlessly over her bosom. Fair skinned, her childlike face seemed all big eyes and full lips.

Her eyes were a black so deep, they were almost obsidian. Her hands were crossed over the hilt of a long, slender, golden sword. The point nearly dragged in the dirt. A man walked beside her. He wore a bronze helmet bearing the design of a goblet with a many-boughed tree growing out of it. The same image was worked into the boss of the round shield he carried on his left arm. In his right he gripped a six-foot-long lance.

He pushed the dancers aside, making a path for the tall woman. At the thick stone slab, she raised the sword and struck it three times with the edge. Bell-like chimes rose above the cacophony of music and song, shivering and vibrating through the air.

Abruptly the drummers ceased beating and the pipers lowered their instruments. Utter silence fell as if a gigantic jar had dropped over the stone circle. Everyone dropped to their knees, facing the slab. Nothing moved, only the wavering of shadows from the flames in the surrounding trench.

The silence lasted for nearly a minute. Then a blossom of light sprouted from the center of the stone slab. Threads of blue witchfire streaked along the grooves of the carvings, pulsing like the lifeblood through a circulatory system. In an instant, the entire inscribed surface of the stone blazed with a webwork of dancing light.

The kneeling crowd drew a single breath and then released it in one prolonged gasp of awe.

A bolt of energy erupted like a column of lightning. Instead of shooting straight up, it described a 360-degree parabolic fountain, emerging from and returning to the center of the stone, arcing back on itself in an ever-tightening spiral of energy.

The cascade of light spun like a diminishing cyclone, shedding sparks and thread-thin static discharges. As quickly as it appeared, the glowing light vanished, as if it had been sucked back into the stone. A tall figure stood there, leaning on a long wooden staff.

The kneeling assembly only stared, unmoving, as if transfixed by the light, eyes swimming with multicolored spots, shaken and stunned. The absolute silence was broken abruptly by a sharp crack as the figure rapped on the stone with the end of the staff.

"I greet you, my brothers, my sisters, my children— my warriors of the grail!"

The people leaped to their feet, roaring one name over and over: "Myrrdian! Myrrdian!"

The gaunt man standing inside the stone circle was old, his long, thin face a parchment of tiny furrows. The long hair that spilled from beneath the edges of a dark gray helmet was the color of aged ivory. The incurving jaw guards of the helmet framed the slash of his mouth. The forepart swept down his forehead like a widow's peak made of silver. Right above the peak, a sphere of metal bulged outward like a blind third eye.

Despite his white hair and seamed face, Myrrdian's eyes were a compelling, opalescent golden color. A faint interlocking pattern of scales ringed his brow ridges, extending over and meeting at the bridge of his nose.

He wore an ankle-length cloak of midnight-blue caught at the throat by a golden-jeweled torque. The illumination from the full Moon struck dancing highlights on the shiny metal strands that wove a pattern of arcane symbols throughout the fabric of the cloak. Beneath it he wore a scarlet tunic and a vest of light chain mail.

An unpolished yellow crystal topped Myrrdian's gnarled staff, seeming to have grown out of a setting of fibrous roots.

Although he looked about seventy, he radiated the aura of a past age and time, but the cheering, the chanting of his name continued.

A smile creased the man's thin lips. "For years I suffered in the dark places, in the land of Skatha, the kingdom of shadows. But while there, I found the lost secrets of the Tuatha de Danaan. I claimed those secrets, and with them we shall begin a new era for our people. Lest anyone still doubt my words—"

Turning toward the raised center of the stone slab, he tapped it with the crystal tip of his staff. "Behold."

A finger of incandescence fluttered up from the surface of the stone. The crowd felt rather than heard a pulsing vibration against their eardrums, as of the distant beating of great wings. Then the entire slab erupted in a blinding explosion of white light.

The people cried out, clapping their hands over their eyes. When they lowered them, blinking, they saw Myrrdian still standing there, but atop the slab lay a collection of weaponry—pistols, carbines, even boxes of ammunition.

"With these tools," Myrrdian announced, "we shall build a new world for ourselves, but be mindful of their true purpose. Else what I have given can be taken away—as can your lives."

He swept the staff in a semicircle over the guns, and a creature flickered into view. The animal dimly resembled a hound, like a monstrous cross between a mastiff and wolfhound, but the bristles along its spine ridge topped Myrrdian's waist.

The heavily muscled neck drooped with the weight of its massive, shovel-jawed head. Muzzle slavering, its long fangs glistened cruelly in a flickering firelight. The two round eyes held a red gleam. It growled, a sound like distant thunder.

The people shrank away in murmuring fear, many of them crossing themselves frantically.

"The hound of Cullan will sniff out any betrayers," Myrrdian said flatly. "And will gnaw on the marrow of their souls for eternity."

He waved the staff again and the phantom hound vanished, as if it had been no more substantial than a shadow cast by the flames. Facing the people, he drew in his breath and declared, "But I have not returned to threaten my own kind. I have come to lead you, as was prophesied long, long ago, when our people were still young."

Myrrdian's voice grew louder, stronger, more passionate. "There will be much bloodshed as we reclaim our old lands, but when it is over and the Celtic people are once again united, I shall give new life to all those who have fallen in service to me. The wounded, the sick and even the dead will be renewed. Once we regain the grail, there will be no more infirmities of age or sickness or death!"

The kneeling people gaped up at him in utter adoration, their eyes shining in the moonlight, mouths open and wet as if with hunger and thirst.

"Soon I will prove my words," Myrrdian went on. "No one need doubt me or fear me."

A cheer burst from the crowd, and with it came the beating of drums and skirling of pipes in a deafening uproar. They danced in triumph.

Myrrdian gestured with his staff, and by degrees the babble died away. "Where is my sword carrier…where is my darling Rhianna?"

The black-robed woman stepped forward her head bowed, still clasping the hilt of the weapon. "I am here, my lord."

"Rhianna, my child," he murmured in a rustling voice, "you have done well. You will receive many blessings from me." He took three steps to the edge of the slab and reached out and caressed her cheek. "Special blessings."

Rhianna smiled but still did not look at him directly. "Thank you, Lord Myrrdian."

He gestured with his staff at the weapons on the stone slab. "My children, my warriors, all of you who are in my service—take what you need."

Then there was bedlam as the crowd, shouting and cheering, rushed forward. A blond-haired woman stepped forward and curtseyed clumsily before Myrrdian. Past her prime and running to fat, she had hastily loosened her skirt and cinched the black sash tighter around her waist before speaking.

In a theatrical voice she called forth, "My lord, we are all at your service. We all wrought the manifestation ritual."

Myrrdian gazed at the woman for a long moment before responding. "Is that so, Eleyne? I will reward you in the manner most befitting you."

The woman smiled and curtseyed again. "Thank you, my lord."

Myrrdian returned the smile, but it seemed stitched-on. "I grow fatigued. Take me to a place of rest."

Bowing deeply, Rhianna allowed Myrrdian to take her arm and step down from the slab. She handed the sword to the man in armor and walked on without a second glance.

Hefting the weapon, the man in armor stepped up beside Eleyne. "Bloody hell, I didn't really think it would work!" he whispered.

"Nor I!" she replied, surprise quavering in her voice.

After a moment, she added smugly, "We are far more powerful than we thought. The ancient ways are still strong here, Conohbar."

He stared at her incredulously. "You don't believe he's actually who he says he is—"

She shook her head. "Of course not. He's a trickster."

"Even so," Conohbar said softly, "I think we should be very careful around him."

They fell into step with the others, walking across the moonlit moor. The drums struck up a slow and solemn beat as the procession marched away from the stone circle.

Eyes flashing with resentment, Eleyne hissed, "That little slut Rhianna…she might as well be naked. I hope she catches the croup."

Conohbar thought Eleyen had spoken in the faintest of whispers, but he saw Myrrdian's shoulders stiffen. Ducking his head, he kept his gaze fixed on the cowpath at his feet and remained silent for another hundred yards.

When he dared to glance up again, the group was strung out along the field. Rhianna and Lord Myrrdian were far out of earshot.

"All I'm saying is, you don't know what you're dealing with here," Conohbar whispered. "Or who. I didn't like the way he looked at you."

Eleyne's lips quirked in an arch smile. "Jealous, Conohbar? I thought you'd gotten over that."

The armored man didn't answer her. He had seen the

light of triumph in her eyes at the thought of being the
cause of his worry. He bit back the response that it had
been a while since any man in the group had cared to
have her, including himself. Eleyne might have been
pretty twenty years before, but now she was fat and
dumpy with thick ankles and a triple chin.

They reached a footpath just as the Moon was setting.
The path skirted a thick wood and curved down between
embanking hedges. The retinue crossed an expanse of
meadow blanketed by heather and bracken and entered
an area where cultivated fields intersected with marsh-
land.

Rhianna led Myrrdian into a small village full of
thatch-roofed cottages. Cattle and horses stirred rest-
lessly as the group made its way past. Only a few of the
houses had lights showing through the shuttered
windows, the cook fires banked for the night.

The village spread out across a shallow valley for at
least an eighth of a mile. The cottages were scattered in
no particular order from one end of the vale to the next.
The areas between the buildings were cluttered with small,
fenced gardens, two-wheeled carts and hobbled ponies.
The group quickly dispersed under the stars as Rhianna
led Myrrdian to a timber-walled great house up a side lane.

It was a fortified place, surrounded by a stockade of
sharpened logs. Several of the group seemed inclined
to linger, but Eleyne shooed them away with brushing
motions. She and Conohbar pulled the heavy plank
door closed behind them.

The interior of the council lodge was cavernous, with an earthen floor strewed with flattened reeds, straw and sand. A high-backed chair with armrests carved in the form of dragons occupied a raised dais against the far wall. Beside it was large sideboard laden with cold meats and white bread.

A fire reeking of fish oil sputtered in a massive hearth. The flames cast a flickering radiance over masses of piled and jumbled objects spread out on a pair of heavy trestle tables.

Myrrdian rushed to the nearest table and pawed through the collection of silvery wheels, golden buckles, helmets, metal rods and artifacts that were completely unidentifiable to the people in the council hall. All they knew was that they were relics of the Tuatha de Danaan, of an ancient time that should have been long dead, but in this part of the world, the past still breathed.

Eleyne strolled to the hearth and stood with her hands behind her back, watching as items fell from the table and clattered to the floor.

"Where is it?" Myrrdian hissed. "Where?"

Rhianna, standing near the door, paused as she slid one arm into the sleeve of voluminous robe. Her eyes reflected confusion. "My lord?"

"The harp!" Myrrdian snapped. "I don't need this other ruck to unlock and activate the grail, but I do need the harp! Where the hell is it?"

"Rhianna never found it, my lord," Eleyne stated

matter-of-factly. "You should have never charged such a silly chit of a girl with a task so important."

Moving with amazing speed for a man of his years, Myrrdian whirled to face her, his cloak swirling about him. "It was a simple task—I told you where it could be found!"

He gestured to the collection of relics with a contemptuous sweep of his staff. "You found this garbage, did you not?"

Rhianna opened her mouth, groping for something to say, but Eleyne said boldly, "The girl did not find it…but *I* did."

Eleyne brought her hands out from behind her back. Resting between them was an object about two feet long. It resembled a lopsided wedge made of iridescent gold. The leading edge was elongated, like the neck of a glass bottle that had been heated, rendered semimolten and stretched. A set of double-banked strings ran its entire length.

Myrrdian smiled, showing the edges of his teeth. "Clever, clever girl, teasing your master. Give it to me."

He reached for the harp, but Eleyne stepped back toward the hearth. "Not so fast, my lord."

Conohbar's eyes widened, his face draining of blood. "Eleyne—no!"

"I know what I'm doing." She smiled at Myrrdian defiantly. "I found this when your favored harlot could not. I was the one who crept through the vaults laid down by the Priory of Awen. I risked much for you and now I demand a reward."

"You risk death now," Myrrdian intoned. "A very painful one."

"I think not." Eleyne laughed mockingly and thrust the harp over the fire, holding it over the flames. "Shall we put it to the test?"

Myrrdian stepped toward her, and she moved as if to toss it into the hearth. He came to a halt. "Flames cannot harm it, you stupid bitch," he growled. "It was crafted by the Danaan."

"Make up your mind, my lord," Eleyne challenged. "My arm is getting tired."

"What do you want?" Myrrdian demanded in a whisper.

"When you find the Grailstone, the Cauldron of Rebirth, I want to be one of the first to benefit from its restorative powers. I want to be young and beautiful again."

An expression of surprise crossed his face. "That's all?"

She nodded. "That is all I ask."

He chuckled, a sound like dry bones rattling in a tin cup. "My dear, you didn't need to go these lengths. I would have offered the cauldron to you in return for your many services to me."

The mocking smile on Eleyne's face became a relieved simper. "Oh, my lord…I should have known. You are kind and caring. Forgive me."

Myrrdian extended his left hand. "The harp, if you please."

She moved toward him, handed him the object and curtseyed. "Forgive me," she said again. "And when I have regained my youth and beauty, I will give you much pleasure."

He grinned and said softly, "You will give me much pleasure now, you treacherous bitch."

She gaped up at him, first in shock, then in uncomprehending fear. The forepart of his helmet swirled, then it formed a cone and stretched out a pseudopod, tipped by the sphere. Like an eyelid, the metal peeled backward, revealing a round gem that pulsed with a cold white light. A shimmering blue nimbus sprang up around it. Between one heartbeat and another, the radiance turned a deep, deep red.

Eleyne opened her mouth to scream but no sound came forth. A blood-colored spear of energy jetted from the orb and shot between the woman's jaws. For an instant, her body swayed. Then her hair burst into flame and her flesh bubbled like wax, falling away as semi-liquid sludge, splattering the floor. Her skull burst open with a sound like a handclap. Her headless body toppled backward. The smell of roasting flesh hung thickly in the air.

Myrrdian spun to face Conohbar. The sphere no longer glowed red, but rather with a steady blue-white radiance. "Get rid of that cow's carcass!"

Conohbar, sweating and terrified, only nodded.

Myrrdian turned toward Rhianna. "Bring me food and drink."

With the harp tucked under one arm, he stamped toward the rear of the council hall and the chair.

Rhianna and Conohbar exchanged stricken, terrified looks.

"What now?" the girl whispered hoarsely. "How could she have been so stupid?"

Conohbar bent over Eleyne's smoldering corpse. "I'll attend to this while you distract him. I've got to figure out a way to send word to the priory without alerting him."

Rhianna nodded grimly. "Sister Fand must know that what she feared the most has come to pass...*he* has returned."

Chapter 1

Manhattan Island, the Upper West Side

The wind sweeping over the roof of the office building carried a chill autumnal bite. Lying flat on a cornice overlooking the walls of the narrow concrete canyon, Kane tugged up the collar of his jacket, but he didn't shiver. He was more concerned about the effect the sudden temperature change might have on the trigger spring of the OICW rifle cradled in his arms.

The stiff breeze gusting up from the dark waters of the Hudson had to be considered for trajectory deflection. He would only have one chance to make the shot before he lost the element of surprise and drew the attention and the wrath of Baron Shuma's followers.

Reaching up behind his right ear, Kane made an adjustment on the Commtact's volume control. The little comm unit fit tightly against the mastoid bone, attached to implanted steel pintels. The unit slid through the flesh and made contact with tiny input ports. Its sensor circuitry incorporated an analog-to-digital voice encoder embedded in the bone.

Once the device made full cranial contact, the auditory canal picked up the transmissions. The dermal sensors transmitted the electronic signals directly through the skull casing. Even for people who went deaf, as long as they wore a Commtact, they would still have a form of hearing. However, if the volume was not properly adjusted, the radio signals caused vibrations in the skull bones that resulted in vicious headaches.

Lifting a compact set of night-vision binoculars to his face, Kane switched on the IR illuminator and squinted through the eyepieces. Viewed through the specially coated lenses that optimized the low light values, the street seemed to be illuminated by a lambent, ghostly haze. Where only gloom had been before, his vision was lit by various shifting shades of gray and green. He squinted against the light of the Sun in the west where it touched the facade of the building on the opposite side of the boulevard.

"Edwards?" he subvocalized.

"Sir?" came the immediate response. The man's voice sounded tense.

"In position?"

"Yes, sir."

"Good. Move in as close to the street as you can. Get prepped when you hear them coming."

Kane couldn't see the shaved-headed ex-Magistrate, but Edwards had proved his competence many times since joining Cerberus nearly a year earlier.

Another voice filtered into his ear. "Commander?"

"Yes, Brady?"

"I can spot 'em fine, Commander."

"Hell, *I* can spot them," Kane snapped. "I want a perfect triangulation."

"I've got the shot, if that's what you're worried about it."

"It is, but you wait for my order."

Kane thumbed the tiny stud on the Commtact, opening another channel. "Domi?"

"Yeah?" The girl's sharp, high-pitched voice made him grimace.

"Any problems?"

"I'm ready to join the pack."

"Acknowledged. In your rig, they won't give you a second glance."

"Hope not." There was a pause. "Kane?"

"Here."

Her tone a bit softer, Domi said, "Aim good. You be very careful."

"Aren't I always?" he retorted.

The transceiver accurately conveyed Domi's snort of derision. "Hell, no. That's why I mentioned it."

A trifle annoyed, Kane said, "Just make sure the target is where he's supposed to be…and be aware of all our people's positions."

"Gotcha."

Kane knew Domi intended to blend in with the group of Farers, flowing unnoticed among their number in her patched denims and long, hooded coat that concealed the girl's white hair and skin, Detonics Combat Master autopistol, grenade-laden harness and her signature knife, with its nine-inch-long, serrated blade.

Kane had been reluctant to put Domi in the midst of the Farers because of her inability to get along with others, but under the circumstances, she was the least conspicuous of the Cerberus rescue team.

He opened another Commtact frequency. "Baptiste?"

"Here," Brigid Baptiste responded in her characteristically calm tone.

"Status?"

"Hanging out with some Roamer stragglers, half a klick north-northwest of your position. "

Kane turned his head in that direction and squinted. "Sun is in my eyes."

"In the convoy's, too," Brigid replied. "I'm keeping a street between us."

"Any sign of Grant?"

"None so far." Someone who didn't know her would not have detected so much as a hint of concern in her crisp tone, but Kane heard the worry underscoring her voice.

"He's still alive," he said reassuringly. "Baron Shuma won't pass up the chance of show off his prize pig to the citizens."

"Assuming," Brigid replied, "nothing has gone wrong in the past few hours."

"You're always such an optimist," Kane said sarcastically.

"About as much as you are…which is to say, not much."

"Aren't you the one who always tells me to watch my overconfidence?"

"Only when you need it," she answered. "Like now."

Kane smiled crookedly and adjusted the Commtact, opening all the individual channels simultaneously. "Status reports every two minutes now, people."

"Yes, sir," Edwards said.

"Yo," Brady announced.

"Gotcha," Domi stated.

"Acknowledged," Brigid said.

Kane took a deep breath. The stock of the OICW rifle felt smooth and warm in his hands. He eyed the sky, noting that in a few minutes the autumn sunset would plunge the narrow concrete valley below into deep gloom. The laser optical scope would help, but he prayed Shuma's triumphant procession arrived while it was still daylight. If anything went wrong on the op, light levels wouldn't matter.

A faint, faraway rumble of a distant engine reached his ears. Hitching around, Kane shifted position. A tall man built with a lean, long-limbed economy, most of his muscle mass was contained in his upper body, much like that of a wolf. The cold stare of a wolf glittered in his blue-gray eyes, the color of dawn light on a sharp steel blade. A faint hairline scar showed like a white thread against the sun-bronzed skin of his clean-shaved left cheek. The wind ruffled his thick hair, its color a shade between chestnut and black.

He resisted the urge to stand up, not wanting to risk being spotted by any of Baron Shuma's advance scouts. Shuma was a known killer who operated for hire, using the bombed-out ruins of Newyork City as his base of operations. Manhattan Island no longer held even the ghost of a thriving metropolis, only the hecatomb of a vanished civilization. The fields of devastation stretched to the horizon in all directions. The few structures that still held the general outlines of the buildings they had once been rose at the skyline, then collapsed with ragged abruptness.

All of the skyscrapers and towers had been broken by titanic blows combining shock and fire. Entire city blocks were nothing but acres of scorched and shattered concrete, with rusting rods of reinforcing iron protruding from the ground like withered stalks of some mutated crop.

Why anyone would want to stake out Newyork as an empire was beyond Kane's understanding, but he knew a number of self-styled and self-proclaimed tyrants had rushed in to fill the power vacuums in the former baronial territories. Shuma was not unique in his dreams of ruling over others. He was, however, a scalie, so by virtue of his pedigree, he stood high on the rung of the unusual ladder.

But even taking overweening ambition into account, Newyork seemed a singularly unappealing place to build an empire of any sort, situated as it was in the longest hellzone in the country.

Manhattan had never been claimed as part of a baronial territory, partly due to its inaccessibility. All the bridges connecting it to the mainland had fallen during the massive quakes in the first few minutes of the nuke-caust.

In the company of Brigid Baptiste, Grant and Domi, Kane had visited the shockscape of ruins over five years earlier, when they found it inhabited mainly by the peculiar mutie strain known as scalies.

The engine rumble grew louder and Kane peered over the edge of the building. Lights bobbed along the dark ribbon of the road, already cast into shadow by the structures rising on either side. Faint cheers and shouted laughter were audible through the mechanical roar.

"On his way," Brigid's voice whispered.

"Acknowledged," Kane replied as he checked the direction of the wind with a moistened forefinger.

He eyed the sky, noting that in less than fifteen minutes, sunset would give way to dusk, then full night. A shot would be exceptionally risky, depending on where Grant was positioned in the promenade.

Brigid's voice came again. "Shuma himself just passed. Big as life and about five times as ugly."

"Did you see Grant?"

"Yes." Her tone quavered slightly. "It's going to be close, I'm afraid."

"It's what I figured. Stand by. Edwards?"

"Yes, sir," the man calmly responded. "Target coming into sight."

"Brady?" Kane inquired.

"Got them in my crosshairs, Commander," Brady stated.

"Acknowledged. Wait for my signal."

A single shaft of sunlight slipped over the top of the building and cast a shifting yellow halo on the road below. A thunder of drums, a rhythmic engine throb and sharp voices echoed between the walls of the concrete canyon. Kane crept closer to the cornice edge and peered through the rifle's scope.

Straight down the potholed street came the procession, and on either side milled the Farers and Roamers, lean people wearing rags, but their faces were those of predatory animals. They yelled and shouted and waved at the vehicle chugging slowly over the potholed blacktop. In a previous incarnation, some two centuries earlier, the long automobile had been a bright yellow Cadillac convertible. Garlands of artificial flowers festooned the bodywork, from the gleaming grillwork to the sharp tail fins. Four men marched beside the vehicle, hammering on drums made of old metal containers.

Although he had never seen him before, Kane had no problem identifying Baron Shuma. An enormous man stripped to the waist stood upright in the rear seat, his arms folded over his thick chest. His hairless head was small in proportion to his massive torso. He resembled a toad more than a lizard. His blunt-featured face was coated in overlapping scales of a dark gray-green. His nose was a blob, a lighter shade of gray. His pendulous lips drew back over yellowed teeth in a savage grin. His black-rimmed eyes glittered brightly even in the dim light.

Kane recalled that Lakesh had speculated the scalies were the descendants of humans modified for war. Most likely the first generation were little more than expendable fighting machines, with their brains modified to ensure that they remained under the control of those guiding their actions.

With a sudden surge of disgust, Kane realized that Shuma was under no one's control. He made that very clear by parading his captive down the street in full view of his subjects.

Grant lay spread-eagled on the broad hood of the Cadillac, arms and legs held at painful angles by taut lengths of rope. His olive-drab T-shirt was ripped and stained. Kane was unable to tell if the gleam on his brown-skinned body was from perspiration or blood.

Grant was a big man with a heavy musculature. His black hair was sprinkled with gray at the temples. Beneath the fierce, down-sweeping mustache, black against the dark brown of his skin, his teeth were bared either in a silent snarl or a rictus of pain.

Kane adjusted the scope and sighted through the lens, carefully pushing a cartridge home into the chamber, gauging the distance at 250 yards. He gave the small figure sitting hunched over in the back seat beside

Shuma only a brief visual appraisal, dismissing him as a servant.

His Commact buzzed and Domi's voice whispered urgently, "Kane?"

"Here."

"The car is about twenty yards from me…" Domi's voice trailed off.

"What is it?" Kane demanded impatiently.

"Not sure…. I see something that—"

The Commtact squirted out a burst of static and Kane squinted against the needle of pain boring into his skull. "Domi?"

There was no reply.

"Domi!"

Nothing.

He opened the channel to Brigid. "Baptiste, can you see Domi?"

"No…why?"

"She was cut off."

"Cut off how?"

"How the hell do I know? That's why I'm calling you."

"Do you think something has happened to her?"

Kane inhaled a slow, thoughtful breath before answering, "I guess we'll find out."

"That's no answer," came Brigid's sharp, reproving response. "Until we know what's happened to her, we should scrub the mission."

"There's no time for that."

"Dammit, Kane—"

Edwards's voice blared through the comm unit. "Sir, I've got Shuma dead center. I haven't heard from Domi."

Brady announced, "Commander, I just tried checking in with Domi, but she didn't respond. Do we scrub?"

"Stand by," Kane said flatly. "Everybody, just *stand by*."

Brigid said curtly, breathlessly, "We need to pull back and regroup before—"

"Shut up, Baptiste," Kane snapped.

The Cadillac lurched as the tires rolled into a rut and Shuma reached out a claw-tipped hand to steady himself. Kane settled the rubber-cushioned stock of the OICW into the hollow of his shoulder and held his breath. The skin between his shoulder blades seemed to tighten and the short hairs at the back of his neck tingled.

He squeezed the trigger.

Chapter 2

When the crowd first glimpsed Shuma, a simultaneous roar erupted from every Farer and Roamer throat. All of Manhattan seemed to echo with it.

Standing at the mouth of a litter-choked alley, Domi narrowed her ruby eyes and tugged the hood of her long coat farther over her face, casting it into shadow. She had visited the ruins of Newyork before, but back then it had been strictly a place of the dead. To see it filled with screaming, roaring people unnerved her.

According to the intel briefing, people had been pouring into Newyork across the river for the past two years, coming from the distant Adirondacks and the barren lands south of the Atlantic seaboard. Domi recognized and could easily tell the difference between the Farers and the Roamers, even though they dressed alike.

Farers were essentially nomads, a loosely knit conglomeration of wanderers, scavengers and self-styled salvage experts and traders. Their territory was the Midwest, so Farer presence in and around Newyork was very unusual.

Roamers, on the other hand, were basically marauders, undisciplined bandit gangs who paid lip service to defying the ville governments as a justification for their depredations.

The reports of both groups assembling in such great numbers on Manhattan Island was alarming enough to dispatch the Alpha Away Team from the Cerberus redoubt. They returned in full rout, beaten and bloody and minus of one of their members, a woman named Wright. She had been captured four days before by Shuma's followers and all contact with her was lost.

Activating her Commtact, Domi whispered, "I'm ready to join the pack."

"Acknowledged," Kane responded. "In your rig, they won't give you a second glance."

"Hope not." She took a deep breath. "Kane?"

"Here."

"Aim good. You be very careful."

"Aren't I always?"

Domi snorted derisively. "Hell, no. That's why I mentioned it."

Sounding irritated, Kane shot back, "Just make sure the target is where he's supposed to be…and be aware of all our people's positions."

"Gotcha."

Domi cut the connection and stepped away from the mouth of the alley. She didn't care for crowds on general principle. Her senses had developed in the savage school of the Outlands, and it felt to her that the wind gusting through the ruins carried with it the whiff of blood about to be spilled.

An albino by birth, Domi's skin was normally as white as milk. She was every inch of five feet tall and barely weighed one hundred pounds. On either side of her thin-bridged nose, eyes glittered grimly like polished rubies. The hood of her long beige coat concealed her short, bone-white hair.

As the laboring of the engine grew in volume, she stepped out of the alley onto the cracked sidewalk and she was immediately jostled and elbowed. Although her temper flared she managed to keep it in check, although she did shove a man who stepped on her toes.

The bellowing crowd surged and swayed as if it were a single-celled organism she had fallen into. The repellant odors of unwashed bodies, as well as the acidic reek of home-brewed liquor, assaulted her sensitive nostrils.

Gritting her teeth, tamping down her disgust, Domi wriggled through the bodies, seeking a closer vantage point to the street. Before she could decide on a course of action, she needed to identify Shuma. She had only seen him once, glimpsed him from afar the previous night in flickering, uncertain firelight. If anything went wrong, it wouldn't matter that Shuma was a murderer or organizing an army of the disenfranchised. As far as she was concerned, the important thing was that Shuma had captured Grant during the dark territory probe. In her mind, Grant's rescue had become the mission objective, taking priority over all other considerations.

She recalled the briefing within the vanadium-sheathed walls of Cerberus. Baron Shuma was like many other self-styled and self-proclaimed dictators who popped up in the Outlands more often than she and her friends cared to think about.

Rather than ignore them, Cerberus had established a policy to conclusively overthrow their empires before their influences spread beyond small, contained fiefdoms. Most of the time, the little pocket-sized tyrants were content to rule over isolated settlements in the hinterlands. Very often, their own subjects assumed the responsibility of ending their reigns. Once the barons became too overbearing, their subjects either moved away or joined forces to kill them.

But every once in a while, one of the local lords expanded his influence and gained enough resources to become a formidable power. Shuma was one of those, but he was also a showman and a politician. He knew that true, lasting strength derived from developing a political movement more than operating a mere criminal enterprise. He called his group the Survivalist Outland Brigade and invited the homeless, the down-trodden—and the ruthless—to join the SOB, promising them a future of soft beds, food and endless luxuries.

The brigade consisted mainly of a loose confedera-tion of bandits, but enough poor outlanders had sworn allegiance to Shuma to swell the ranks of the SOB sig-nificantly.

Outlanders were born into a raw, wild world, accustomed to living on the edge of death. Grim necessity had taught them the skills to survive, even thrive, in the postnuke environment. They may have been the great-great-great-grandchildren of civilized men and women, but they had no choice but to embrace lives of semibarbarism.

In the Outlands, people were divided into small, regional units. Communications were stifled, rivalries bred, education impeded. The people who lived outside the direct influence of the villes were reviled and hated. No one worried about an outlander, or even cared. They were the outcasts of the new feudalism, the cheap, expendable labor forces, even the cannon fodder when circumstances warranted. Generations of Americans were born into serfdom, slavery in everything but name. Whatever their parents or grandparents had been before skydark, they were now only commodities and they cursed the suicidal foolishness of their forebears who had brought on the nightmare.

Recently, the numbers of the SOB had grown large enough to be noticed by other groups, like renegade Magistrates who had turned to the mercenary trade or the Millennial Consortium. Neither possibility was comforting, so Domi, Grant, Kane and Brigid traveled to Newyork through the mat-trans gateway network. They set out to scout the area and ascertain if the reports about Shuma's Survivalist Outland Brigade had any foundation.

Posing as Farers, the team hadn't experienced much

difficulty in blending in at first, and the easy acceptance made them careless, although Domi was alert from the start. As an Outlands child born and bred, Domi had learned how to hunt and had been taught the way of the hunted.

Still, the ambush had caught her almost completely unaware. She and Grant had scouted out the area around Shuma's headquarters, in the tangled fastness of Central Park. Domi suspected that something they had done or not done had given them away, but whatever the case, she and Grant had been set upon by shadowy figures wielding ropes and clubs.

Although her first impulse was to remain and fight by the big man's side, she realized they were severely outnumbered and couldn't hope to shoot, slug or slash their way clear. When Grant ordered her to run, she had done so—reluctantly and shamefully, but she had obeyed him, melting into the gloom and the overgrowth.

Domi had never considered herself a soldier, as someone dedicated to fighting for a cause, but over the past few years she had accepted the need to prevent an unstable world from being overrun by human and inhuman tyrants alike.

Now, as she squirmed between the shouting people toward the curb, Domi closed her right hand over the checkered walnut grip of her Detonics Combat Master, holstered at the small of her back.

Kane's voice suddenly whispered in her head, "Status reports every two minutes now, people."

"Gotcha," Domi stated.

She inched her way to the edge of the sidewalk, pushing in front of a short, flat-faced man wearing a ragged mackinaw and beat-up bottle-green derby. Judging by his clothes, he was a Farer. Roamers tended to prefer clothes made of animal hide, which reflected their more barbaric mind-sets.

"Watch it, you li'l bitch," he growled in a voice slurred by liquor.

Domi ignored him. Her belly slipped sideways as she sighted the yellow Cadillac and the big man spread-eagled across the hood like a hunting trophy. Word had traveled fast through Shuma's followers that he had captured Grant, one of the renegade baron blasters.

The term "baron blaster" was old, deriving from the rebels who had staged a violent resistance against the institution of the unification program a century before. Domi knew that neither Kane nor Grant enjoyed having the appellation applied to them. Their ville upbringing still lurked close to the surface, and they had been taught that the so-called baron blasters were worse than outlaws, but were instead terrorists incarnate.

Regardless, the reputations of the core Cerberus warriors had grown too awesome, too great over the past five years for even the most isolated outlander to be ignorant of their accomplishments, even if it was an open question of just how many of the stories were based in truth and how many were overblown fable.

With a conscious effort, Domi tore her gaze away from Grant, at once relieved that he did not appear to be seriously hurt but enraged that he was injured at all. Beneath the overhang of her hood, she watched Shuma intently, only vaguely aware that there was something not right about him beyond his obvious physical deformity. ·

She had seen and even killed scalies before, but her belly still roiled with nausea and her hand automatically went to the hilt of her long knife, fingering the pommel. For six months she had been enslaved by Guana Teague, the Pit Boss of Cobaltville, and she had never forgotten the greenish tint of his skin and its odd, faintly scaled pattern. A number of people had suspected that Guana had a scalie in the family—hence his nickname. The loathing for her former master still ran deep within Domi, even years after slitting his throat with the very knife sheathed at her hip.

Shuma's reptilian appearance didn't trigger a mental alarm, since he looked pretty much like the other scalies she had seen. Her eyes focused on the figure slouched in the seat beside him. He was a very small man, probably no more than four feet five. However, a massive, almost rectangular head rose from between a pair of down-sloping shoulders.

The pale flesh of his freakishly high forehead showed a blue-and-red network of broken blood vessels spreading up to his hairline. His mouth was a short, lipless gash. His ash-gray hair was thin, almost downy, stirred slightly by the breeze atop his flat skull. A great shelf of bone jutted above his eyes.

They were unusual in shape and color—disproportionately large, completely round with tiny irises and pupils totally surrounded by the whites. They seemed to glow, like two pinpoints of fire.

His eyes swept the crowd disinterestedly, and they rested momentarily on Domi. In that instant she felt a faint touch on the surface of her mind, as if it had been brushed by a cobweb. His eyes moved on, but she instantly realized what the little man was.

She reached up for her Commtact. "Kane?"

"Here."

"The car is about twenty yards from me…." She hesitated when the little man's round eyes flicked back toward her as the Cadillac rolled past. A thick, ropy vein pulsed along his the right temple.

"What is it?" Kane asked impatiently.

"Not sure…. I see something that—"

Domi caught only the most fragmented impression of an arm whipping toward her from behind. She ducked, but still a hard object struck the side of her head, just under her ear. She staggered and would have fallen into the street if not for the press of bodies all around her.

Senses reeling from the impact of the blow, fighting off unconsciousness, Domi moved on pure animal instinct. She drew her knife and lashed out blindly. A vague figure jerked away from the nine-inch serrated blade.

Blinking through the amoeba-shaped floaters swimming across her vision, Domi saw the flat-faced man in the derby flail at her with a metal truncheon. She sidestepped and slashed again, feeling the point of the knife catch and drag through cloth and flesh.

She heard the profanity-seasoned howl of pain and as her eyes cleared she saw the man stumble backward, clutching at his right arm. Blood seeped between his fingers.

When a hand closed in a painful grip on the back of her neck, Domi leaned forward, her left leg flashing up in a back kick. She felt a solid, satisfying impact against the toe of her combat boot. A heavyset man uttered a muted squeal and doubled over, clutching at his groin.

More people shuffled toward her, arms spread wide to prevent her from bolting into the crowd. Domi backed away, weaving and swaying, reaching under her coat for her autopistol. Then she pivoted on her heel and ran full-out up the boulevard, in the opposite direction from which Shuma and his entourage had come.

Coattails flying, Domi ran as fast as she could, hearing shouts and the sound of pounding feet behind her. She knew she wouldn't get far, but she didn't intend to. She reached for her combat harness, her hand closing around a small, metal-walled sphere.

The rifle shot sounded like a distant firecracker going off under a tin can and she smiled grimly. She yanked the M-33 fragmentation grenade free of the harness and its safety lever.

Chapter 3

What you fear the most rarely comes to pass.

That refrain cycled through Brigid Baptiste's mind on a continuous loop as she stood with her flank against the crumbling brick wall. Her heart pumped and her throat constricted as the screams of the crowd reached her.

Brigid forced herself to calm down, knowing that Domi and Kane were supremely competent in almost any situation. Still, she felt almost relieved something was finally happening. For the past two hours she had been loitering along a narrow side street, separated by the ruins of two buildings from the main activity of the city.

Brigid had visited Manhattan in the twentieth century, during an abortive time-travel mission a few years earlier. What she saw now was scarcely recognizable as the remains of one of the one largest metropolises in the world. Centuries of human history had been reduced to hundreds of square miles of smoldering rubble within a handful of minutes. Some of the towers still stood, shattered and cracked, yet with an indomitable appearance.

A tall woman with a fair complexion, Brigid's high forehead gave the impression of a probing intellect, whereas her full underlip hinted at an appreciation of the sensual.

She wore black denim slacks, loose enough in the leg for free movement, the cuffs tucked into thick-soled combat boots. A camouflage jacket covered her torso. Her waist-length mane of red-gold hair was now a short, tightly bound sunset-colored club hanging at her nape. A TP-9 autopistol was snugged in a cross-draw rig strapped around her waist, and a Copperhead subgun hung from a harness beneath her coat.

Under two feet long, the Copperhead had a 700-round-per-minute rate of fire, the extended magazine holding thirty-five 4.85 mm steel-jacketed rounds. The grip and trigger units were placed in front of the breech in the bull pup design, allowing for one-handed use.

Optical image intensifier scopes and laser autotargeters were mounted on the top of the frames. Low recoil allowed the Copperheads to be fired in long, devastating, full-auto bursts.

On the other side of the crumbling heaps of masonry and massive chunks of fallen concrete Brigid listened to the chorus of voices chanting Shuma's name, and she shivered despite the jacket. Carefully she touched the dabs of soot applied to her face to conceal her peaches-and-cream complexion. She knew she would pass a quick visual inspection by a Farer or a Roamer, but she also knew she didn't smell as rank as they did.

However, her devotion to the masquerade had its limits. As it was, her nostrils recoiled at the potpourri of odors wafting on the wind. To Brigid, whose nose had sampled aromas from all over the world, the place simply stank.

A gangling Roamer youth with a scraggly brown beard made decorative by the addition of little silver beads twisted into the whiskers slid along the brick wall and stood beside her. She ignored him until he reached out and rubbed her right shoulder.

"I been watchin' you, big sister," he said in a husky whisper. "You got me swoll up."

"Fade, little brother," Brigid retorted in a flint-hard voice, employing the Roamer pattern of speech.

"You be a beaut babe," he said, rolling his shoulders beneath the tattered, patchwork coat that hung nearly to his ankles.

"Skid off, kid off."

"And them eyes, they's like emeralds. You be for me, big sister."

Brigid stared directly into his face, catching the acidic whiff of home-brewed whiskey that hung around him like a cloud. "I told you to skid off, little brother. I want to see Shuma."

The Roamer's lips stretched back over cavity-speckled teeth, and his right hand drifted from her shoulder to breast. "We got the time."

"Your hand," Brigid said.

The youth blinked. "What about it?"

"Take it off or I'll break it off."

The Roamer's grin widened. "Tough, you be tough. I likes my big sisters tough. Helps get me more swoll."

"Dandy," Brigid replied. "Then this should help, too."

She jacked her knee up into his groin. The youth grunted, doubling over at the waist, his hands leaving Brigid's body to clutch convulsively at his crotch. Swiftly, Brigid gripped him by his greasy hair and pulled him hard against the wall, the crown of his head striking the brick with a sound like two concrete blocks colliding.

As he slumped bonelessly to the ground, Brigid stepped casually away from him. No one else in the vicinity noticed the scene. As far as the Roamer definition of violence was concerned, the little struggle barely qualified as a harsh word.

The rumbling of a big engine grew louder and Brigid crossed the side street, peering past broken walls and over the heads of the assembled Farers and Roamers. The long yellow vehicle rolled into sight. The crowd chanted "Shuma! Shuma!" like a religious mantra.

"On his way," Brigid whispered over the Commtact.

"Acknowledged," came Kane's quick response.

Homemade drums beat a discordant fanfare. Brigid joined the other Roamers thronging toward the parade. Despite herself she felt the tingling warmth of excitement at the prospect of danger spread through her.

For a very long time, she was ashamed of that anti-

cipation, blaming her association with Kane for con-
taminating her. Now she had accepted the realization
that his own desire for thrill-seeking hadn't infected her,
but only forced her to accept an aspect of her person-
ality she had always been aware of but refused to con-
sciously acknowledge.

In her years as a baronial archivist, Brigid Baptiste
had prided herself on her intellect and logical turn of
mind. She was a scholar first and foremost. Back then,
the very suggestion she would have been engaged in
such work would have made her laugh. Now she was
a veteran warrior, and at some point during her time
with Cerberus she realized the moments of danger no
longer terrified her but brought a sharper sense of
being alive.

Her life in Cobaltville's Historical Division had not
been a full life, but only an artifice, a puppet show she
had performed so the string-pullers wouldn't become
displeased and direct their grim attention toward her.
Of course, eventually they had. Over the past few
years, she had left her tracks in the most distant and
alien of climes and breasted very deep, very danger-
ous waters.

The crowd clogging the alley was too densely packed
to move among easily, so rather than force her way
through the shouting mob, Brigid chose to run parallel
to the parade route. As she picked her way through the
rubble, she absently noted the ripple pattern spreading
across the asphalt. Weeds sprouted from splits in the

surface. She had seen the rippling effect many times, mainly in the Outlands. It was a characteristic result of earthquakes triggered by nuclear-bomb shock waves.

When Brigid came to a knitted mass of wreckage that appeared to be several buildings that had toppled atop one another, she paused to study it, looking for a way through it or over it rather than around.

A series of concrete slabs formed something of a crude staircase over the top of the rubble and she began clambering up them, leaping from one to the other until she pulled herself to the summit. Breathing hard, she looked toward the street, just as the yellow Cadillac rolled behind a pile of bricks. She saw the broad dark bulk of Shuma standing in the rear of the vehicle, waving to the shrilling mob. She caught only a glimpse of the big black man spread-eagled across the hood and her heart jumped in her chest.

Quickly she opened the Commtact channel to Kane. "Shuma himself just passed. Big as life and about five times as ugly."

"Did you see Grant?" he demanded.

"Yes." Her tone quavered ever so slightly. "It's going to be close, I'm afraid."

"It's what I figured. Stand by."

Brigid knew Kane was in contact with the other members of the away team, Brady and Edwards, so she did not linger. Swiftly, she bounded down the face of the rubble heap. The footing wasn't treacherous, but it wasn't particularly trustworthy, either. Twice, stones turned beneath her feet and she nearly pitched headlong to the ground below.

When she reached the base, she started running, hoping to get ahead of the Cadillac and provide support for Brady, Edwards and Domi, although she knew all three people were experienced. Domi, of course, had lived most of her young life in the wild places, far from the cushioned tyranny of the baronies. She had spent years cautiously treading the ragged edge of death, and her inner fiber had been forged into an iron strength and an implacable stoicism.

Edwards and Brady were, like Kane and Grant, former Magistrates and were now trusted members of the Cerberus away teams. Lakesh had initially opposed the formation of the three Cerberus away teams, made uncomfortable by the concept of the redoubt's own version the Magistrate Divisions, ironically composed of former Magistrates. However, as the scope of their operations broadened, the personnel situation at the installation also changed.

Kane, Grant, Brigid and Domi couldn't always undertake the majority of the ops and therefore shoulder the lion's share of the risks. Over the past year and a half, Kane and Grant had set up Cerberus Away Teams Alpha, Beta and Delta. CAT Delta was semipermanently stationed at Redoubt Yankee on Thunder Isle, rotating duty shifts with the New Edo's Tigers of Heaven, and CAT Beta was charged with the security of the redoubt and surrounding territory.

A number of former Magistrates, weary of fighting for one transitory ruling faction or another that tried to fill the power vacuum in the villes, responded to the outreach efforts of Cerberus.

Diplomacy, turning potential enemies into allies against the spreading reign of the overlords, had become the paramount tactic of Cerberus. Lessons in how to deal with foreign cultures and religions took the place of weapons instruction and other training.

Over the past five years, Brigid Baptiste, Domi, Kane and Grant had tramped through jungles and ruined cities, over mountains and across deserts. They had found strange cultures everywhere, often bizarre re-creations of societies that had vanished long before the nukecaust.

Due in part to her eidetic memory, Brigid spoke a dozen languages and could get along in a score of dialects, but knowing the native tongues of many different cultures and lands was only a small part of her work. Aside from her command of languages, Brigid had made history and geopolitics abiding interests in a world that was changing rapidly.

She and all the personnel of Cerberus, more than half a world away atop a mountain peak in Montana, had devoted themselves to changing the nuke-blasted planet into something better. At least that was her earnest hope. To turn hope into reality meant respecting the often alien behavior patterns influenced by a vast number of ancient religions, legends, myths and taboos.

Brigid ran through a scattering of machine parts, her

Copperhead bumping in an irritating rhythm against her left hip. Most of the rusted hunks of metal were so corroded as to be unidentifiable. Brigid continued along the front a row of roofless brownstones. As she crossed an overgrown strip of gravel alley between a pair of buildings, she heard the roar of the crowd as Shuma's vehicle hove into view.

Vaulting over a web of rusty iron pipes, Brigid sprinted to a low brick wall and knelt down behind it, catching her breath. Urgency vibrated along all the sensitive nerve endings of her body. Kane's voice suddenly entered her head.

"Baptiste, can you see Domi?"

From a jacket pocket Brigid withdrew a small monocular and pressed it against her right eye. She swept the crowd swarming on both sides of the street, but she saw no one standing out to attract her attention.

"No…why?"

"She was cut off."

"Cut off how?"

"How the hell do I know?" Kane snapped impatiently. "That's why I'm calling you."

"Do you think something has happened to her?" Brigid demanded, still peering through the lens of the monocular.

"I guess we'll find out."

Brigid focused on the dark bulk of Shuma's figure. "That's no answer. Until we know what's happened to her, we should scrub the mission."

"There's no time for that."

"Dammit, Kane—"

"Stand by," Kane broke in tersely. "Everybody, just *stand by*."

Brigid's gaze was drawn to the strange figure hunched down beside Shuma. He looked shrunken, almost dwarfish. A chill finger of dread stroked the base of her spine as she studied his features. His eyes were his most disquieting characteristic. They were wide, unblinking and not completely human. Tiny red pinpricks blazed brightly within the pupils. The eyes fixed on her, and she felt a sudden pressure in her temples.

Heart trip-hammering in her breast, feeling out of breath, Brigid jerked the monocular down and said into the Commtact, "We need to pull back and regroup before—"

"Shut up, Baptiste," Kane snapped.

Her face filmed with cold sweat, Brigid did not reply. The gunshot was sharp and sudden. Even at such a distance, she saw the spark flaring from the Cadillac's polished grillwork. A plume of steam jetted from the radiator, obscuring Grant from sight.

Pushing herself up from behind the wall, she reached for her TP-9. A sudden explosion behind the Cadillac sent a cloud of black smoke billowing into the air. The sound boomed back and forth, and Brigid felt the concussion like the slap of a languid hand across her face.

She recognized the characteristic crump of an M-33 fragmentation grenade, and she had no doubt at all who had thrown it.

Chapter 4

When Grant awoke that dawn, he tasted blood in his mouth. The blood had dried on his lips and he licked them, his tongue exploring the lacerations on the tender lining of his cheeks. He came out of unconsciousness like an exhausted swimmer pulling himself ashore, and he became aware of a consuming pain in his head and a burning thirst. He remained motionless, listening to the sound of voices speaking in low tones below him. The abraded flesh around his left eye felt swollen and raw.

Grant lay in a wooden cage, a bit under five feet tall at its apex, six feet in diameter. The slats were lashed together by rawhide thongs and many turns of a heavy-gauge wire. The entry gate was sealed by a length of rust-flecked chain and an old-fashioned iron padlock.

All things considered, the cage hanging from the cross-brace framework ten feet above the ground wasn't the worst place he had ever been imprisoned, but it was a long way from the most comfortable.

The events that had led up to his imprisonment were only a set of disjointed images, fragmented memories of ugly dreams.

Grant remembered how he and Domi sauntered into the camp of the Survivalist Outland Brigade without being challenged by sentries, mainly because none was posted. They hadn't seen any pickets, nor did there appear to be a clear-cut perimeter of the camp. The place was a sprawling mess of people and slapdash structures.

Tar-paper shacks, lean-tos, huts and tents stood jumbled in Central Park, spread out like a spilled garbage can. Four huge fires sputtered redly in the drizzle. In front of some of the dwellings stood poles of stripped saplings with skulls mounted on top, not all of them animal.

The people they saw in the camp ranged from youths with wispy beards to sharp-eyed, hard-bitten warriors. The clothing styles were varied and eclectic—colorful wool serapes, wide-brimmed cowboy hats with snake-skin bands and scruffy fur caps.

Grant easily differentiated between the Roamers and the Farers—the Roamers were festooned with weaponry, bandoliers crisscrossed over their chests, with foot-long bowie knives and big, showy handguns at their hips.

The Farers dressed a bit more sedately, and their weapons of choice were utilitarian longblasters, bolt-action rifles and a few autocarbines.

But neither Roamer nor Farer gave Grant or Domi so much as a second glance, which, he realized in ret-rospect, should have aroused his suspicions. Despite being dressed in standard Farer wear—patched denim jeans and leather hip jacket over a khaki shirt—he still stood four inches over six feet and much of his coffee-brown face was cast into sinister shadow by the broad brim of an old felt fedora. Walking side by side with a petite albino girl barely five feet tall should have drawn some curious glances, even from the most jaundiced member of the SOB.

He had almost no memory of being buffeted on all sides by a surging mass of bodies that overwhelmed him with such swift efficiency he had no chance to draw his weapon. As he was borne to the ground under the weight of many men, he heard Domi blurt in wordless anger. He shouted for her to run, then a flurry of blows fell on him and hands ripped the big revolver from his shoulder rig beneath his jacket.

A soft, lisping voice said, "Move aside, let me see him. Move aside, let him up so I can see him."

When the crushing weight obligingly left Grant's body, he lunged upward—then he felt as if an immense fist slammed into the back of his head. The impact drove all light and consciousness from his eyes. For a long time, he saw nothing but black and heard only silence.

He regained his senses in piecemeal fashion when a cup of icy water dashed into his face roused him. He blinked, trying to clear his vision. Agony tore his skull apart. He tasted the salt of his own blood in his mouth.

Then the pain ebbed, fading to a steady throb. Grant

squinted around, trying to focus through a series of what seemed to be gauzy veils draped over his face. Finally, he realized he was surrounded by planes of pale gray smoke. He made a motion to touch his head, but he couldn't move his arms. He sat tied to a heavy, wooden, straight-backed chair, arms and legs bound tightly by strips of rawhide. Glancing down at himself, he saw he wore only his T-shirt and jeans. Everything else, including his boots and socks, had been stripped from him.

The acrid fumes of the smoke seized his throat and dragged a cough from him. Lying on a far table were several long-stemmed clay pipes, the bowls discolored and smoldering. The place reeked of marijuana and overcooked meat, of stale and sweaty bodies.

The fact that he could even smell the stink of the room told him just how powerful the stench was. His nose had been broken three times in the past and always poorly reset. Unless an odor was extraordinarily fragrant or fearsomely repulsive, he couldn't smell it; he was incapable of detecting subtle aromas unless they were literally right under his nose.

Grant coughed again, then cleared his throat.

"You may speak if you wish."

The voice was a low, ghostly whisper, touched with a faint lisp. He remembered hearing the voice before, and he turned his head toward a shadowy figure looming on his right.

He felt a quiver of revulsion at the sight of Shuma

and his enormous scaled belly bulging over his sweat pants. He glanced up into his face, expecting to see it twisted in a triumphant smirk. Instead, Shuma's expression was vacant, his eyes hooded and distant as if they were focused on another scene entirely. His flaccid lips hung open, slick with saliva.

The voice spoke again and Shuma's lips did not move. "Do you find your host revolting, Mr. Grant?"

Not responding to the question, Grant rumbled in his lionlike voice, "Who the hell are you?"

Shadows shifted behind Shuma's bulk, and Grant caught a whistling, asthmatic wheeze. "I am the voice, the mind, the spirit behind the Survivalist Outland Brigade."

Grant hawked up from deep in his throat and spit on the floor. "Bullshit."

The voice tittered, sounding somewhat like an out-of-breath owl. "Why are you so sure?"

Straining against the rawhide bindings, Grant tried to peer around Shuma. "Let me see you."

"All in good time, Mr. Grant…all in good time."

"How do you know my name?"

"Oh, your spy—Wright was her name?—was most forthcoming about everyone and everything."

Grant did not allow his sudden apprehension to show on his face or be heard in his voice. "I don't know who you're talking about."

There was another breathy giggle. "Oh? What a pity…because *I* definitely know what she was talking about."

The note of certainty, of complete confidence in the speaker's voice sent a tingle of fear up Grant's spine. He gusted out a weary sigh. "All right. But she wasn't a spy."

"She was here on an intelligence-gathering mission, correct?"

"More or less. We wanted to find out more about Shuma and this SOB of his."

"Of *his?*" A mocking lilt touched the voice, but Grant detected an edge of anger there, as well.

"Who else?" He eyed Shuma surreptitiously, looking for a glimmer of intelligence in his eyes. They were covered by a dull sheen, the lids drooping.

"What's wrong with him?" he asked.

"Nothing," came the dismissive response. "That is, nothing that's isn't wrong with any other addict of jolt and various other opiates."

Grant knew that jolt was a combination of various hallucinogens and narcotics, like heroin. To sample it once was to virtually ensure addiction.

He hesitated, started to ask a question, then closed his mouth, shaking his head.

"You were about to ask how a jolt-brain could command his own bowels, much less an army."

Grant nodded. "Something like that, yes."

"I command Shuma and he commands the SOB."

"Which brings me back to my first question—who the hell are you?"

"My name would mean nothing to you…but if you must call me something, you may call me Esau."

Grant inhaled a deep breath, held it, then released it slowly. "*What* are you?"

"I believe you have already guessed."

When Grant declined to respond, he heard a shuffle of movement and a small figure stepped out from behind Shuma. At first Grant thought it was a crippled child, leaning as it did on a pair of crutches. But when the figure lurched closer he knew with a rise of nausea he was vastly mistaken.

Esau stood a little more than four feet tall, his emaciated body lost in a baggy flannel shirt and pants several sizes too large for him. An old extension cord cinched the waistband tight. The frayed cuffs of the trousers dragged on the floor, but Grant couldn't see any sign of feet.

Esau's face was dominated by a thick shelf of bone bulging above his huge eyes. The forehead rose like a marble wall, angling upward to join with the flat crown of his skull. A mat of thin gray hair covered it.

Grant struggled to keep his expression neutral, to disguise the fear swelling within him.

Esau's small mouth twitched in a parody of a smile. "I revolt you more than Shuma, do I not?"

Grant didn't respond for a few seconds, visually examining the blue-and-red mapwork of broken blood vessels spreading over Esau's forehead. "Not exactly. I've come across your type a time or two."

Esau's smile widened in mock ingenuousness. "And what type is that, Mr. Grant?"

"Doomies," he retorted matter-of-factly. "You're a doomseer. I didn't think there were many of you left."

In the Outlands, people with enhanced psionic abilities were called doomseers or doomies, their mutant precognitive abilities feared and hated.

Most of the mutant strains spawned after the nuclear holocaust were extinct, either dying because of their twisted biologies, or hunted and exterminated during the early years of the unification program. Doomseers weren't necessarily mutants, but norms with true telepathic abilities were rare in current times.

Extrasensory and precognitive perceptions were the most typical abilities possessed by mutants who appeared otherwise normal.

Esau uttered a scoffing, contemptuous laugh. "Hardly a doomseer. I can't foretell the future any more accurately than you can."

"Then what do you call yourself?"

Casting a sideways glance up at Shuma, Esau answered confidently, "A mastermind. I call myself a mastermind."

Grant cocked his head in puzzlement. "A what?"

"I can master minds not my own…like Shuma's here."

His gaze narrowed, Grant asked, "How can you do that?"

Esau's shoulders jerked in what appeared to be a nervous tic but was an attempt to emulate a shrug. "By a variety of measures. The drugs help, of course."

"Of course."

"But I have the ability to stimulate certain parts of his brain so I can flood his nervous system with endorphins." Esau paused for a handful of thoughtful seconds, then asked, "Do you know what those are?"

Grant nodded. "I do."

"Then you know that when the nervous system is exposed to endorphins, a biochemical reaction takes place. The reasoning parts of the brain are inhibited."

"And therefore easy to control," Grant interjected.

Esau's smile widened. "It doesn't work the same for everybody. It helps if you're a self-indulgent voluptuary in the first place, like Shuma."

"I gathered that," Grant replied dryly. "So you're really the boss and Shuma is just the front man?"

"Something like that. Clever, wouldn't you say?"

Grant nodded in grudging agreement. "I suppose so…Roamers would never take orders from a crippled little pissant like you."

Esau's lips tightened and he stepped closer to Grant, staring at him unblinkingly, as if challenging him to look away. Grant did not. "Are there any further questions?"

"Plenty of them, but first, where is the Wright woman?"

Esau's brow acquired a line of concentration. "Oh, I do apologize. I should have reunited you much sooner. She can actually answer most of your other questions."

"You don't even know what they are."

In a voice barely above a whisper, Esau stated, "You would ask me to reconsider leading the Survivalist Outland Brigade and join with Cerberus in an alliance against these so-called overlords…whatever they are."

Grant stirred uneasily. "How do you know that?"

"Because that is what the Wright woman asked."

"And what did you tell her?"

Esau turned toward Shuma. On the right side of his massive head, a thick vein pulsed. Shuma lumbered forward, grasped the back of Grant's chair and lifted it clear of the floor without apparent effort. He turned it and set it down at a different angle.

Peering through the gloom, Grant saw heavy wooden beams supporting the ceiling. Four chains dangled from a block-and-tackle assembly attached to the rafters. The ends of the chains were tipped with sharp meat hooks of the type used in slaughterhouses.

From two of the hooks hung a naked body, gutted like the carcass of a pig he had seen once since in a butcher's shop. One of the big hooks had been inserted through the underside of the chin, and the tip of another pierced the left armpit.

Through the fog of horror clouding his vision, Grant looked into the glassy, dead eyes of Wright.

Teeth clenched, a wordless snarl of rage vibrating in his throat, Grant hurled himself against his bonds, rocking the chair back and forth, hoping to tip it over on Esau. Shuma's huge hands fell onto his shoulders, pressing him down, holding him motionless.

Esau lurched into view on his crutches, staring levelly into Grant's eyes. "She told me quite a bit, but not everything. You'll do that for me, Mr. Grant."

"Goddamn you to Hell, you little mutie piece of shit." His voice was so guttural with fury it sounded more like the growl of an animal.

Esau leaned forward, stroking the side of Grant's face with tiny baby fingers. "God has done enough to me already, Mr. Grant. I do the damning to Hell here."

His unnaturally large eyes suddenly seemed to increase in size, as if they were squirming from their sockets. Tiny red flames flickered within the pupils. Grant sensed rather than heard a multitude of tiny voices, all chittering like faraway crickets. The sound slid along the edges of his awareness, and terror pushed away his rage. His heartbeat thundered in his ears.

A nova of pain exploded within the walls of his skull and he heard himself crying out, as from a million miles away. His body spasmed, thrashed. He felt his mind being pulled into a whirlpool of dark energy that sucked his blood and bones and soul out through the pores of his skin, and turned them to dust.

He whirled, orbiting every instant of his life, spiraling through memories of joy, of loss, of grief, of victory and defeat. He spun through a sea of images, and no matter how hard he tried to stop them from flying to the forefront of his mind, he knew Esau saw them, rifled through them, memorized them.

The most intense pain gradually abated but didn't

fade completely. There was a ringing in his ears and numbness in his extremities. He felt blood inching from his right nostril and flowing over his lips. He breathed shallowly because of the bile burning in his throat. Then he doubled over and vomited between his legs. He felt as if a violent tornado had ripped a mile-wide path of destruction through the field of his mind.

Slowly raising his head, he squinted through his watering, blurred eyes toward Esau. The vein on the little man's temple pulsed violently as if a worm squirmed just beneath the thin layer of flesh. The network of broken blood vessels on his forehead appeared to be even more livid. His arms trembled as if he was having difficulty maintaining his balance on the crutches.

"Interesting," he said in a faint, tremulous voice. "Far more interesting than I thought it would be. I'm going to keep you alive a while longer, Mr. Grant…at least until your friends come to rescue you, an eventuality of which you seem certain. But it wouldn't be so if our situations were reversed."

A small, bronze-hued curve of metal clinked to the floor at Grant's feet. He recognized it as the Commtact.

"You are quite isolated, my large friend," Esau went on. "You live only at my sufferance and my continuing interest in your memories. Many of them are intriguing to the point of fascination.

"Shuma, I think he needs some fresh air. Take him to the cage."

Chapter 5

A cold rain pattered down through the leaves that formed a loose canopy over the top of the cage. Grant shivered in the early-morning chill, but he turned his face upward so the raindrops fell into his open, as-dry-as-dust mouth.

The water soothed the cuts on his lips and cheek lining and eased his thirst somewhat. When the drizzle intensified, his torn T-shirt was quickly soaked through and plastered to his skin.

"Well, here I am," he rasped, a little dismayed by how hoarse and weak his voice sounded.

Grant retained little memory of being half dragged, half carried to the cage by Shuma. His arms and legs refused to function, the muscles feeling as if they were filled with half-frozen mud. He wasn't sure if the impaired movement was due to his being in a chair or an aftereffect of Esau's psionic rape.

He tried to dismiss the concept, but he felt violated. Esau had virtually torn open his mind and ransacked its contents. Although he didn't know exactly how the little man had accomplished it, he knew with a grim certainty there would be a final reckoning.

When the sun came up and filtered feebly through the interwoven branches, he moved carefully to the entry gate of the cage. Sliding his hands between the wooden slats, his fingers explored the iron padlock. He briefly considered ripping loose a splinter of wood and using it to pick the lock, but he discarded the idea when he saw a pair of armed men approaching him.

Grizzled, bearded Roamers, they didn't warn him not to touch the lock. All they did was glare, and he withdrew his hands.

Biting back a profanity, Grant sat down and listened to the camp stirring around him, watching dim shapes hustle back and forth between shacks and cook fires. He grew cold in his wet clothes, but he maintained his stoic exposure. As a Magistrate, he had been taught techniques to manage pain and discomfort, but he wasn't a Mag anymore. He realized with bleak humor that he had experienced more periods of physical suffering in the five years since his exile than during his entire two decades as a hard-contact Magistrate.

In his first few years as a Mag, as he rose up the ranks, he had undergone periodic training exercises to toughen him and increase his stamina, and that included exposure to extremes of temperature.

Even now he recalled those exercises with loathing. They were days of pure, unadulterated torture, of walking naked in a desert or clambering among rocky mountains, waiting for the commander to ration out just enough food and water to survive from one dawn to one sunset.

But Grant learned to live by instinct, reflex and training, to focus solely on putting one foot in front of the other and slogging on. Those of his fellow Mags who didn't learn didn't survive.

Despite the twinges of protest from his knee joints, Grant sat cross-legged and stared at a white spot on the floor of the cage, where the bark had peeled back from the wooden slat. He tried to relax his neck and shoulder muscles, working his way down to his bare, cold toes. He concentrated on regulating his respiration, putting himself into a quasihypnotic state.

He was trying to achieve the "Mag mind," a technique that emptied his consciousness of all nonessentials and allowed his instincts to rise to the fore. He had been trained to do it while serving the Magistrate Division of Cobaltville. He used it for handling pain and dealing with exhaustion. Brigid Baptiste had referred to it as a form of yoga, but Grant still thought of the process as Mag mind.

After memorizing the white spot, he closed his eyes, visualizing it. He struggled to superimpose a mental image that matched the actual spot, but he was unable to do so. His concentration was scattered.

Grant wasn't sure if it was due to the pains of the injuries inflicted by the SOBs or whether he was emotionally drained. Rather than seeing the white mark in his mind, he kept seeing Esau's huge eyes with their red pupils, like a vid tape on continuous replay.

Despite his situation, worry about his friends

consumed him. He felt sure the Cerberus personnel knew he still lived—in fact, they were probably aware of his general state of health, due to his biolink transponder.

All permanent residents of the Cerberus redoubt had been injected with subcutaneous biolink transponders that transmitted heart rate, respiration, blood pressure and brain-wave patterns. Based on organic nanotechnology, the transponders were composed of nonharmful radioactive chemicals that bound themselves to an individual's glucose and the middle layers of the epidermis. The constant signal was relayed to the redoubt by the Comsat, one of the two satellites to which the installation was uplinked.

The telemetry transmitted from Grant's subdermal biolink transponders would be directed down to the Cerberus redoubt's hidden antenna array. Sophisticated scanning filters combed through the telemetric signals using special human biological encoding.

Although most satellites had been little more than free-floating scrap metal for well over a century, Cerberus had always possessed the proper electronic ears and eyes to receive the transmissions from at least two them. One was of the Vela reconnaissance class, which carried narrow-band multispectral scanners. It could detect the electromagnetic radiation reflected by every object on Earth, including subsurface geomagnetic waves. The scanner was tied into an extremely high resolution photographic relay system. Conceivably, they could fix Grant's present position in Central Park—not that it would do him any good.

Kane was far too canny a tactician to try to penetrate the SOB's camp in broad daylight. As it was, Grant knew he and Domi had somehow been identified and allowed to get as far as they had before being jumped. He assumed Esau's mental powers were responsible.

He also assumed Esau planned to use him to lay a trap for Kane, Brigid, Domi and whoever else participated in a rescue attempt. He didn't know if the little man wanted to capture them or kill them, but he had seemed exceptionally intrigued by what he had seen in Grant's mind. He guessed the information about the Annunaki overlords was of special interest, since it was connected to the fall of the united baronies.

Humankind's interaction with a nonhuman species had begun at the dawn of Earth's history. That relationship and communication had continued unbroken for thousands of years, cloaked by ritual, religion and mystical traditions.

According to information gathered by the Cerberus personnel over the past few years, most myths regarding gods and aliens derived from a race known in ancient Sumerian texts as the Annunaki, but also known in legend as the Dragon Kings and the Serpent Lords.

A species of bipedal reptiles that appeared on Earth at the dawn of humanity's development, the Annunaki arrived from the extrasolar planet of Nibiru. They reared great cities, built civilizations and spaceports and influenced the evolution of humankind.

The Annunaki were also consumed by abounding pride and arrogance, and more than a few maintained an insatiable appetite for conquest and control. The faction led by Enlil had developed and imposed complex, oppressive caste and gender systems on early human cultures to solidify that control.

As far as Enlil was concerned, the nukecaust was a radical form of remodeling and fumigation. The extreme depopulation, as well as the subsequent atmospheric and geological changes, approximated Nibiruan conditions. Earth would become the new Nibiru.

Before that occurred, Cerberus was determined to build some sort of unified resistance against Enlil and the other overlords, but the undertaking proved far more difficult and frustrating than Grant had imagined. Even long months after the disappearance of the barons, the villes were still in states of anarchy, with various factions warring for control on a daily basis.

Grant heard a murmur of many voices rising around him like the sound of rushing water. Opening his eyes, he saw a crowd of about twenty people gathered below the cage, clustered around it like a swarm of bees.

Most of them were Roamers, a rough-looking gang—bearded, wild haired, wearing a variety of rags and furs.

A tall woman strode up to the cage and leaned forward to stare between the slats. She stood well over six feet tall, naked to the waist except for crisscrossing cartridge belts over her blue-tattooed breasts. Tattoos writhed all over her bare arms and torso, like a formfitting body suit imprinted with fantastic designs.

She wore green camouflage pants and high-topped boots. Her black hair was cropped to her scalp except for a crest that sprouted up six inches from the center of her skull. The ends of it were dyed a bright purple. Silver-studded red leather bands encircled her wrists. She cradled a heavy Stoner M-207 machine gun in her muscular arms.

At one time her blue-eyed face might have been pretty, but that was before it was disfigured by the wide cicatrix scar indenting her left cheek like a fault in snowy terrain.

She stared speculatively at Grant, and Grant gazed at her. Neither person spoke for a long moment, then the woman turned and nodded to her companions. "Yep, it's him all right. It's Grant, just like Shuma said."

Grant stirred uneasily. "You know me?"

The woman turned back to him. "We've never been formally introduced. We traded shots about eighteen years ago, in the Great Sand Dunes hellzone. You 'member that?"

Grant did, and the memories weren't pleasant. He and a Magistrate squad had been ambushed by a group of surprisingly well-armed Roamers. He touched his left cheek. "I give you that?"

She uttered a spitting sound of derision. "Shit, no. My first husband did, back when I was a sprout. Claimed I was steppin' out on him. Hell, I was only fourteen. But I kilt him for it all the same. Had me six more husbands since then."

A bell of recognition chimed faintly in Grant's memory. "Didn't you used to be called the Merry Widow?"

The woman grinned in genuine amusement. "Called that still. Glad to find out I still have a rep…wasn't sure with all this fuss made over that Shuma bastard and this SOB of his."

The derogatory tone in the woman's voice caught Grant's attention. "You're not a part of it?"

The Merry Widow shook her head. "Not yet. Brought my people here to check the whole thing out. Lot of other clans I have problems with are here. Can't say I'm too inclined to take orders from a mutie, neither, much less a fuckin' scalie."

Grant inched closer to the bars. "You're only about half right."

Lines furrowed her brow. "What do you mean?"

Grant eyed the Roamers standing behind the Merry Widow and asked, "Are all these your people?"

She nodded.

"Can you trust them?"

"Trust 'em to do what?"

"Not to sell you out."

"Why would they do that?"

Dropping his voice to a whisper, Grant said, "Because I've got some information that you might find pretty interesting. But I think it should it be for your ears only."

The Merry Widow opened her mouth to retort, closed it, then turned, sweeping the ragtag band with a challenging stare. She made a brushing gesture with her right hand. "Fade."

Reluctantly, the Roamers shuffled away, some of them casting Grant resentful glares, others looking merely puzzled.

The woman turned back to Grant. "Spill, sec man."

Grant felt the back of his neck heating with a flush of anger. "Sec man" was an obsolete term dating back to preunification days when self-styled barons formed their own private armies to safeguard their territories. It was still applied to Magistrates in the far hinterlands beyond the villes.

He swallowed his irritation and said lowly, "Shuma is just the puppet. A crippled mind-mutie named Esau really pulls the strings."

The Merry Widow eyed him skeptically. "I thought that little slug was his ass-wipin' servant or something."

"That's what he wants you to believe. He's really the brains of the whole outfit."

Taking a deep breath, Grant told the Roamer chieftain everything he had witnessed and been told by Esau. He didn't embellish or even try to conceal the reasons he and his friends were in Manhattan. He spoke directly and honestly. He knew the Merry Widow distrusted him and didn't blame her.

His own work with the Cerberus exiles kept him in a shadow world of danger and eternal suspicion, of sudden crisis and alarm, where human beings died in a covert war that ranged from the sands of the Black Gobi to the utter remoteness of a forgotten colony on the Moon.

When he was done, the woman's scarred features were drawn in a troubled frown. "I don't like that," she murmured. "Not a'tall. But…"

She trailed off and after waiting a few seconds Grant demanded, "But what?"

The Merry Widow shrugged. "But Shuma has made plans for you, and everybody is lookin' forward to it."

Grant felt his stomach lurch. "Plans?"

The woman nodded. "Yeah, a big parade down the street with you as the main trophy. A lot of people in this camp don't like you, Grant."

The corner of her mouth quirked in a wry smile. "Go figure, huh?"

"Yeah," he echoed. "Go figure."

Contemplatively, she continued, "But a lot of people in this camp don't like taking orders from a scalie in the first place, and they sure as shit won't like it if they find out they're really taking orders from a little runt of a doomie on crutches."

Gusting out a sigh, the Merry Widow ran a hand over the purple-dyed tips of her hair. "Mebbe there's something we can do about that. Lemme think on it."

Chapter 6

Kane ran across the rooftop with a long-legged stride. As soon as he had seen the geyser of steam burst from the Cadillac's radiator, he dropped the OICW, leaped to his feet and started running.

A chorus of outraged screams and panicked yells erupted from the crowd below, and he smiled in grim satisfaction.

"Kane," came Brigid's voice into his head. She sounded more indignant than confused or concerned. "What the hell is going on?"

"Keep standing by," he told her.

"I've *been* standing by. I need to know—"

Reaching up to the Commtact, he cut the channel. He knew she would heap vituperation on him when next they spoke, but he couldn't afford a distraction. He heard the distant whip-crack of a rifle shot, and the angry yells from the crowd hit a fever pitch of fear. Either Edwards or Brady was taking the initiative.

Kane wasn't concerned about leaving the OICW behind. His first priority was reaching street level as soon as possible, and so he concentrated on running.

The Sin Eater snugged in its forearm holster weighed considerably less than the rifle, although the four grenades attached to the combat webbing beneath his jacket bounced painfully against his ribs.

Racing across the roof, he leaped nimbly over haphazard heaps of unidentifiable junk. He angled away from the cupola enclosing the stairway. He had no inclination to be trapped in the stairwell by enraged Roamers who he was sure were on their way up.

Obeying an impulse triggered by his point man's sense, Kane had decided to stop Shuma's vehicle rather than snipe at live targets. He wasn't sure why he had reached his decision, but he put a great faith in his instincts as a general rule.

When Kane's point man's sense howled an alarm, he usually paid attention. His point man's sense was really a combined manifestation of the five he had trained to the epitome of keenness. Something about Shuma and his big-headed companion—some small, almost unidentifiable stimulus—had triggered the mental alarm.

Sprinting across the flat surface of the roof, he reached the edge and took an alleyway yawning before him in a single leap. He misjudged the distance to the adjacent building and landed too hard, falling onto his right side and rolling over and over. He came to a halt when he slammed up against the brick facade of a chimney.

Biting back a curse, he quickly examined the scrapes on the palms of his hands, then rose to a knee. Across the alley he heard a door slam open and he cast a glance over his shoulder.

A pair of bearded Roamers bulled their way out of the cupola, looking this way and that. Both men cradled lightweight deer rifles in their arms. Kane gauged the weapons to be .22-caliber, and therefore they had little stopping power unless the shooters were very accurate. He assumed the Roamers would be, so he sidled out of sight on the opposite side of the chimney.

The two men glared around with wild, angry eyes and when they spotted the OICW lying on the rooftop, they jogged toward it. Kane took advantage of their distraction to stand up and start running again.

He heard a wordless bellow of rage behind him, then the snapping of a rifle shot. A bullet drilled into a stack of lumber on his right, throwing up a little cloud of splinters. Increasing his speed and the length of his stride, he reached the far edge of the roof and dived off it, to the building fifteen feet below.

Kane landed on the balls of his feet, and he threw himself forward into a somersault. The layer of rotting wood and roofing material sagged beneath his weight and collapsed inward. He dropped amid a seething cascade of plaster, drywall, boards, insulation and broken rafters.

Fortunately, he didn't fall far, but the impact still very nearly jolted all the wind from his lungs. Gasping, his vision blurred, Kane dragged himself to his hands and knees, hearing splintery shards and timbers crashing down all around him. The swirl of dust and dirt particles stung his eyes and coated his tongue.

Coughing, fanning the air in front of his face, he staggered to his feet, glancing up at the ragged hole his hurtling body had made in the ceiling. Faintly, he heard the Roamers yelling in frustration, but he doubted they would risk following him. They no doubt hoped he had broken his neck or at the very least his back in the fall.

Kneading the small of his back, Kane squinted through the dust, seeing a hallway piled high with the detritus of two centuries. Though the light was dim, he moved toward the mouth of a stairwell. Dark doorways yawned on both sides of the passage. He saw only shambles inside the rooms and evidence they were used as nests for vermin. The interior smelled stale and musty.

Carefully, he went down the steps, wincing as the risers creaked and sagged alarmingly beneath his boots. The banister wobbled whenever he touched it. He could only dimly hear the sounds of commotion out in the street, more screams and sporadic gunfire.

Activating his Commtact, he opened the channel to Brigid. "Status?"

Her tone of voice flat, Brigid responded, "Shuma threw himself over that weird little man. Edwards and Brady have been shooting into the crowd, keeping anybody from getting too close to Grant. I haven't seen Domi, but I know she was the one who—"

Brigid broke off, then said crisply, "Stand by."

"Baptiste—"

"It's *your* turn to stand by."

THE GRENADE ROLLED ONLY a few feet before detonating with a brutal thunderclap. A hell-flower bloomed, petals of flame curving and spreading outward. Spewing from the end of every petal was a rain of shrapnel, ripping into bodies and the facades of buildings.

Fragments rattled violently against the half-fallen wall behind which Domi had taken cover. The explosion was followed by the shattering of glass and several keening screams. Domi caught glimpses of men staggering backward with their hands clapped over their ruined faces. Other people stared in wide-eyed shock, frozen in horror.

Two rifle shots, sounding like the snap of dry twigs, cut through the echoes of the detonation. A pair of men standing on opposite sides of the street fell thrashing to the ground, their heads misshapen by the high-powered bullets. Domi knew the bullets had been fired by Brady and Edwards.

The crowd ran in a howling, panicky rush that bowled people off their feet and trampled more than a few of them. Domi stayed behind the wall until the main mass of the crowd had passed. She resheathed her knife then rose to her feet.

She lunged back in the direction she had come, plunging through the smoke. As she ducked beneath an outstretched arm, she drew her Combat Master, appreciating the feel of the checkered walnut grip against the palm of her right hand.

A Roamer, blood streaming from a shrapnel-inflicted gash on his cheek, jumped in her path, his discolored teeth bared in a snarl of rage. With neat precision, she clubbed him across the mouth with the barrel of her autopistol. He reeled away, spitting scarlet and crumbs of his shattered teeth.

As Domi stepped around him, she saw a dark-complexioned man wearing a yellow turban racing toward Grant with a three-foot-long sword held over his head, readying himself to deliver a decapitating blow. Because of the roar of the crowd, she couldn't hear what he said, even though his lips worked as if he was shrieking a stream of imprecations.

Moving on impulse, almost without thought, Domi leveled her autopistol and swiftly brought the turbaned man into target acquisition. Twenty yards was long range for the handgun, especially aiming at a moving target, but she had made far more difficult shots. When the sword-wielding figure was framed within the weapon's sights, she adjusted for elevation and windage, then she squeezed the trigger two times.

The big automatic pistol bucked in her hands, sending out booming shock waves of ear-shattering sound. The first .45-caliber bullet hit the man directly in the center of his turban and the other struck his neck. He catapulted backward amid a spouting of blood.

The people around him scattered at the sound of the shots, running in all directions. Because the majority of the crowd was composed of hard-bitten, violence-prone Roamers, they didn't indulge in a panic-stricken flight. They took cover either in the ruins or they dropped flat to the street, eyes and guns seeking targets.

Domi glimpsed the huge dark bulk of Shuma hustling away from the Cadillac, a limp shape cradled protectively in his arms. She guessed the scalie was ferrying his small companion away to safety, but she couldn't understand why he would care.

She didn't devote any further thought to the matter. She kept her gaze fixed on Grant as he strained against the bonds that held him to the hood of the vehicle. Wisps of steam from the punctured radiator still curled around him, like an early-morning fog.

Through a part in the vapors, Domi a saw a scar-faced woman with a bizarre purple-tinged Mohawk haircut shouldering her way through the press of bodies, using the stock of a Stoner machine gun to hammer a path. Her narrowed eyes were turned toward Grant.

Domi came to a halt and sighted down the length of her pistol, aiming at a spot between the woman's exposed, tattooed breasts. Too late she sensed a rushing body behind her. Arms encircled her in an agonizingly tight grip, lifting her from the ground. She smelled stale sweat and hot, rancid breath washed over her cheek.

As she tried to bring up her pistol, the arms tightened around her in a crushing embrace, pumping all the air from her lungs. Gasping, she kicked backward, the edge of her boot heel striking his shin. Her next tactic was to butt the man with the back of her head. This move was marginally more effective because he swore in pain, but the pressure of his pinioning arms increased, closing like the jaws of a vise.

Through blurry eyes, Domi saw the bare-breasted woman raising her Stoner, resting the stock against her hip, the hollow bore staring at her like a cyclopean eye. Domi struggled wildly.

A short tongue of flame lipped from the muzzle. The sound of the single shot was like a muffled handclap. Domi squeezed her eyes shut. She felt the man holding her jerk violently as if he received a blow. His grip loosened and his arms fell away altogether. Domi stumbled when the man dropped, but she saw the neat red-rimmed hole in the middle of his forehead and the far-from-neat cavity in the rear of his skull.

She threw the Mohawked woman an uncomprehending stare. She smiled at Domi in amusement, inclined her head in a nod and gestured with her autorifle toward Grant.

"He's all yours, sweetheart!" she called.

Then she turned and merged into the bustling crowd.

Breathing hard, Domi reached Grant, drawing her knife. He turned his head toward her and demanded, "What kind of rescue plan is this—to parboil my ass?"

As the edge of the blade sliced through the ropes encircling his right wrist, she answered, "The Kane kind."

Grant gusted out a weary sigh. "Why did I even have to ask."

Domi couldn't help but grin as she cut the big man free. Although he looked bruised and battered, the fact that he could complain and criticize meant he wasn't hurt too severely.

As Grant pushed himself off the hood of the Cadillac and stood massaging his wrists, Brigid Baptiste pounded up, holding her TP-9 in a two-fisted grip. Her green eyes glinted, bright with worry.

"Are you all right?" she asked, looking Grant up and down and wincing slightly at the abrasions and contusions on his face. "Do you need medical treatment?"

He shook his head. "Later, maybe."

Brigid turned toward Domi. "We lost contact with you and almost scrubbed the op."

Gingerly, the girl touched the Commtact behind her ear and when she withdrew her hand, her fingertips glistened with wet crimson. "Took a wallop there," she said with a wry smile. "Mashed it up pretty good but probably kept me from a broken head."

She glanced toward the nearby buildings rising from the skyline. "Where's Kane and everybody else at?"

"I just spoke to him," Brigid said. "He, Edwards and Brady are on their way to us. Once we rendezvous, let's get to the jump chamber and gate back to Cerberus."

She paused and smiled without humor. "I've pretty much had my fill of New York, New York."

Grant matched her humorless smile. "Yeah, it's a hell of a town. But we can't leave it right now."

A voice from behind them asked, "Why the hell not?"

They turned as Kane jogged up. His dark hair was white with plaster dust, his face and clothes coated with a pale film. With every footfall, little clouds of dust puffed up around him.

"What happened to you?" Brigid asked sarcastically. "Too much standing by?"

Kane threw her a fake sweet smile. "Lucky guess."

"Why didn't you just shoot Shuma?" Grant asked impatiently.

Kane regarded him with wide-eyed innocence. "And I'm so happy to see you, too."

Grant scowled. "Thanks for saving my life, okay? Now tell me why you saved it the way you did."

Kane opened his mouth to reply, then closed it and shook his head. "I'm not really sure. I had him in my sights, but then I got the feeling he wasn't the real brains behind this whole SOB deal. I also got the feeling that if I blew his brains out in front of this crowd of scum, I'd be making a martyr, not ending a threat."

He paused and added nonchalantly, "Not to mention that every Roamer in the vicinity would've tried to carve the best pieces off you in retaliation."

Grant stared at him levelly. "I'm impressed. That actually makes sense, unlike most of your make-shit-up-as-we-go-along plans."

Kane nodded in mock humility, then stiffened when the snare-drum rattle of automatic gunfire and screams rose from behind the ruins. "If nothing else, I think we jump-started some old Roamer clan feuds."

Domi snorted. "What else is new?"

Grant, Kane and Brigid understood her oblique reference. It often seemed that wherever the Cerberus team went, violence and death were only moments away. It was rarely planned that way, but terrible and bloody events always happened and the body count soared. Brigid had once opined that they were avatars, catalysts, triggering eruptions and explosions of savagery that had simmered at a low boil for a long time

"If Shuma isn't the guiding intelligence behind the SOB," Brigid broke in irritably, "then who is?"

"Little big head man," Domi piped up promptly. "Right?"

Grant threw her a fleeting, appreciative smile. "You don't know *how* right. You say Edwards and Brady are with you?"

"Yeah," Kane replied. "They'll be along. Did you find Wright?"

The smile fled Grant's lips. "I did, I'm sorry to say. Let's go get her."

Chapter 7

Shuma's headquarters were situated between a pair of overgrown knolls on the far side of Central Park. Rather than expend time and effort on stealth, the Cerberus warriors opted to proceed the Magistrate way—head-on and determined to shoot, stab and slug their way through any obstacles.

Brady and Edwards walked flanking point, wielding their OICW rifles and glowering at everyone who glanced in their direction. Both ex-Magistrates, the two men were of a type. The shaved-headed Edwards stood over six feet tall, very broad of build with overdeveloped triceps, biceps and deltoids.

Brady was equally bulked up, but slightly shorter. His blond hair was little more than bristles covering his scalp. He and Edwards were dressed similarly in black T-shirts, green-striped camo pants and high-laced jump boots. In addition to their rifles, the two men carried H&K VP-70 autopistols in belly holsters.

Kane, Grant, Domi and Brigid marched purposefully side by side through the nearly deserted camp of the Survivalist Outland Brigade. All four people knew walking in such a fashion was tactically unwise, but they also knew by doing so they were making a theatrical, defiant statement to any Roamers or Farers they might meet.

Anyone who lived near any of the baronies had heard tales of Kane and Grant, the two rogue Magistrates who had continually escaped and outwitted all the traps laid for them by various barons of different villes. No two men over the past two hundred years had reputations to equal theirs, even if it was an open question of just how many of the stories were based in truth and how many of them were overblown fable. For their part, Kane and Grant found that blurring the lines of demarcation between legend and fact had proved very useful on occasion.

They were credited with killing Baron Ragnar in his own bed, and although no one knew how they had managed it, they were also held responsible for the fall of the villes and disappearance of the barons.

The four of them strode through the camp grimfaced and single-minded and weren't confronted. The few people they encountered either scuttered behind trees or sank to the ground, as if hoping they would be mistaken for lumps in the terrain. Some of them were so dirty, they blended in almost perfectly.

"Doesn't look like anybody is inclined to interfere with us," Brigid noted softly.

"We're pretty scary when we want to be," Domi replied in a side-mouthed whisper, her pistol hanging from her right hand. "Sometimes even when we don't want to be."

Grant found it difficult to maintain an implacable facade, since he walked in his bare feet and occasionally stepped on a sharp object. When he hopped on one foot and swore under his breath, Kane tried hard to keep from smiling.

The majority of the people who had made up the SOB had already packed up their belongings and departed from the sprawling camp. Unlike the Roamers, the Farer element of the SOB wasn't enthusiastic about participating in clan feuds. The Farers were too fixated on mere survival to engage in random and gratuitous acts of violence.

More sounds of strife reached them—gunfire, screams and a loud female voice shouting orders.

"Good thing the Merry Widow didn't hold a grudge," Brigid remarked.

"Too soon to say about a Roamer," Domi stated contemptuously. "Most of 'em only came here for the chance of free food or findin' underage slaves. They were already primed to start slaughterin' one another."

Kane nodded in agreement. "Grant's parade was just a diversion. This whole enterprise would've fallen apart anyway. It wasn't worth the life of Wright."

He cast Grant a penetrating glance. "I'd say we did what we set out to do. The Survivalist Outland Brigade has disbanded."

Grant scowled. "You wouldn't say that if you'd met

Esau. If we don't stop him here, he'll start up some-place else."

"He's just one more mind-mutie with an attitude," Kane argued. "We've dealt with his type before."

"He's a mind-mutie with an attitude who knows a whole hell of a lot about us, about Cerberus, about our tech and our defenses. That makes him damned danger-ous."

"The more he knows about us," Brigid pointed out, "then the less he would want us to pay any attention to him."

Grant pursed his lips, considering her words, then shook his head. "No. There's something about that little son of a bitch. He's powerful, he's ambitious and he's flat-out evil."

Kane regarded him with surprise, since Grant very rarely spoke in moral absolutes. The fact that he done so meant Esau had shaken him profoundly, to his emo-tional core. Although he looked too huge and solid to have many abilities beyond sheer strength, Grant was an exceptionally intelligent and talented man.

Behind the man's fierce, deep-set eyes, down-sweeping mustache, granite jaw and broken nose lay a mind rich with tactics, strategies and painful experience.

By the time they sighted the building that served as the SOB headquarters, night had fallen. They gazed silently at the structure, noting it was far larger than any of the huts, long and rambling, with a covered veranda running its entire length.

"I think this place used to be a restaurant. A pretty famous one, too," Brigid said softly.

Kane grunted disinterestedly and with hand gestures indicated that Brady and Edwards were to take up positions on either side of the main entrance. When the two men were in place, Kane waited and listened.

The trees in the vicinity swayed a little in the slow breeze. The underbrush rustled. The far-off shrieking of humans in pain or in anger reached his ears.

He stepped forward and whispered, "I'm going in first."

Neither Grant, Domi nor Brigid objected. Kane always assumed the position of point man. It was a habit he had acquired during his years as a Magistrate and he saw no reason to abandon it. His three teammates had the utmost faith in Kane's instincts.

During his Mag days, because of his uncanny ability to sniff out approaching danger, he was always chosen to act as the advance scout. When he walked point, Kane felt electrically alive, sharply tuned to every nuance of his surroundings and what he was doing.

When he reached the steps leading up to the veranda, he fell into a crouch, stiffening his right wrist tendons. Sensitive actuators clicked and with a faint, brief drone of a tiny electric motor, the butt of his Sin Eater slapped into his hand.

The official sidearm of the defunct Magistrate divisions, the 9 mm autopistol had no safety or trigger guard, so when the firing stud came in contact with a crooked index finger, it fired immediately. However, Kane kept his finger extended and out of contact with the trigger stud.

Through his Commtact, he subvocalized, "I'm going in. Keep alert."

"Yes, sir," Brady said.

"Got it, Commander," Edwards said.

Creeping up the sagging steps, he entered the open door of the building. By the amber beam of his Nighthawk flashlight strapped around his right wrist, he saw a big open space full of rickety-looking chairs and tables. The cloying stench of human sweat, marijuana and an untended latrine clung to the air.

Back pressed against the wall just inside the door, he waited, casting the flashlight around, straining to hear even a hint of sound or catch even a flicker of movement. When he saw and heard nothing, he whispered, "Brady, Edwards—move on in. Baptiste—you, Domi and Grant can come up, too. I think this place is deserted."

As Edwards and Brady entered, Kane moved deeper into the room. He found a flare-topped kerosene lantern on one of the tables. The fuel well was full, so he lit the wick with a simple flint-and-steel lighter he carried. The two ex-Mags carefully scanned the area, walking heel to toe.

The pale yellow radiance showed very little except rough-hewed furniture and a very dirty floor. He saw a table holding Grant's clothing and his boots. When

Brigid, Domi and Grant came in, he pointed out
the items.

Uttering a grunt of triumph, Grant sat on a stool and
pulled on his boots. As he quickly laced them up,
Edwards returned and said, "Nobody is here. They
cleared out with the rest of the scum."

"They didn't take Wright with them. Look at the far
end of the room," Grant said flatly.

Brady and Edwards moved in the direction he indicated, sidling among the tables. They used their Night-
hawks to illuminate their way. The amber glow cast a
sickly illumination on the maimed body of the woman,
still dangling from the meat hooks.

Reflexively, Brigid put a hand to her mouth, but she
didn't turn away and neither did Domi. Both of them
had witnessed any number of atrocities over the years,
and although they weren't inured to them, they no
longer overtly reacted with horror to the sight.

Placing the lamp on a table and stepping closer to her
body, Kane growled between clenched teeth, "Why the
fuck would he do that to her?"

Grant stood up, stamping down to settle his boots.
"Because he could."

"Like you said," Domi bit out. "Evil."

Brigid called in an unsteady voice, "Can't you get
her down from there?"

Brady and Edwards cast Kane questioning glances
and he nodded. "See what you can do."

The two men leaned their rifles against the wall in a

corner and walked around the woman's hanging body, examining how deeply the hooks were sunk into it. Both of their faces remained dispassionate masks, as per their training. Like Grant and Kane, they had been taught the technique of detaching themselves from their emotions in the performance of ghastly chores.

Edwards pulled up a chair and climbed atop it while Brady took hold of Wright's legs and pushed upward. Quickly, Edwards detached the sharp points of the hooks from the woman's flesh and muscle.

Working together, they disengaged her and carefully lifted her down, carrying her over to a large table. With a surprisingly gentle touch, the pair of ex-Mags laid her down and folded her arms over her chest. Edwards pulled her lids down over her glazed eyes.

"Thank you," Brigid said quietly.

Brady nodded. "Yes, ma'am."

He returned to the corner to retrieve their weapons. As he turned to retrace his steps, he stopped suddenly, a frown creasing his forehead. Looking down, he stamped his foot on the floor.

"What is it?" Kane called.

Brady lightly rapped the floorboards with the butt of a rifle. Everyone heard an unmistakable hollow echo. "I think I've found something."

Setting aside the rifles, Brady shone his flash down, illuminating a thread-thin outline of a trapdoor. "This is how the bastards got away."

Unsheathing his combat knife, he jammed the steel

blade into the narrow slit between the edge of the hatch and the flooring. "It's locked from the underside, but I can jimmy it."

Cold suddenly brushed Kane's spine and alarm jerked through the nerve endings of his body. Loudly, he said, "Brady, get away from there—"

An explosion flamed orange and yellow. The blast filled the air with broken wood and flying debris, the concussion feeling like a fist of hot air. Kane staggered, shielding his eyes as splinters rained around him like grapeshot.

Chapter 8

The eruption of flame dazzled everyone's eyes and the detonation nearly deafened them. The concussion was like a battering ram of hot, almost solid air swatting Kane backward, cartwheeling him head-over-heels. The heat seared his face. He slammed against the floor with a body-numbing jolt.

Kane lay motionless for a moment, eyes stinging from the smoke, the stink of scorched human flesh and the chemical reek of kerosene and high explosives thick in his nostrils. His stunned eardrums registered little more than a surflike throb. A fine rain of pulverized wood pattered onto him.

Dizzy, ears ringing, Kane fought to his feet, clearing his vision with swipes of his hands. He peered through the scraps of smoke, settling dust and swirling wood particles. He barely made out a welter of smoldering, splintered floorboards, punched up from below. There was no sign of Brady.

The explosion had overturned the lamp but had snuffed out the wick before it could ignite the spilled kerosene. Kane cast his flash toward his friends, but at first he couldn't see them through billowing smoke. As his hearing recovered, he heard Domi swearing fiercely.

He squinted through the haze, his body feeling like a gong that been struck with a sledgehammer. His entire skeleton seemed to shiver and vibrate in the echoes of the explosion.

He saw Grant, Domi, Brigid and Edwards slowly staggering to their feet, looking around dazedly. Except for a couple of raw nicks on Edwards's bare arms, nobody looked injured.

"Booby-trapped," Grant announced, his voice sounding eerily muffled in the wake of the detonation. "Should've figured."

"I did," Kane bit out. "But about two seconds too late. Is everybody all right?"

Brigid slapped at her clothes, brushing away splinters and dust. "Think so. Domi?"

"Yeah," the albino girl said hoarsely, shaking fragments of wood out of her hair. "Where's Brady?"

Edwards stumbled through the planes of smoke, kicking rubble out of his way, stepping over Wright's body. The beam of his flashlight cut pale threads through the roiling vapors. He coughed and said quietly, "Here he is."

Kane, Brigid, Grant and Domi went to his side, fanning away smoke. They saw Edwards kneeling beside a blackened, man-shaped scarecrow. Brady's face was covered by red raw patches and he breathed in shallow, whistling gasps. His shirt hung in tatters, clinging to the third-degree burns on his torso.

"He's still alive," Edwards said in surprise. "Just barely and God knows how, but he's still alive."

Kane gazed down at what was left of Brady's face, and anger built inside him. It was an impersonal kind of anger, subsumed by resolve. He knew with a great and irrevocable certainty that neither he nor Grant nor Brigid would leave Manhattan until they found the men responsible for setting the trap and for murdering Wright.

Brigid touched his arm. "We need to get Brady to the gateway and back to Cerberus as soon as possible, if there's any chance of saving his life."

Kane nodded curtly. "Edwards, give Grant your sidearm."

Edwards peered at him in confusion, then unholstered the VP-70 and handed it to Grant butt-first. "I don't understand."

"You and Domi can rig up a litter to carry Brady to the gateway," Kane continued. "I'm afraid we'll have to leave Wright where she is for the time being."

"What are you going to do?" Domi demanded.

With a wave of one hand, Kane indicated himself, Brigid and Grant. "We're going to track down Shuma and Esau."

Edwards stared at him incredulously. "Just the three of you?"

"The three heads of Cerberus," Kane declared.

Edwards nodded grimly in understanding and attended to Brady. Grant checked the action of the VP-70. "You'd better get moving before it gets much darker."

"I'll make sure Brady gets home," Edwards declared matter-of-factly. "Don't worry about that."

Both Grant and Kane knew that the bond between Magistrates could sometimes be closer than those shared by family members. For most Mags, the divisions in which they served took the place of conventional family units, and their fellow enforcers were brothers and shield mates.

A century before, the Magistrate Divisions were formed as a complex police machine that demanded instant obedience to its edicts and to which there was no possible protest. Over the past century, both the oligarchy of barons and the Mags who served them had taken on a fearful, almost legendary aspect. Kane and Grant had been part of that legend, cogs in a merciless machine.

All Magistrates followed a patrilineal tradition, assuming the duties and positions of their fathers before them. They did not have given names, each taking the surname of the father, as though the first Magistrate to bear the name were the same man as the last. The originators of the Magistrate Divisions had believed that family names engendered a sense of obligation to the duties of their ancestors' office, ensuring that subsequent generations never lost touch with their hereditary roles as enforcers. Last names became badges of social distinction, almost titles.

But old Magistrate habits died very hard, particularly because of the rigorous discipline to which they had submitted themselves. Casting aside their identities as Mags and accepting new roles as rebels and exiles hadn't been easy for either Kane or Grant, and it was doubly difficult for former enforcers like Edwards and Brady, who had been driven from their respective villes after the infrastructure of baronial authority collapsed.

Although they never admitted it to each other, Kane and Grant sometimes yearned to return to the regimentation and routine of their former lives. If nothing else, the world had made more sense back then.

Kane examined the splintered ruin of the trapdoor, toeing aside the flinders. "A grenade was most likely wired to the catch."

Brigid shone her flash into the dark aperture, looking past the jagged fragments of wood that edged it. The light did not penetrate very far, but a faint, foul odor rose from the opening, carrying with it fetid reek of sewage. Faintly they heard the trickle and drip of water.

The metal rungs of a ladder ran down one side of the shaft into the dimness. The walls were made of heavy, mortared concrete blocks. The shaft was a perfect circle, six feet in diameter.

"This goes down into the sewer system," Brigid remarked uneasily.

"Appropriate," Grant replied, tucking the VP-70 into the waistband of his pants.

Brigid glanced from him to Kane. "You two are taking this very personally. Don't get reckless."

Kane smiled coldly, but he didn't disagree. Although in his youth he had been a hellion who laughingly charged headlong into danger, now he was less the happy lunatic than a seasoned warrior who had a natural tendency to hesitate before climbing down into a foul-smelling black hole.

"I'll go first if you want," Grant offered.

Kane shook his head. "Why break with tradition?"

As he sat down on the edge of the aperture and inched his legs over the hole, Domi called out, "If you're not back in Cerberus within an hour after we get there, I'm coming back here with enough firepower to level this whole fuckin' island. So if I were you, I wouldn't sightsee."

Kane grinned crookedly. "That's the kind of time-table I like to work under, thanks."

Before she turned her attention to Brady, Domi touched her right index finger to her nose and snapped it away in a wry "one percent" salute. It was a private gesture Grant and Kane had developed during their years as hard contact Magistrates and reserved for undertakings with small ratios of success. Over the years of working with the two men, Domi had borrowed the gesture.

Kane returned the salute, eased over the edge and began to climb down. Grant waited until he had descended halfway before swinging his legs over and out. Brigid followed him.

The ladder rungs descended about twenty feet. At the bottom of the shaft, they sank ankle deep in mud and algae, staring into a tube made of rusty metal, featureless except for ridges where the sections of pipe were welded. It stretched out as far as they could see.

Brigid, Kane and Grant put on dark-lensed glasses. The electrochemical polymer of the lenses gathered all available light and made the most of it to give them a limited form of night vision.

Kane eased out into the shaft, Sin Eater in hand, walking heel to toe in the characteristic way of a Mag penetrating a potential killzone. Brigid followed, with Grant bringing up the rear. The tube was narrow, its diameter not permitting them to walk side by side or to stand fully upright. The passageway was very quiet, as if upon entering it they had stepped into a vault that hoarded only silence.

The metal walls dripped with slime. Now and then they curved, first left, then right. Casting the amber beams of their flashlights ahead of them, they walked as quickly as the slippery footing allowed. The shaft sloped sharply upward and water dripped down steadily from splits in the welds.

"That's not a good sign," Brigid murmured.

"Why not?" Grant asked.

"We could be walking under the East River...or a reservoir."

Kane tamped down a surge of claustrophobia, but he kept moving forward through the putrid quagmire, his back beginning to ache from being bent over. The tunnel leveled out, and he thought he saw a glimmer of light far in the distance. It wavered like a ghostly candle flame.

The shaft opened onto a ledge overlooking a concrete channel sunk ten or so feet below it. On either side reared high bulwarks of stone. The brickwork and concrete blocks were coated by damp green moss. The man-made canal stretched to a circular grating made of rusted metal slats, through which water flowed slug-gishly.

The three people climbed down a short ladder to the edge of the channel and walked toward the grate. Rats, some of them as big as domestic cats, scuttled away at their approach. A few of the bolder ones stopped after their initial fright and reared up on their hind legs to sniff at them as they passed by.

Brigid did a very poor job of repressing a shudder of revulsion. Her loathing for rodents went far deeper than a simple antipathy for filth-wallowing vermin. A few years before, she had undergone a nightmarish experi-ence with plague-infected rats in the bayous of Loui-siana.

They walked swiftly toward the grate. The dark water bubbled and roiled as they went past, as if some-thing very large stirred on the bottom, aware of their presence.

When they reached the grate, Grant put his shoulder against it, pushing hard, digging his toes into the concrete. It didn't budge. Kane pulled on it, but the barrier was firmly fixed in place. Grant shook it experimentally. Metal clanked and rattled on the exterior.

Inserting his hands between the iron slats, Kane touched a heavy chain and a padlock. "It's buttoned up, but I can probably pick the lock open."

A faint rustling and clicking sound came from behind them. Brigid turned toward it and saw a surging motion in the shadows on either side of the channel. The amber beam of her light glinted from tiny red sparks that seemed to ooze out of the gloom. The flashlight beam illuminated a multitude of beady eyes, whiskered snouts and champing incisor teeth.

She couldn't help but draw in her breath sharply and cringe against the wall. Puzzled, Grant and Kane turned their heads toward her. In a voice tight with tension, she whispered, *"Rats."*

"What about them?" Kane demanded, his hands still exploring the lock and chain on the outside of the grate.

A rat launched itself toward them. Grant squeezed off a shot from his VP-70, and the rodent went twisting backward, trailing bits of skull bone and brain matter.

Kane withdrew his hands from between the slats of metal, his Sin Eater popping into his palm. He threw Grant a fleeting wry grin. "Too bad I didn't have any jack riding on you making that shot."

During his many years as a Magistrate, Grant had

often dumbfounded his colleagues with his snap shots, as accurate as they were uncannily swift. He had won a number of contests, competing with his fellow Mags and always outshooting any self-styled marksmen that the academy produced.

A chittering squeal arose from the mass of rats, high-pitched, angry and threatening. Unlimbering her Copperhead and placing the butt against her shoulder, Brigid said, "This brings back memories…not very nice ones. They're regrouping for an attack."

"How the hell can that be?" Kane snarled.

"Esau," Grant stated. "He's controlling them…has to be."

"Even so, a couple dozen rats aren't going to give us much trouble," Kane said, aiming his Sin Eater at the rodents.

Suddenly, the dark water in the channel erupted. With a hissing bellow, a huge shape heaved itself out of the muck. Despite the mud clinging to its scaled and armored form, the hide was pale, almost a fish-belly white. Fang-lined jaws opened with a pop.

"Oh, for the love of—" Kane exclaimed. "Don't tell me—"

"Afraid so," Brigid said. "One of the legendary alligators in the sewers."

Chapter 9

"And under the control of Esau," Grant interjected dolefully. "Just like the goddamned rats."

The alligator looked to be about ten feet long, with splotches of yellow running along its thick, glistening body. With several lumbering steps of its stubby legs, the reptile climbed completely out of the channel. Its jaws gaped wide, showing the dark ivory points of many teeth.

Kane's stomach jumped in adrenaline-fueled spasms. Although he had always prided himself on being free of phobias, he had developed a fear of things reptilian over the past few years. It wasn't an irrational fear, but one derived from terrifying firsthand experience.

Brigid switched on the Copperhead's laser autotargeter and centered a pinpoint of blood-hued light between the creature's eyes. "You'd think it would be more interested in eating rats than us."

"Wouldn't you?" Kane snapped sarcastically, sliding his Sin Eater back into the forearm holster. He drew his combat knife and put his hands through the metal slats again. His fingers fumbled with the lock, probing at it with the point of the blade. "Just keep it off my ass long enough for me to get this open."

The rats milled around them in a crescent, chittering and squealing in agitation.

"Keeping the gator off your ass is one thing," Grant said. "The rats are another."

"Just do the best you can—" Kane broke off when a callused hand suddenly closed around his right wrist, squeezing it in powerful grip.

"Is Grant with you?" a woman's vibrant voice demanded.

Kane squinted between the slats, seeing a tall, scar-faced woman sporting a ridiculously high crest of hair. He answered, "Yeah, he's right behind me. Can I tell him the Merry Widow is inquiring about him?"

She chuckled and released him. "You're Kane, right?"

"That's me. Pleased to make your formal acquaintance after all these years."

"Step back," the Merry Widow commanded, settling the stock of a Stoner machine gun at her shoulder. "I'm going to shoot the lock off."

"Up against the wall," Kane said to his friends.

Brigid and Grant obeyed, their eyes and gun barrels still trained upon the hissing alligator and the squealing rodents.

The staccato jackhammering of autofire echoed hollowly in the shaft, punctuated by the keening whines of ricochets. Stray slugs punched into the mass of rats, scraps of fur and blood spraying in all directions. With a snuffling grunt, the alligator snapped its jaws shut on the morsels. Bones crunched loudly.

When the barrage ceased, Kane hazarded a quick glance through the slats of the grate and saw the Merry Widow pound at the chain with the stock of her weapon.

Metal clattered and clanked to the ground. "Done!" she announced. "Push it open!"

Grant and Kane threw their bodies against the heavy metal portal, which swung open ponderously on squealing hinges. At the movement, the alligator lunged forward, blood-rimmed jaws gaping wide.

Brigid stroked a 3-round burst from her Copperhead, and the bullets plunged into the reptile's dark gullet. Emitting a hissing screech, the alligator went into convulsions, writhing and thrashing, its body spasming wildly. The muscular tail whiplashed and sent rats flying.

The creature flipped and flopped madly, as if its brain refused to admit that its body was dying. Rolling over and over, it crushed several rats beneath it, then fell into the channel with a great splash. The heavy flailing tail sent spuming sheets of muddy water cascading over the concrete floor.

The Cerberus warrior rushed out into a deep culvert. The Merry Widow and two of her men stood nearby. One of them wore a scarlet headband, and the other had a single loop of silver hanging from his nose. Both men glared at the three people with thinly disguised hatred.

"Thanks," Kane panted, glancing behind him to make sure no rats scuttled in pursuit.

The Merry Widow chuckled. "Don't mention it. You're after Shuma, right?"

"Right," Grant replied. "And that sick little mind-mutie, Esau."

"I know where they are," she declared matter-of-factly. "Do you want me to lead you to them?"

Brigid eyed her suspiciously. "Why are you making the offer?"

The woman shrugged. "I don't like muties and I 'specially don't like muties with 'tudes."

Grant smiled sourly. "There's a little more to it than that. A hell of a lot of scummy Roamers and slag-assed Farers are suddenly without a leader to rally around, right?"

The woman matched Grant's smile with a wintry one of her own. "Wouldn't you rather have somebody like me in charge than Shuma?"

Kane shrugged. "I haven't really thought about it. But if you know where Shuma and Esau have holed up, why didn't you smoke them out yourself?"

"I tried," the Merry Widow answered. "I chased 'em down and I'm pretty sure I winged Shuma, but he was shielding Esau with his own body. I decided to let you three have a crack at him."

"Not to mention," Brigid interposed, "that if we three take care of him, none of his followers will hold you responsible for his death."

The woman's smile widened, but it didn't reach her eyes. "Something like that."

Kane gestured grandly. "Point taken. Lead on."

The six people struggled up the sloping side of the culvert, their feet slipping on the slimy slabs of concrete. The climb was strenuous, and the various pains in Grant's body returned with a vengeance. The concrete was smooth, and footholds were hard to come by. Most of the handholds were mere slits between slabs of the concrete, but he wedged his fingers in and pulled himself along.

Once they were out on the street, the Merry Widow and her men marched between buildings that were little more than hollow shells. Bricks had fallen from the walls, and none of the windows had glass. Pieces of rotten wood lay about the foundations like detritus from a dead forest.

The mounds of dirt and rubble on either side of the avenue had been leached over the years by the elements, so they had spread, smothering the pavements and sidewalks and making a new, mulchy floor for the dead city. Huge cracks seamed the pavement.

They walked through the concrete gullies of overgrown and blackened bricks. They passed the remains of several trucks and smaller automobiles. The bodywork had long ago been stripped bare of paint and they were only husks of flaking rust.

The Merry Widow came to a halt and pointed to a sprawling flat-roofed brick structure that looked very old. Inscribed on a pediment above a flight of stone steps were the words Gate House No. 5, Jerome Park Reservoir.

"They're holed up in there," the scar-faced woman announced, saluting the building. "He had a couple of men with him."

Kane visually inspected the structure, then glanced her way. "Are you going in with us?"

The Merry Widow regarded him with a look of feigned innocence. "The big-bad baron blasters don't need the help of any scummy Roamers, do they?"

"No," Brigid snapped, pushing past her.

Grant favored the woman with a slit-eyed stare. "Stay out here, then. But if this is a trap you're part of—"

He said nothing more. There was no need. She nodded curtly that she understood the implicit threat.

The Cerberus warriors circled the building, their shadows lost among the shadows of the brush. A little stream of water tricked from somewhere, turning the ground to sludge. Now and then they stopped to listen but they heard no sound from within the building.

"I think we've been had, girls," Kane murmured.

Then, for an instant so brief it was almost a subliminal impression, they saw the faint flicker of a flame from within the building.

"Somebody is in there," Brigid whispered.

"We might as well assume it's Shuma and Esau," Grant said. "If you face Esau, don't make eye contact."

"I don't plan on getting that close," Kane intoned.

They backtracked to the front entrance. Taking the point, Kane went up the steps at an oblique angle from the dark doorway. Motioning the people behind him to stop, Kane went to one knee, taking a slow visual assessment of the murky area beyond the doors. Fresh blood glistened in spatters on the stonework. He saw no signs of movement within. Standing up, he gestured for his companions to come forward.

"Standard deployment," he said to them quietly.

The three people fanned out in a wedge as they stepped inside the building. Brigid held her TP-9 in a two-fisted grip, the barrel as steady as stone. Next to her, Grant held the VP-70 with both hands, bore downward.

The beam from his Nighthawk showed Kane a foyerlike room and short corridor beyond. He moved in fast, shifting the barrel of his Sin Eater back and forth. The others came in behind him, moving to his right and left.

Kane crept down the hallway, walking heel to toe. When he reached the open doorway at the end, he came to a halt and cocked his head, listening. He thought he heard someone take a deep breath, but he wasn't sure. He decided to take no chances. He had been sandbagged too often in the past when he entered unlit rooms.

He unclipped an Alsatex flash-bang grenade from his combat webbing, tweaked away the pin, slipped the spoon and lobbed the cylinder underhanded into the room. It struck the floor and bounced. A male voice yelled in wordless fright. The echoes were swallowed up by an eardrum-piercing bang. The eruption of white light turned the dark room into high noon for a split second.

Almost at once Kane rushed in low and saw two men writhing on the floor, hands clapped over their eyes. They howled in pain. A revolver lay between them, and Grant kicked it away. A flight of metal stairs stretched up into the darkness, and from above they heard the scuff and scutter of running feet. A shout of alarm reverberated through the building.

Kane ran to the staircase and took the risers three at a time. Grant and Brigid followed closely. On a landing, they paused to look through an open door and glimpsed the yellow glare of a lantern deep in the gloom.

The Cerberus warriors sprinted along a narrow catwalk. Foul smells wafted up from below, the stench of dead animals rotting away in pools of stagnant water. At the end of the catwalk Kane paused to catch his breath. In a room beyond, a torch sputtered in a wall sconce.

Kane moved toward it, then he heard a snort, a thump of running feet, and a huge bulk collided with him with enough force to pick him up and slam him against the wall. Massive paws caught at his throat.

Smelling blood and sweat, Kane fought off the great scaled arms that tried to crush him. Shuma's enormous weight pinned him to the wall, pressing his Sin Eater crossways against his midriff.

Grant hammered at the back of his skull with the barrel of the VP-70. Shuma paid no attention. He was already in so much pain from the bullet wounds inflicted on him that additional blows were little more than pinches.

He struck out blindly behind him with a beam-sized arm, sending Grant staggering into Brigid. His movement freed Kane's arm and he whipped up the bore of his pistol, planting the muzzle under Shuma's chin. He depressed the trigger stud. Three rounds exploded through the top of the scalie's head as if a grenade had detonated within it. The acrid stink of powder-burned flesh cut into Kane's nostrils.

Shuma's great body toppled sideways, as if his bones had suddenly turned to soft tallow. A slurry of blood and brain matter oozed from the cavity in his cranium.

Kane stood over him, breathing hard, noting the three bullet holes in his upper torso. "He was dying anyway…the Merry Widow was a lot more accurate than she thought."

Brigid nodded, her face looking paper-pale in the light cast from the Nighthawk. "More than likely Esau kept him going."

"That's *exactly* what Esau did," said a soft lisping voice from the darkness behind them.

The Cerberus warriors whirled. At first they saw only a dim, malformed outline, then two pinpoints of red flamed in the darkness. Swiftly, they aimed their pistols at the figure, but their index fingers didn't constrict around the triggers. Kane, Brigid and Grant felt their joints locking in place, seizing tight. At the same time, blinding pain drove into their heads like white-hot railroad spikes.

Clenching his teeth so hard he heard them squeak, Kane watched Esau shamble forward, propelled by his crutches. Veins pulsed and swelled on his high forehead.

Esau's voice purred with amused triumph. "I'm more powerful than you could have imagined. You may have killed Shuma, but I can find other figureheads, other puppets."

His small mouth curved in a smile as his huge eyes stared unblinkingly at the three of them. "My ambitions have just begun. Perhaps I'll visit this New Edo place that holds such a prominent place in Mr. Grant's mind."

Grant growled deep in his throat, funneling all of his concentration and willpower on his hand, commanding his finger to squeeze the VP-70's trigger. His entire arm trembled.

Esau's smug smile faltered and the mapwork of broken veins spreading down from his hairline gleamed with a fine sheen of sweat.

Hoarsely, Brigid bit out, "All of us…*focus*…working together…we can beat him."

Esau's eyes flicked toward her. Brigid's breath suddenly became a series of labored wheezes. She swayed, her back arching as if she had received a violent blow between her shoulder blades. Her eyes rolled, showing only the whites. Threads of blood inched from her nostrils.

"Stop it, you little bastard," Kane husked out.

"I've barely begun," Esau whispered. "You need an example of the extent of my abilities, and since Miss Baptiste drew my attention, she will suffice."

Tendons stood out in relief on Brigid's slender neck and her lips drew away from her teeth in a rictus of agony. She cried out sharply.

Kane tried to depress the trigger stud of the Sin Eater, but his hand froze, the metacarpal bones and the tendons locking in a painful cramp. He managed to gasp out, "Stop it!"

Esau tittered. "Save your breath, Mr. Kane. You have very little left to you. I shall make certain of that."

A gun roared, echoing like thunder in the corridor. The top of Esau's scalp lifted, red spraying out around it in fine mist. He blinked in confusion, right before a cascade of blood flowed down over his eyes. An unintelligible garble came from his mouth. He uttered a sorrowful sigh. Instantly, the barrels of the pistols in Kane and Grant's fists spit flame, their fingers convulsing on the triggers at the same time.

Six bullets punched into Esau's misshapen body, bowling him backward, the crutches clattering beneath him.

Brigid sagged and would have fallen if Kane hadn't stretched out an arm to catch her. She put a hand to her face to staunch the flow of the blood from her nostrils, then she bent her head and vomited onto the floor.

Sweat pouring down his face, Grant kept his gun trained on the crumpled form of Esau, watching for any sign of life. Only when the tall figure of the Merry Widow stepped out of the shadows, her Stoner machine gun at her shoulder, did Grant look away from the corpse.

She marched up to Esau, aimed carefully at his head and fired once more. The echoes of the cracking report bounced back and forth.

The Merry Widow stared steadily at the three out-landers. "You made a mistake not killing him the first time. I wasn't about to repeat it."

Brigid straightened, wiping her mouth with the back of her hand. In a strained, raw voice she said, "Thank you."

The woman grinned lopsidedly. "I guess the big, bad baron blasters needed the help of a scummy Roamer after all, didn't they?"

For a long moment no one answered. Then Kane replied genially, "As a point of fact, they did. First time for everything, I guess."

Chapter 10

Brigid clenched her teeth but didn't flinch as Reba DeFore shone the pencil flash first into her right, then her left eye. The brightness felt like a blade stabbing at her retina.

The medic grunted softly and clicked off the light. With a gentle touch, she eased Brigid's head back. "You're not in any pain?"

Brigid hesitated. "Well—"

"And if you say, 'Think I'd tell you?' I'll prescribe a brine-and-lye suppository."

Sitting on the edge of an examination table, Brigid forced a chuckle. "I *do* have a headache…ringing in my ears, too."

"I don't doubt it." DeFore's full lips pursed. A stocky, buxom woman with deep bronze skin, ash-blond hair braided at the back of her head and liquid brown eyes, she had served as the Cerberus chief medical officer for the better part of a decade.

"Why do you say that?" Brigid asked.

DeFore eyed her critically. "You display all the signs of suffering from a concussion, except for head trauma."

Brigid shifted uneasily. "Like I explained, it was a psionic assault, not a physical one, although I was affected physically…hemorrhaging and extreme nausea. Kane and Grant were affected, too."

DeFore gave her an appraising stare. "You're the only one showing these kind of symptoms, though. Could be a byproduct of the head injury you suffered a few years back."

Brigid nodded but said nothing, remembering the duel with the vicious Otto Skorzeny in Antarctica. The only visible sign of the wound that had laid her scalp open to the bone and put her in a coma for several days was a faintly red horizontal line on her right temple that disappeared into the roots of her red-gold hair.

Stepping to a cabinet, DeFore removed a small bottle filled with yellow capsules. Uncapping it with a thumb, she shook out two of them into Brigid's hand and gave her a cup of water. "Swallow these and let me know how you feel in an hour."

As Brigid did as she said, Kane appeared in the doorway, dressed much like her in a black T-shirt, jeans and white sneakers. "How are you doing, Baptiste?"

Brigid indicated DeFore with a nod. "Ask the doctor."

DeFore turned toward him. "She's showing signs of a concussion, including a case of tinnitus, but I can't find any sign of a trauma to her head. If the symptoms don't go away in twelve hours, I think we should perform an EEG. But in my estimation, her condition isn't serious."

Brigid frowned. "Too bad the same can't be said for Wright and Brady."

Kane sighed, folding his arms over his chest. "Yeah, it was a bad break. But our casualties could've been worse."

DeFore scowled toward him. "That's your standard response. Killing back what killed our people doesn't change anything, Kane. Our people are still dead."

He lifted a shoulder in a shrug. "Every day you're alive is just another spin of the wheel. Winning is just breaking even."

"Yeah, I've heard that macho crap before," DeFore said irritably. "Save it for your new Cerberus away team recruits."

Kane kept his expression composed, even though DeFore glared at him angrily. At one time, the medic had been openly antagonistic toward him—or rather what he represented. As a former Magistrate, Kane embodied the totalitarianism of the villes, glorying in his baron-sanctioned powers to dispense justice and death.

For a couple of years DeFore had believed that due to his Mag conditioning he was psychologically conflicted and therefore couldn't be trusted. Although she had reevaluated her attitude, DeFore was still quick to take offense at his offhand philosophizing about life and death.

Brigid didn't comment on Kane's apparent callous attitude. Brady had died while Domi and Edwards were carrying him to the mat-trans unit. Kane, Grant and Brigid had retrieved Wright's body, and both people lay in the morgue adjacent to the infirmary, awaiting burial.

Cerberus had lost a number of personnel over the past couple of years, but repetition did not make the losses easier to deal with. Kane adopted a stoic demeanor about casualties, but Brigid wasn't fooled by it.

"Lakesh is waiting for us to join the debrief. He's pretty impatient," Kane said blandly.

"What else is new?" Easing off the table, Brigid grabbed the edge as the floor tilted beneath her feet. Kane reached for her, but she waved him off. She smiled wanly as the surge of dizziness passed. "I'm all right."

Straightening up, she tugged down her T-shirt, thanked DeFore and stepped out into the twenty-foot-wide main corridor of the Cerberus redoubt with Kane by her side. They had returned to the installation less than three hours before, arriving barely in time to head off a rescue expedition led by Domi.

As they strode down the corridor, they noticed heads of men and women turning toward them, the glances respectful and even embarrassingly admiring. Kane, Brigid, Grant and even Domi were considered something special among the personnel. The actions performed by the four of them had quite literally saved the world, more than once.

"Just an FYI," Kane muttered dourly. "Lakesh isn't happy about what he's heard so far about the Newyork op. He's of the opinion we might've left loose ends that could endanger the redoubt."

Brigid shook her head in exasperation. "He's a good one to talk, with some of the stuff he's pulled over the years."

Although Cerberus had been constructed to provide a comfortable home for well over a hundred people, it had pretty much been deserted for nearly two centuries. When she, Kane, Grant and Domi arrived at the installation over five years before, there had been only a dozen permanent residents. Like them, all of the personnel were exiles from the villes recruited by Lakesh because of their training and abilities. For a long time, shadowed corridors, empty rooms and sepulchral silences outnumbered the Cerberus personnel.

Over the past three years, the corridors had bustled with life, the empty rooms filled and the silences replaced by conversation and laughter. The immigrants from the Manitius Moon base had made the installation their home, although some of them divided their time between Earth and the Luna colony. Since the fall of the baronies and the rising threat of the overlords, most of the émigrés had shown a disinclination to wander too far from the Cerberus redoubt. As the installation became more crowded, Kane felt less content to stay there for any length of time. The pull of adventure, of exploring the remote places, grew stronger with every passing day. Despite the sense of danger, he also experienced a profound sense of peace while in the wild regions. Regardless of his growing sense of claustro-phobia, he still considered the Cerberus facility his home.

The three score people who currently lived in the Cerberus redoubt, regardless of their skills, acted pri-marily in the capacity of support personnel. They worked rotating shifts, eight hours a day, seven days a week. For the most part, their work was the routine maintenance and monitoring of the installation's envi-ronmental systems, the satellite data feed, the security network. However, everyone had been given at least a superficial understanding of all the redoubt's systems, so they could pinch-hit in times of emergency.

Constructed in the mid-1990s, no expense had been spared to make the redoubt, the seat of Project Cerberus, a masterpiece of concealment and impenetrability. The Cerberus process, a subdivision of Overproject Whisper, had been a primary component of the Totality Concept. The researches to which Project Cerberus and its personnel had been devoted were locating and trav-eling hyperdimensional pathways through the quantum stream.

Once that had been accomplished, the redoubt became, from the end of one millennium to the begin-ning of another, a manufacturing facility. The quantum interphase mat-trans inducers, known colloquially as "gateways," were built in modular form and shipped to other redoubts. Most of the related overprojects had their own hidden bases. The official designations of the redoubts had been based on the old phonetic alphabet code used in military radio communications. On the few existing records, the Cerberus installation was listed as Redoubt Bravo, but the handful of people who had made the facility their home for the past few years never referred to it as such.

Built primarily of vanadium alloy, the Cerberus redoubt was designed for a self-sufficient community of at least a hundred people, although Lakesh preferred to think of the trilevel, thirty-acre facility as a sanctuary. The installation contained a frightfully well-equipped armory and two dozen self-contained apartments, a cafeteria, a decontamination center, an infirmary, a swimming pool and even detention cells on the bottom level.

The Cerberus redoubt had weathered the nuclear holocaust of 2001 and all the subsequent earth changes. Its radiation shielding was still intact, and its nuclear generators still provided an almost eternal source of power. The facility also had a limestone filtration system that continually recycled the complex's water supply.

When Mohandas Lakesh Singh secretly reactivated the installation over thirty years earlier, the repairs he made had been minor, primarily cosmetic in nature. Over a period of time, he had added an elaborate system of heat-sensing warning devices, night-vision vid cameras and motion-trigger alarms to the plateau surrounding the redoubt.

He had been forced to work completely alone, so the upgrades had taken several years to complete. However, the location of the redoubt in Montana's Bitterroot Range had kept his work from being discovered by the baronial authorities.

In the generations since the nukecaust, a sinister mythology had been ascribed to the mountains, with their mysteriously shadowed forests and hell-deep, dangerous ravines. The wilderness area was virtually unpopulated. The nearest settlement was located in the flatlands, and it consisted of a small band of Indians, Sioux and Cheyenne, led by a shaman named Sky Dog.

Planted within rocky clefts of the mountain peak beneath camouflage netting were concealed the uplinks from an orbiting Vela-class reconnaissance satellite and a Comsat.

The road leading down from Cerberus to the foothills was little more than a cracked and twisted asphalt ribbon, skirting yawning chasms and cliffs. Acres of the mountainsides had collapsed during the nuke-triggered earthquakes nearly two centuries earlier.

"Lakesh is raising the issue of discontinuing the away-team program again," Kane said.

Brigid nodded, then winced. "It doesn't take much for him to want to talk about that."

Kane eyed her intently. "Are you sure you're all right?"

"I'm *always* all right," she replied curtly. "After five years of being shot at together, you should know better than to ask that question."

When Kane didn't respond, she smiled wryly to let him know she was only joking. When she and Kane were first thrown together, their relationship had been volatile, marked by frequent quarrels, jealousies and resentments. The world in which she came of age was primarily quiet, focused on scholarly pursuits.

Kane's was a world of daily violence and was supported by a belief system that demanded a ruthless single-mindedness to enforce baronial authority. Both people had their gifts. Most of what was important to people in the twenty-third century came easily to Kane—survival skills, prevailing in the face of adversity and cunning against enemies. But he could also be reckless, high-strung to the point of instability and given to fits of rage.

Brigid, on the other hand, was compulsively tidy and ordered, with a brilliant analytical mind. However, her clinical nature, the cool scientific detachment upon which she prided herself, sometimes blocked an understanding of the obvious human factor in any given situation.

Regardless of their contrasting personalities, Kane and Brigid worked very well as a team, playing on each other's strengths rather than contributing to their individual weaknesses. Despite their differences, or perhaps because of them, the two people managed to forge the chains of partnership, which linked them through mutual respect and trust.

Only once had the links of that chain been stretched

to the breaking point. More than a year earlier Kane had shot and killed a woman, a distant relative of Brigid's, whom he perceived as a threat to her life. It took her some time to realize that under the confusing circumstances, Kane had no choice but to make a snap judgment call. Making split-second life-and-death decisions was part of his conditioning and training in the Magistrate Division, as deeply ingrained as breathing.

What conflicted her during that time was not the slow process of forgiving him, but coming to terms with what he really was and accepting the reality rather than an illusion. He was a soldier, not an explorer, an academic or intellectual.

When she finally understood that about him, the two people achieved a synthesis of attitudes and styles where they functioned as colleagues and parts of a team, extending to the other professional courtesies and respect.

Brigid and Kane turned down a side passageway and entered the cafeteria.

They saw Lakesh, Domi and Grant seated at a table near the serving station with a pot of coffee between them.

When Lakesh caught sight of them, he made an exaggerated show of consulting his wristwatch and staring at them reproachfully. Kane responded by making an exaggerated show of extending the middle finger of his right hand.

Chapter 11

"How surprisingly mature of you, Kane," Lakesh said. His cultured voice, underscored by a lilting East Indian accent, was frosty with sarcasm. "Your achievements in personal growth continue to surprise me."

"I'm glad I still can," Kane replied with an insincere smile, pulling a chair away from the table and dropping into it. "You, for one, are becoming very predictable."

Grant blew out an exasperated sigh. "Can we get on with this? Some of us have a life outside this place."

Domi cast him a sideways glance full of resentment, but the big man affected not to notice. Of the five people in the cafeteria, she had the least patience with the routine of briefings and debriefings.

Although the redoubt had an officially designated conference theater, most of the Cerberus briefings took place in the small and more intimate dining hall. The miniauditorium had been built to accommodate the majority of the installation's personnel, back before the Nuke when military and scientific advisers visited. The auditorium hadn't been used for its official function since the last installation-wide briefing a couple of years before. Generally, the big room served as a theater, a place where the personnel watched old movies on DVD and laser disks found in storage.

Kane pushed a chair out for Brigid and reached for the coffeepot. One of the few advantages of living as a Cerberus exile was unrestricted access to genuine coffee, not the bitter synthetic gruel that had become the common, sub-par substitute since skydark, the generation-long nuclear winter. Tons of freeze-dried packets of the real article were cached in the redoubt's storage areas. There was enough coffee to last the exiles several lifetimes.

Lakesh fixed his penetrating blue eyes on Brigid. "I presume Dr. DeFore gave you a clean bill of health?"

Brigid nodded. "She did. She said I show symptoms of a concussion, but it's nothing serious."

Lakesh nodded. "I'm relieved to hear that. None of us is getting any younger."

"Yeah, you ought to know about that," Kane said in a sardonic drawl, pouring coffee into a mug.

Lakesh ignored the gibe. A well-built man of medium height, with thick, glossy, black hair and a long, aquiline nose, Lakesh looked no older than fifty, despite strands of gray threading his temples. In reality, he had observed his 250th birthday a short time before. He wore a one-piece white zippered bodysuit, the unisex duty uniform of the Cerberus redoubt.

Lakesh had been born back before nuclear winter had cloaked the world in more than two decades of night. As a youthful genius he had been recruited and finally indoctrinated into the complex web of technology and treachery known as the Totality Concept.

Lakesh had seen the Earth before it had disappeared under scorching mushroom clouds, and retained vivid memories of times well before the nukecaust. He had slept in cryonic stasis in the Anthill, the master Continuity of Government center located within and beneath Mount Rushmore, for more than a century.

"Dearest Domi and friend Grant have already told me their experiences in Manhattan," Lakesh stated. "I'm interested in hearing your perspectives."

Kane shrugged and took a sip of the black coffee. "My perspective is probably identical to theirs. The whole Survivalist Outland Brigade deal was just a smoke-and-mirrors play. Even if the Merry Widow manages to reorganize it in some fashion, it won't pose much of a threat, except to other Roamers."

Lakesh nodded as if he had expected Kane's response and cut his gaze over to Brigid. "And I presume you feel the same way?"

Brigid ran nervous fingers through her tousled mane of sunset-colored hair. "To a point. I don't think we should have gone there in the first place."

Domi's eyes flashed like rubies reflecting sunlight. "What?"

Brigid shrugged. "As vile and as evil as he was, I don't think Esau posed much of a threat."

Grant stared at her incredulously. "He was a god-damned mind-mutie!"

"And as such," Lakesh said, "a rarity. Genuine human mutants are virtually extinct, you know. The few that survive should be studied. Esau sounds like a fascinating subject, since we've never run across any specimen with the kind of abilities he displayed."

The general supposition had always been that the muties were the unforeseen byproducts of radiation and other mutagenics. But Lakesh claimed that genetic codes scrambled at random could not have accounted for the many different monstrosities and deformities among men, women and animals. According to Lakesh, most of the hordes of muties that once roamed the Outlands were the result of pantropic sciences, the deliberate practice of genetic engineering to create life-forms able to survive and thrive in the postholocaust environment.

The population of muties had been dwindling for a century, partly due to the long campaigns of genocide waged by the baronies, but primarily because most of the human mutations had reached developmental dead ends generations before.

However, one breed of human mutant that had increased since skydark was the so-called psi-mutie, a person born with augmented extrasensory and precognitive mind powers. As Lakesh had said, these abilities weren't restricted to muties, since a few norms possessed them, as well, but generally speaking, nonmutated humans with advanced psionic powers were in the minority.

"If you'd seen the little son of a bitch for yourself," Grant rumbled, "the last thing you would've thought about doing is fetching him back here for study."

"That's for damned sure," Domi agreed fervently.

Lakesh blew on his coffee and shook his head, his expression sorrowful.

"What?" Grant challenged. "You're not really wishing we'd brought that monster here, are you?"

"Only a little bit of that, friend Grant. Obviously your safety took precedence. But his death is regrettable. His kind are very few and far between."

"Yeah, well," Kane said negligently. "The fewer the better. Anything else you need to know?"

"We need to screen our CAT applicants to find replacements for Wright and Brady," Domi declared.

Lakesh grimaced. "I think what we really need to do is reevaluate the entire Cerberus away team program."

"We've had this discussion many times," Brigid pointed out, impatience edging her voice.

"The issue was never conclusively resolved," Lakesh countered.

"Not as far as you were concerned," Grant snapped.

"We took a vote, following the nice and neat democratic process," Kane said. "You were outvoted and that's what really burns your ass."

Lakesh swallowed a mouthful of coffee, struggling to tamp down his anger. When Brigid, Domi, Grant and

Kane first arrived at the Cerberus redoubt, Lakesh held the position as the primary authority figure in the redoubt. Within a few months, a minicoup had dramatically changed the situation.

Lakesh hadn't been totally unseated from his position of authority, but he became answerable to a more democratic process. At first, he bitterly resented what he construed as the usurping of his power by ingrates, but he grew to appreciate how the burden of responsibility had been lifted from his shoulders. With the removal of that burden, the risk that his earlier recruitment methods would be exposed also diminished.

Before the arrival of the Manitius personnel, almost every exile in the redoubt had joined the resistance movement as a convicted criminal. Lakesh had set them up, framing them for crimes against their respective villes. He admitted it was a cruel, heartless plan with a barely acceptable risk factor, but it was the only way to spirit them out of their villes, turn them against the barons and make them feel indebted to him.

This bit of explosive and potentially fatal knowledge had not been shared with anyone other than Grant, Kane, Domi and Brigid. Grant's grim prediction of what the others might do to him if they learned of it still echoed in all their memories: "I think they'd lynch you."

The argument regarding the formation of the away teams had not been protracted, but it had been acrimonious with Lakesh and the redoubt's medic, Reba

DeFore, leading the opposition among the eight senior members of the Cerberus command staff.

Lakesh had opposed the formation of the three Cerberus away teams, feeling distinctly uncomfortable at the concept of the redoubt's own version of the Magistrate Divisions. Ironically the away teams were composed of former Magistrates. However, as the canvas of their operations broadened, the personnel situation at the installation also changed.

Both Kane and Grant had been through the dehumanizing cruelty of Magistrate training, yet had somehow managed to retain their humanity. But vestiges of their Mag years still lurked close to the surface, particularly in threatening situations. In those instances, their destructive ruthlessness could be frightening.

Now the Mags who had joined Cerberus were learning the same painful lesson as Kane and Grant. They also had to confront the fact they had spent most of their adult lives supporting a system that was nothing more than old-fashioned fascism.

Most Magistrates were egotistical, testosterone-saturated thugs who aspired to be nothing more than tools in the hands of an authority figure, to be used to batter and terrorize. It hadn't been easy training them to think or to behave in any way other than as blunt instruments.

Massaging her temples with the heels of her hands, Brigid asked quietly, "Is there any other business we need to attend to? Any overlord activity or Millennial Consortium movement?"

Lakesh's scowl gave way to a solicitous, sympathetic smile. "Are you all right, dearest Brigid?"

She smiled wryly. "I still have a headache, thanks to Esau. I'm sure it'll pass." She angled a questioning eyebrow at Lakesh. "So?"

Lakesh shrugged. "So, believe it or not, there is no other pressing business. Nothing of note has registered, either locally or internationally. According to Mr. Bry, even the voyeur channel has been quiet."

Donald Bry, who acted as Lakesh's lieutenant and apprentice in matters technological, had developed an electronic eavesdropping system through the communications linkup with the Keyhole Comsat. It was the same system and same satellite they used to track the telemetry from the subcutaneous transponders implanted within the Cerberus personnel.

Bry had worked on the system for a long time and finally established an undetectable method of patching into the wireless communications channels all of the baronies used. The success rate wasn't one hundred percent, but he had been able to listen in on a number of baron-sanctioned operations in the Outlands.

He monitored different frequencies on a daily basis, but ever since the fall of the baronies, all of villes had been in a state of anarchy, with various factions seizing power, then being supplanted by others. The radio transmissions were equally chaotic. He referred to it as the "voyeur channel."

"Perhaps our actions over the years have finally

yielded positive results," Lakesh continued. "Or, more than likely, we're experiencing the proverbial calm before the storm."

"For once," Kane said a bleak smile, "I agree with you. Nothing ever stays quiet for long."

"If it's something pessimistic," Domi said bitterly, "then you two are in total agreement. If it's about something nice, then you go at each other's throats—"

The transcomm on the wall suddenly emitted a harsh buzz, and from the op center, Bry's voice shouted in alarm, "We've got unscheduled gateway activity and an unidentified jumper!"

Hitching around in his chair, Lakesh faced the voice-activated unit and demanded loudly, "Jumping in from where?"

"That's the problem—I can't trace the jump line!"

"So much for the calm," Grant muttered, swiftly pushing his chair back from the table and standing up. "Goddammit."

Kane rose just as quickly. "Stop complaining. You wouldn't have it any other way."

Chapter 12

Klaxons blared in a discordant rhythm, echoing throughout the redoubt. People ran through the corridors to preappointed emergency stations. Domi, Brigid, Kane and Grant had to dodge and sidestep to keep from being bowled over as they rushed to the operations center. Lakesh followed as swiftly as he could.

The central command complex was a long, high-ceilinged room divided by two aisles of computer stations. Half a dozen people sat before the terminals. Monitor screens flashed incomprehensible images and streams of data in machine talk.

The operations center had five dedicated and eight shared subprocessors, all linked to the mainframe computer behind the far wall. Two centuries before, it had been one of the most advanced models ever built, carrying experimental, error-correcting microchips of such a tiny size that they even reacted to quantum fluctuations. Biochip technology had been employed when it was built, protein molecules sandwiched between microscopic glass-and-metal circuits.

The information contained in the main database may

not have been the sum total of all humankind's knowledge, but not for lack of trying. Any bit, byte or shred of intelligence that had ever been digitized was only a few keystrokes and mouse clicks away.

A huge Mercator-relief map of the world spanned the entire wall above the door. Pinpoints of light shone steadily in almost every country, connected by a thin, glowing pattern of lines. They represented the Cerberus network, the locations of all functioning gateway units across the planet. As the four people entered, they cast quick over-the-shoulder glances at the map. They didn't see any lights blinking, which normally meant that none of the mat-trans units were in operation.

On the opposite side of the operations center, an anteroom held the eight-foot-tall mat-trans chamber, rising from an elevated platform. Six upright slabs of brown-hued armaglass formed a translucent wall around it. From the emitter array emanated a sound much like the distant howling of a gale-force wind, rising in pitch. Bright flares showed like bursts of heat lightning on the other side of the walls, but they were safely contained.

Armaglass was manufactured in the last decades of the twentieth century from a special compound that plasticized and combined the properties of steel and glass. It was used as walls in the jump chambers to confine quantum-energy overspills.

Farrell, a shaved-headed man who affected a goatee and hoop earring, sat at the main ops board. The slightly built Donald Bry was bent over the mat-trans control console. He held the earpiece of a headset against his right ear, listening intently.

"What's going on here?" Lakesh demanded.

"The signal began as a standard gateway carrier wave," Bry replied distractedly, "like a unit-to-unit transmission. But the jump point of origin doesn't register on the network, and at the exact same time we started receiving a telemetric signal over the sat download."

Bry and Lakesh had tied the satellite's data into sophisticated computer programs that could parse and analyze the data and alert them when something out of the ordinary occurred.

"So it's coming from one of the mass-produced modular gateway units," Domi said waspishly. "What's the big deal about that?"

"The big deal about that," Lakesh stated, "is that whoever is coming over the jump line has this unit's destination code."

Waving his hand, Bry raised his voice and said impatiently, "Be quiet, will you? I'm getting some kind of organized audio signal over the sat feed."

"Are the two events connected?" Brigid asked.

Lakesh tugged absently at his long nose. "It can't be a coincidence."

"Shh!" Bry glared at them from beneath a mass of coppery curls badly in need of a trim. "The signal is tied with the mat-trans carrier wave. I'm trying to read it."

"Patch it in with the comm channel," Kane said, "so we can all hear it."

Bry tapped a pair of keys and then a stuttering tone filtered out of the speaker.

"Dots and dashes," Brigid declared. "The international radio alphabet. Morse code."

Lakesh cocked his head, eyes narrowed in concentration. "Dash...dot-dot-dot...that's *B* for Bravo. Someone is definitely trying to contact us."

"More than that," Bry said tensely. "We've got a materialization cycle."

The small man turned in his chair, back toward the four-foot VGA monitor screen. "This is crazy," he muttered, his fingers flying over the keyboard. "Now I'm getting a trace...*after* the materialization cycle kicks in!"

All of them turned to look at the red light pulsing on the large Mercator map. The strident electronic buzz continued.

"This is something new," Lakesh said wonderingly.

"What do you mean?" Brigid asked.

"Hush!" Bry said loudly. "Cut the backchat!"

Brigid stiffened at his peremptory tone, but she quickly turned her attention to the screen before her, crowding next to Bry to get a closer look, as did Lakesh.

Strands of her long red-gold hair obscured her view of the screen as Brigid bent over Bry's shoulder, and she impatiently pushed it behind her ears as she struggled to make sense of the data. The monitor screen displayed a drop-down window in the left-hand corner. A jagged wave slid back and forth across a CGI scale.

Gazing at the scale, Bry stated, "Every piece of matter, whether organic or inorganic, that has been ever been transported to or from our gateway here has a computer record in the database. The image processor scans for patterns corresponding with those in the record and allows for materialization unless we physically locked out that pattern, redirecting it to a holding buffer."

"What we've got here is not organic," Brigid said, nodding to the readout on the drop-down window. "It's metal."

"I'm shunting the pattern to the holding buffer, then," Bry announced, fingers spreading over the keyboard.

"Hold on that," Lakesh said.

Bry twisted his head to stare at him incredulously. "Somebody could have gated a nuclear warhead in here to us! The overlords and maybe even the Millennial Consortium have access to that kind of tech."

"That tactic is a little too subtle for the overlords," Grant commented dryly.

"And the consortium, even if they got their hands on an atomic weapon, are too damned cheap to waste it on us," Kane said.

The Millennial Consortium was, on the surface, a group of organized traders who plied their trade selling predark relics to the various villes. In the Outlands, it was actually the oldest profession.

Looting the abandoned ruins of predark cities was less a vocation than it was an Outland tradition. Entire generations of families had made careers of ferreting out and plundering the secret stockpiles the predark government had hidden in anticipation of a nation-wide catastrophe.

Most of the redoubts had been found and raided decades ago, but occasionally one hitherto untouched would be located. As the stockpiles became fewer, so did the independent salvaging and trading organizations. Various trader groups had been combining resources for the past couple of years, forming consortiums and absorbing the independent operators.

The consortiums employed and fed people in the Outlands, giving them a sense of security that had once been the sole province of the barons. There were some critics who compared the trader consortiums to the barons and talked of them with just as much ill favor.

Since first hearing of the Millennial Consortium a couple of years earlier, the Cerberus warriors had learned firsthand that the organization was deeply involved in activities other than seeking out stockpiles, salvaging and trading. The group's ultimate goal was to rebuild America along the tenets of a technocracy, with a board of scientists and scholars governing the country.

Although the Consortium's goals seemed utopian, the organization's method of operations was very pragmatic and cold-blooded. Their influence was widespread, very well managed and they were completely ruthless when it came to the furtherance of their agendas.

"It's possible that one of the Supreme Council managed to decrypt this unit's destination code," Brigid commented. "But it doesn't seem likely. The last time any of the overlords came calling, they sent a remote probe."

"We will still observe due diligence," Lakesh conceded.

Turning to Farrell, who watched anxiously from the ops console, he ordered, "Lower the security shields. Lock us down."

The man's hands flew over a series of buttons on his keyboard. The alarm fell silent but the hooting was replaced by the pneumatic whoosh of compressed air, the squeak of gears and a sequence of heavy, booming thuds resounding from the corridor. Four-inch-thick vanadium-alloy bulkheads dropped from the ceiling to seal off the living quarters, engineering level and main sec door from the operations center, completely isolating it from the rest of the redoubt.

Kane, Domi, Grant and Brigid moved quickly into the anteroom. A couple of years before, after the mad Maccan's murderous incursion into the installation through the gateway, it had become standard protocol to have at least one armed guard standing by during a materialization.

To simplify matters, a weapons locker had been moved into the ready room. Opening the locker door,

Domi removed a lightweight SA-80 subgun and tossed it to Grant. She threw two more to Brigid and Kane.

All of the Cerberus personnel were required to become reasonably proficient with firearms, and the lightweight "point and shoot" subguns were the easiest for the firearm challenged to handle.

The four people took up positions all around the room, shouldering the subguns, barrels trained on the door of the jump chamber, making it the apex of a tri-angulated cross fire if one was necessary. They waited tensely as the unit droned through the materialization cycle. Because of the translucent quality of the brown-tinted armaglass shielding, they could see nothing within the chamber except vague, shifting shapes without form or apparent solidity.

The chamber was full of the plasma bleed-off, a by-product of the ionized waveforms that resembled mist. Within seconds, the electronic whine melded into a smooth hum.

Over her shoulder, Domi shouted, "We're set! Unbutton her!"

"Unbuttoning!" Lakesh activated the remote control from the console.

Solenoids clicked and the heavy armaglass door swung open on its counterbalanced hinges. Mist swirled and thread-thin static electricity discharges arced within the billowing mass.

The laser autotargeters mounted atop the subguns pierced the thinning planes of vapor with bright red threads and cast kill dots on hexagonal floor plates. Kane and Grant moved in warily.

They froze just inside the chamber door, staring silently at the floor.

Anxiously, Brigid asked, "Well? What is it?"

"It's not a warhead, but I'm not sure what to make of it," Kane answered flatly.

Brigid stepped between the two men and followed their downward gaze. The last wispy scraps of white vapor dissolved like early-morning mist. A small disk of black enamel and silver lay on the hexagonal floor disk. Inscribed in silver on the obsidian surface of the disk were glyphs resembling two scalene triangles flanking an isosceles. The points of the three triangles were topped by small circles.

"I'd say it's a calling card," Brigid intoned, repressing the quiver of dread in her voice. "From the Priory of Awen."

Chapter 13

The silver-and-black disk rested on the center of the trestle table in the long chamber that served as the testing facility and workroom of the Cerberus redoubt. Rows of drafting tables with T-squares hanging from them lined one wall. Upright tool lockers, a bandsaw, a drill press, lathes and various chassis of electronic equipment, including a spectroscope, lined the other.

Hands clasped behind his back, Lakesh slowly walked around the table, examining the object from all angles. "The seal of the Priory of Awen," he said softly. "A mysterious message from a mysterious order sent by mysterious means."

"What I find the most mysterious," Brewster Philboyd said darkly, "is why you brought the damned thing in here instead of outside, just in case it blows up."

An astrophysicist in his midforties, Philboyd stood slightly over six feet tall but was very thin and lanky of build. Pale blond hair was swept back from a receding hairline, which made his high forehead seem very high indeed. He wore black-rimmed eyeglasses and his cheeks appeared to be pitted with the sort of scars associated with chronic teenage acne.

Philboyd was one of a number of space scientists who had arrived in the Cerberus redoubt from the Manitius base over the past three years. Like Lakesh, he was a "freezie," postnuke slang for someone who had been placed in stasis, although conventional cryonics was not the method applied.

Domi glanced toward him, mockery and a challenge glinting in her eyes. "Or mebbe it'll turn into a cyber-spider and try to take over the place, huh?"

Philboyd flushed with embarrassment at the patronizing reminder of a past incident. He didn't respond to Domi's taunt. As the leader of CAT Beta, internal and external security of the redoubt fell to her.

"I doubt anything will explode," Brigid said dryly. "I'm getting no readings from it whatsoever. It's apparently exactly what it looks like."

She stood at one end of the table, consulting the LCD gauge of the power analyzer in her right hand. The rectangular device was designed to measure, record and analyze energy emissions, quality and harmonics. She swept the extended sensor stem back and forth above the seal in short left-to-right arcs.

"Also, the Priory of Awen has no reason to bring us harm," Lakesh interjected. "They've been our allies for a number of years now."

"You've said they were, but the priory sure as hell

has kept a low profile since I've been here," Philboyd shot back.

The Priory of Awen was a secret Druidic society that flourished from the fourth century A.D. through the twenty-second. In the ancient Gaelic tongue, *awen* meant "inspiration" and the *awenyddion* solved problems or looked for hidden information.

The priory was allegedly founded by Saint Patrick after he had driven the serpents from Ireland. The basis of the old myth sprang from legends of the Serpent Folk, the Annunaki. Until the twentieth century, the priory existed as a very small, secretive enclave of priests that safeguarded the secrets of pre-Christian Ireland, secrets that flew in the face of accepted religious doctrines—particularly their knowledge of the two extraterrestrial races who had influenced the development of humanity, the Tuatha de Danaan and the Annunaki. Many of the priory clergy boasted descent from the Danaan.

During a mission to Britain and Ireland several years earlier, the Cerberus warriors had come in contact with representatives of the priory and struck an uneasy alliance with them.

"True," Lakesh agreed. "But that doesn't mean they haven't been busy in their part of the world."

Rather than respond to the observation, Philboyd asked, "Why would the priory go to all the trouble of gating that thing here?"

Brigid turned off the power analyzer and placed it on

the table. She eyed the seal closely. "Apparently it wasn't so much gated to us as transported. Whoever the sender was used a parallax point, not a mat-trans unit."

Kane frowned, leaning an elbow against a pedestal next to him. Atop it, encased within a locked transparent Lucite box, was an object resembling a very squat, broad-based pyramid made of smooth, dully gleaming metal. Barely one foot in width, the height of the interphaser did not exceed twelve inches.

"Even if that's so," he said, "how could they have sent it to our jump chamber without an interphaser of their own?"

Brigid's lips quirked in a crooked smile. "Perhaps they have one. Remember, we had to leave the first version of the interphaser in Strongbow's fortress in order to escape."

Grant grunted. "We never did find out what happened to it."

The interphaser had evolved from the Project Cerberus. Several years before, Lakesh had constructed a small device on the same scientific principle as the mat-trans gateways, a portable quantum interphase inducer designed to interact with naturally occurring hyperdimensional vortices.

The first version of the interphaser had not functioned according to its design, and was lost on its first mission. Much later, a situation arose that necessitated the construction of a second, improved model.

During the investigation of the Operation Chronos

installation on Thunder Isle, a special encoded program named Parallax Points was discovered. Lakesh learned that the Parallax Points program was actually a map of all the vortex points on the planet. This discovery inspired him to rebuild the interphaser, even though decrypting the vortex index program was laborious and time-consuming. Each newly discovered set of coordinates was fed into the interphaser's targeting computer.

With the new data, the interphaser became more than a miniaturized version of a gateway unit, even though it employed much of the same hardware and operating principles. The mat-trans gateways functioned by tapping into the quantum stream, the invisible pathways that crisscrossed outside of perceived physical space and terminated in wormholes.

The interphaser interacted with the energy produced by a naturally occurring vortex and caused a temporary overlapping of two dimensions. The vortex then became an intersection point, a discontinuous quantum jump, beyond relativistic space-time.

Evidence indicated there were many vortex nodes, centers of intense energy, located in the same proximity on each of the planets of the solar system, and those points correlated to vortex centers on Earth. The power points of the planet, places that naturally generated specific types of energy, possessed both positive and projective frequencies, and others were negative and receptive.

Lakesh knew some ancient civilizations were aware of these symmetrical geo-energies and constructed monuments over the vortex points in order to manipulate them. Once the interphaser was put into use, the Cerberus redoubt reverted to its original purpose—not a sanctuary for exiles, or the headquarters of a resistance against the tyranny of the barons, but a facility dedicated to fathoming the eternal mysteries of space and time. Unfortunately, Interphaser Version 2.0 had been lost during a mission to Mars to unlock a few of those mysteries.

Brigid Baptiste and Brewster Philboyd had worked feverishly to construct a third one, but with expanded capabilities. They had completed Interphaser Version 2.5 a couple of years earlier.

"We should assume, then, that the seal was phased here from England?" Philboyd inquired.

Lakesh picked up the disk and turned it over in both hands, scrutinizing it, shaking it, smelling. "Friend Bry is still tracing the transit line. Hopefully, he can isolate the origin point."

Kane realized Brigid gazed at him keenly. He met her stare and demanded, "What?"

"You're thinking about Fand, aren't you?" she asked.

Before Kane could reply, Philboyd turned toward him. "Fand? That insane three-way hybrid from Ireland?"

"She wasn't insane the last time I saw her," Kane retorted, refusing to allow his sudden discomfiture to show in either his demeanor or tone. "But she's probably still a hybrid."

Lakesh held the seal up to eye level, rotating it slowly within his hands.

"What are you doing with that thing?" Grant asked suspiciously.

Lakesh uttered a short, self-conscious chuckle. "I half hoped that the seal contained a hidden message, like a cryptex used by a number of secret societies in Europe."

"A what?" Domi wanted to know.

"A portable device used to convey and hide secret messages," Lakesh replied. "If you didn't know how to access the cryptex, then you risked destroying the message."

Philboyd snorted. "That seems like a lot of trouble to go to, even for a secret religious order. Sindri could be responsible party for all we know. We're just speculating the priory is behind it."

"Not anymore." Bry strolled in, a file jacket tucked under one arm.

"You found something?" Kane asked.

"Yeah." Bry opened the file jacket and spread out two satellite photographs on the tabletop. "You might say I have."

From the pocket pouch on the leg of his bodysuit he withdrew a large magnifying glass. "I didn't have time for much in the way of enlargement or rectification work, but I have some multispectral imagery."

Everyone crowded around the table. From the breast pocket of her shirt, Brigid withdrew the symbol of her former office as a Cobaltville archivist. She slipped on the pair of rectangular-lensed, wire-framed spectacles and examined the photographs. Although the eyeglasses were something of a reminder of her past life, they also served to correct an astigmatism.

Bry held his magnifying glass over the largest of the photographs. It displayed an extreme aerial view of the North Atlantic and the northern European continent, overlaid by a longitude-and-latitude map. One square glowed with a tiny yellow dot.

"Definitely the British Isles," Lakesh murmured.

"Cornwall, to be precise," Bry said.

"Near Land's End, to be even more precise," Brigid said, peering intently at the photograph.

"Exactly…and the Vela detected an energy surge in that very place."

"There are several parallax points near there, but I think that's the area of Merry Maidens," Brigid said thoughtfully.

"The Merry Whozits, Baptiste?" Kane tried to keep his voice even, although he was puzzled by her comment. Since Brigid Baptiste had an eidetic memory, it usually wasn't a good idea to challenge her on the facts.

Brigid slid over the second photograph and placed the tip of a forefinger on one section of it. "The Merry Maidens stone circle. The ancient megalithic sites are the geodetic markers for naturally occurring vortex points, remember?"

"Yeah, I remember." Kane squinted at the image and barely discerned several dark gray specks that could have been anything, much less megalithic stones.

"The stone circles and dolmens of Britain can definitely serve as gates between nexus points," Lakesh said. "The maidens are the best known and preserved circle in Cornwall. They are believed to be complete, which is exceedingly rare for prehistoric structures."

Brigid tapped the specks on the photograph. "The nineteen granite stones, although only four feet tall, form a perfect circle seventy-seven feet in diameter. They're also called Dans Maen, or 'Stone Dance,' in Cornish."

Kane rolled his eyes ceilingward. "And I'm sure the legends about them are connected to the Danaan, right?"

Brigid smiled with genuine amusement. "Not exactly. Most legends associated with the site tell of nineteen maidens on their way to Sunday vespers who were distracted by the playing of two pipers...represented by two tall standing stones a quarter mile distant from the main site. The maidens strayed into the field to dance to the music. A thunderbolt transfixed both pipers and maidens to the spot, where they now forever stand, turned to stone for the sin of dancing on the Sabbath."

"I thought so," Kane said sourly.

Bry and Lakesh exchanged smirks. Kane usually

became impatient when Brigid rambled on. Facts would sometimes spew forth from her eidetic memory like data out of a computer.

"If the origin jump point is the stone circle, it means someone familiar with the principles of the vortices transported the seal to us," Grant said. "That narrows the field of suspects considerably, especially since the priory and Cornwall are basically in the same geographic neighborhood."

"The Morse code only kept repeating 'Bravo'," Bry said. "I'd guess it was the sender's way of letting us know the message was intended strictly for us."

Kane glanced from the satellite photographs to the seal still nestled in Lakesh's hands. "Somebody is going the long way around the barn to attract our attention."

Lakesh nodded. "But they *did* attract it. And if that somebody isn't the priory, then it's important for us to find out who can manipulate the parallax points."

Grant dry-scrubbed his scalp in agitation. "Let me guess…Kane, Brigid and I run right over to Cornwall to find out who that might be?"

"Something like that," Lakesh replied, trying to repress a smile and failing. "But 'run' might not be the most applicable of terms."

"The Merry Maidens," Kane muttered. He glanced at Brigid. "You might as well put on your dancing shoes."

He held out his hand to Lakesh. "Let me see that thing for a minute."

Lakesh casually tossed the seal to him underhanded. Kane caught it—and a tidal of wave of blazing light crashed over him.

Chapter 14

Cold white light filled his vision with a flaring radiance. He shielded his face, but his eyes were still overwhelmed by the incandescent blaze.

"Ka'in!"

Startled, blinking furiously, he turned toward Conor, staring at the man, knowing who he was without really recognizing him.

The king was a heavyset, bearded man, a shaggy wolf-skin cloak exaggerating the breadth of his shoulders. The cloak didn't hide the glittering coat of chain mail and the heavy broadsword scabbarded at his hip. A golden circlet confined his mass of curly red hair.

"You warned us not to look at the light cast by the Eye of Balor," Conor said severely, "and here you do it yourself. Can you see?"

"Yes, my king." Ka'in rubbed his eyes with thumb and forefinger, and clarity of vision returned.

"That is good," Corineus said, marching up behind him. "But my knights would follow the mighty Cuchulainn even if you were deaf and crippled."

Corineus, king of Cornwall and cousin to Conor,

was tall and lean, his black hair streaked with silver. Overlaying his coat of chain mail was a magnificent battle harness decorated with silver torques. He carried a slender lance in his right hand.

Ka'in glanced down at himself and felt a faint surge of surprise, but it was faraway and dim. From throat to hip, supple molded leather encased him. The overlapping scales of polished steel on his breastplate caught the reflections cast by the Eye of Balor. In his right hand he gripped the heavy shaft of his war spear, Gae Bolg. Snugged within a leather scabbard at his hip swung a broadsword, the hilt and pommel worked in precious gems and gold filigree.

From beneath the rivet-studded brim of a horned helmet, he gazed around at the field of standing stones. In the darkness beyond, a hunting horn blared one long, belligerent bellow to split the predawn darkness. A wordless war cry followed it, and the Firbolgs, the men of the bog, began to move. They came slowly at first, creeping among the outcroppings of chert and running from one bit of cover to another.

Ka'in sensed rather than heard the assembled warriors and knights drawing up around him in preparation for battle. They brandished swords, bows and lances. Bronze helmets covered manes of black and red-blond hair. He glanced around at the broken ring of cyclopean stone blocks looming on all sides. They rose from an area so flat and bare of vegetation that he knew it had once been a vast courtyard.

Also, on an almost unconscious level, he knew the megalithic stones had nothing to do with religious rites or dancing maidens—they were the bare bones, the foundation of an ancient tower that had once risen toward the heavens, reared on this very spot a thousand or more years ago.

"Where are the Danaan?" Corineus demanded. "Time grows short."

Ka'in did not respond for so long, he drew a sharp look from Conor. "Answer him, Ka'in."

"I do not know," Ka'in replied frankly. "They will come when they are needed the most."

Beyond the milling mass of Firbolgs, light blazed again, hurting the eye with its unwavering brightness.

"Balor holds forth with his evil eye," Conor said with a grim fatalism. "When it turns again in our direction, we must be prepared to look away or die."

"It's not really an eye, your highness," Ka'in stated.

Conor glared at him. "Of course it's not an eye—it's some bit of sorcery created by your friends the Tuatha de Danaan and stolen long ago by the Formorii."

Ka'in knew the Balor who cocommanded the Firbolg force was not the same sea king who had used the evil eye to destroy his enemies millennia before, but he did claim direct descent.

According to legend, the Formorian Balor was notable for his one eye, which could kill anyone it looked upon. Allegedly, he gained this power as a child when watching his father's druids preparing poisonous spells, the fumes of which rose into his eye. As an adult, his eye was normally kept closed, only to be opened on the battlefield by four men using a handle fitted to his eyelid, or, in some versions, a system of ropes and pulleys.

Prophecy stated that Balor was to be killed by his grandson. To avoid this fate, he locked his daughter, Ethlinn, in a tower made of crystal to keep her from becoming pregnant. However, Cian, one of the Tuatha de Danann, with the help of the Druid priestess Birog, managed to enter the tower. She gave birth to triplets by him, but Balor threw them into the ocean.

Birog saved one, Lugh, and gave him to Manannan mac Lir, who became his foster father. He was called Lugh Lamhfada and became a prince of the Tuatha de Danann.

Lugh led the Danaan in the second Battle of Magh Tuiredh against the Fomorians. The warrior Ogma disarmed Balor during this battle, but Balor killed King Nuadha with his eye. Lugh shot a sling stone that drove Balor's eye out the back of his head, where it continued to wreak its deadly power on the Fomorian army.

One tale had it that when Balor was slain by Lugh, Balor's eye was still open when he fell face-first to the ground. Thus his deadly eye beam burned a hole into the earth. Long after, the hole filled with water and became a lake known as Loch na Suil, or "Lake of the Eye."

Ka'in couldn't be sure how much of the legends of

the Formorian Balor were true, but he knew that the evil eye was an artifact separate from the man. The chieftain who claimed Balor's bloodline was far worse than that of a Formorian, as far as Ka'in was concerned— he was traitor to his clan.

History repeated itself with a pact struck between Balor and Eochy mac Erc, king of the Firbolgs.

According to the tales told around the hearths in Tara and Ulster, the Firbolgs claimed to be survivors of a cataclysm that sank their island homeland. They were, however, not the lords of that mysterious land, but a slave race created to till the fields and fish the seas.

When some of the survivors reached Eire, they did constant battle with the Formorii who had established strongholds along the north coast. When the Tuatha de Danaan claimed a large portion of the heartland, the Firbolgs and Formorians struck an alliance to drive them away. Instead, both the Firbolgs and Formorians were defeated by the combined forces of the Danaan and the Gaelic tribesmen.

The Firbolgs left Eire in despair, joining a handful of other survivors in Scythia, where, because of their stunted appearance, they were shunned, oppressed and finally enslaved as in their sunken homeland. But Eochy mac Erc's own grandfather staged a revolt and the Firbolgs returned to Eire in three groups.

The Formorii were long gone, and so the Firbolgs claimed their empty fortresses and a crushing tribute from the surrounding counties. The war between Gael and Firbolg had been waged sporadically for the past fifty years and now it entered its final stage.

When negotiations with King Conor to permit the Firbolgs to live on the Eire's northern coast had failed, Eochy mac Erc and Balor joined forces to invade Cornwall and establish a kingdom there. Corineus beseeched his cousin Conor to help repel the incursion.

However, the war wasn't sword against spear, arrow against shield. From some hidden sea-drowned vault, Balor had retrieved the ancient weapon so associated with his namesake—the evil eye.

When Ka'in learned about the evil eye, he sought out the few remaining Danaan and asked for their aid. He was instructed to gather the combined forces of Conor and Cornieus and make a stand in the field of stones, the site of one of their first structures. They promised they would come at dawn.

As the gray-blue sky began to lighten with streaks of pink and orange, the front ranks of the Firbolgs began moving faster and faster, bent over in animalistic crouches. They were men of short stature with stumpy, bandy legs and barrel-shaped bodies. They wore drab, brown leather armor, crudely cross-stitched over their arms and legs.

Eochy mac Erc shrilled out orders from a safe remove. By squinting, Ka'in could barely make him out, standing atop a rock formation and shaking a sword. The Firbolg king's face was gaunt, with a hooked nose reminiscent of a falcon's beak. The lips formed a thin cruel line above a jutting jaw. Sprouting from his naked scalp were small, cartilaginous masses, like little twisted horns.

"The Firbolgs do not appear to be in much of a hurry," Conor commented wryly.

Ka'in knew why, but he didn't speak. The bright funnel of light sweeping back and forth across the moors suddenly turned the color of freshly spilled blood. The Cornish and Irish warriors had been warned of this phenomenon and how to react. Their officers roared, "Down! Take cover! Down!"

All of the soldiers within the stone circle dropped flat to the ground as a torrent of hell-hued light whiplashed over the bent heads of the Firbolgs. The bolt struck a megalith dead center, and the upper half exploded in a shower of stone shards and pebbles.

Ka'in lay on his stomach, feeling his shoulders, legs and back pelted by the gravel raining down. He heard faint, strangulated screams and curses amid the crash and clatter of falling rock.

Quickly, he levered himself to his feet. "Swiftly now—the eye cannot fire another bolt for some little time. We must attack."

The hunting horn sounded a brassy, bleating note. The Firbolgs howled and swept forward, swinging their bronze swords. Their charge had no military neatness or tactics—they simply ran forward in a milling mass, uttering strident cries.

"Archers!" Conor shouted. "Front and forward!"

The contingent of bowmen rose up from where they knelt and, in practiced unison, drew arrows from quivers, nocked them and drew back on their bowstrings.

"Loose!" Conor cried.

The archers let fly. With each long arrow, squalling Firbolgs tumbled to the ground, clutching at feathered shafts sprouting from their chests, but the main force came on like a tide, a howling horde trampling their wounded underfoot.

The Celtic warriors of Conor and Conerius bounded forward to meet the wiry barbarians, unlimbering great broadswords and leveling their pikes. The outer perimeter of the stone circle instantly became a scene of screaming, bloody chaos. Swords thrust, axes split skulls, knives stabbed into bodies. Both the Celts and the Firbolgs fought with the fury of desperation. The clangor of steel striking steel and the shrieks of wounded quickly rose to a deafening cacophony.

Despite the almost mad urge to join in the slaughter, Ka'in remained beside his king, knowing that Balor would soon dispatch the cream of his soldiery, a unit of trained horsemen. He saw them massing in the near distance, and he glimpsed a giant of a man astride a tall black horse.

Massive of height and breadth, Balor wore his gray beard plaited into two thick braids upon his chest. A scar marred the right side of his pale face, tracking down over a raw, empty eye socket. A five-foot-long broadsword was strapped to his back. Whereas Ka'in invested his war spear, Gae Bolg, with an almost mystical power to slay, Balor did the same with his sword, which he called Riastradh. A double-bladed battle-ax hung by a thong from his saddle.

Ka'in couldn't help but wonder if Balor relied much on swords and axes, now that he gained the evil eye and used it as his forebear had done. The top and sides of his skull were concealed by a helmet wrought of black, gleaming metal. Twisting interlace designs deeply inscribed the jaw guards.

From the crest of the helmet rose a curve of metal, resembling a long-necked dragon in outline. The extended jaws held a smoothly contoured, fist-sized gem that glowed steadily with a blue-white illumination.

A mounted standard bearer lifted a banner and rode with it to the forefront of the horsemen. The helmeted figure of Balor rode behind him. The horn set up a prolonged trumpeting, and suddenly the mass of mounted men surged forward.

Ka'in clutched the shaft of Gae Bolg so tightly the wood creaked within his grasp. He smelled the blood on the wind, the stink of an enemy thundering down to kill him and destroy everything he held dear. The legendary battle madness of Cuchulainn burned through him like a raging wildfire. He hungered to leap into battle and chop at heads, but he had promised the Danaan to wait until they appeared.

Over the thunder of hooves and the clash of steel, at the periphery of his hearing, Ka'in heard a new sound—a faint, high-pitched whine so distant that he couldn't really be certain he heard it.

He had begun to turn when he felt a tingling, pins-and-needle sensation all over his body. The tingling became a prickle. The fine hairs all over his body seemed to vibrate, to bristle. He, Conor and Conerius all exchanged startled glances, then whirled toward the center of the stone circle.

The air pulsed like the beating of gigantic, invisible heart. A hazy, blurred shimmer rose from the ground, reminding Ka'in of a ripple made by a fish just beneath the surface of the river.

He gazed at it, frozen in place. Particles of dirt lifted from the ground, dancing and spinning, growing from a dust devil to a swirling, cylindrical tornado. It glittered as if powdered diamonds were caught within its powerful vortex.

Sounding half-strangled, Conor gasped, "What is happening?"

A waxy, glowing funnel of light fanned up from the center of the megalithic stone blocks, like a spreading, diffused veil of backlit fog. As the three men stared, stunned into speechlessness, the light expanded into a gushing borealis several feet wide, spreading out like the spokes of a chariot wheel, touching all of the looming slabs of rock.

Then a yellow brilliance erupted from the ground.

Ka'in felt the shock wave slapping his breath painfully back into his lungs, pushing him backward. Although not blinded, his eyes stung fiercely.

Through the blurred afterimage of the flare, he glimpsed three dark, shadowy shapes shifting in the fan of light. The sinuous forms leaped from the light and padded past the two kings and the warrior on clawed, padded feet. The fur-covered spine ridges reached Ka'in's waist, and the eyes shone with a fearsome, unnatural light, like freshly minted coins. From the broad, heavy muzzles, saliva-wet fangs glistened. At close quarters, they seemed as large as a pony.

Moving as one, the hounds of Cullan threw back their heads and bayed, mournful, terrifying howls that sent spasms of terror even through Ka'in. The unleashed hounds bounded into the battle, lusting for hot blood and flesh.

"Your guardian beasts go to war," announced a clear, strong female voice. "You must join them, else they will feast on the hearts of your allies."

Ka'in turned to see Fand striding forth from the shimmer of light. His heart jerked in his chest at the sight of the face that was not completely human, but stirringly beautiful nonetheless.

Like most of the Danaan he had met, Fand had huge, slanted eyes as big in proportion to her high-boned face as those of a cat. They were the sparkling blue of mountain meltwater, with feline pupils. Her lips were full, her skin as smooth as alabaster with a tinge of blue. The thick, wavy hair hanging loose on both sides of her face bore tiger stripes of black and blond. Although he couldn't see them, he knew her small ears swept up and back to form points.

Tall and beautifully made, she wore the finery of a Danaan warrior queen—a molded breastplate of a silvery material encased the upper half of her strangely elongated torso, and spurs jangled at the heels of her thigh-high, black leather boots. A crimson cloak belled out behind her. In her right hand, instead of a sword or spear, she gripped a long staff, wrapped with vines and many turnings of silver wire. An ivory knob like an oversize egg topped it.

"Fand," he husked out, wanting to rush to her but also knowing he could not.

She smiled at him sadly. "Go, my beloved. Fight. Recover the eye."

Ka'in permitted himself to stare at her for one moment more, only dimly aware of Conor and Conerius standing in silent shock behind him. Then he wheeled around, shouting to his horse, "Dibhirceach! It is time!"

With a high-pitched neigh that sounded almost joyful, the huge stallion pounded out from where he was picketed. The horse stood eighteen hands high, very broad through the chest and withers. Beneath a glossy, cinnamon-colored coat, long muscles roped his long-legged frame. Much like his master, scars crisscrossed Dibhirceach's body, testifying to the many battles he had already fought.

The horse reared and Ka'in swung astride his back, vaulting into the saddle. Whipping his broadsword free of its scabbard, he drove in his heels and the stallion plunged forward. The hounds of Cullan had already reached the skirmish line and rampaged among the Firbolgs, jaws closing on their limbs, ripping out their throats. The giant dogs tossed the grotesque bodies in the air, playing with them like puppies with rag dolls. Screaming in terror, the Firbolgs dropped their weapons and ran, ignoring the strident commands of Eochy mac Erc to hold the line.

Dibhirceach's steel-shod hooves lashed out and crushed skulls of the warriors in his way, but panic possessed Balor's warriors and they retreated before the giant war horse and vicious hounds. With his sword in his left and Gae Bolg in his right, Ka'in hacked and stabbed his way through the press of bodies.

"Balor!" he roared.

The bearded one-eyed face turned toward him. "Ka'in."

"I'm here to claim your life, you traitorous bastard!"

Balor raised his ax, spurring his black horse into a gallop. "Come and take it!"

Dibhirceach lunged toward him. The gem atop Balor's helmet glowed, but Ka'in did not avert his gaze. He stood in the stirrups, sword and spear held ready. The two horses slammed together breast-to-breast. The Eye of Balor flashed, filling Ka'in's eyes with dazzling, painful brilliance. He slashed with his sword at Balor's helmet. Instinctively, he squeezed his eyes shut….

WHEN KANE OPENED his eyes again he stood in the center of a stone circle under a leaden sky. Glancing down at himself, he saw without much surprise he was naked. He saw the long scar along his left rib cage where the jolt-walker had stabbed him during a sweep of the Cobaltville pits and the smaller weal on his upper right thigh where Quayle had slashed him with a cutlass. There were many more marks of violence scattered over his body—Kane's body, he reminded himself, not Cuchulainn's.

He also knew where he stood. Skatha, the land of shadows, was the region that existed between dreams and waking, the conscious and the unconscious, between life and death.

Wearily he said, "Fand, I know you brought me here. Show yourself."

The ground at his feet began to crack and split, and wedges of light inched upward. Fand rose with the light. She was nearly as tall as Kane, and as naked. As sleek and as beautiful as he remembered from the last time he had seen her, nearly four years earlier.

Unlike the Danaan princess from whom she claimed descent, Fand had the powerful look of a lioness about her, and her golden, unbound hair tumbled down past her hips like a flaxen waterfall. Great physical strength showed in the arching rim of her rib cage and tautly muscled limbs. She carried a staff identical to the one he had seen the Danaan Fand wield in his vision of the past.

"It is good to see you again, my darling Kane." Her liquid voice, vibrant and melodious, caressed his nerve endings.

Stolidly, he said, "So the seal sent by the priory was a message after all."

Fand nodded. "A summons, meant for you. It stored memories of your past life as Cuchulainn. At your touch, the receptacle imparted them to you so you would have an idea of what awaited you. Now it has established a bridge, a psi-link between our two minds."

"Why go to all that trouble?" Kane demanded angrily. "You know how I hate it when you dig into my brain. You could've just come to Cerberus yourself. You know how."

Fand's full lips compressed. "I could not risk alerting our common foe as to my actions. As it is, he may very well know that you have been contacted."

Kane repressed a shiver from a chill that was not physical. "Common foe? You don't mean Balor?"

"Not Balor," Fand replied softly. "He is called Myrrdian."

"Never heard of him," Kane snapped.

"But you *have* contended with him." She took a deep breath, her high, firm breasts lifting. "You knew him as James L. Karabatos. Both of us knew him as Lord Strongbow. He has returned after all these years and he brings with him death and despair and the ancient weapons of the Tuatha de Danaan. He seeks the Grailstone, the Cauldron of Bran, and he will stop at nothing to steal it, even if it means plunging the entire world into war."

Chapter 15

"Myrrdian? You're sure that was the name?"

Kane cast Brigid Baptiste a sour look. "As sure as you can be of something imparted telepathically, which is to say, probably not a whole hell of a lot."

The two people walked side by side down the redoubt's wide main corridor. Great curving ribs of metal and massive girders supported the high rock roof.

"I still think you should let Reba examine you," Brigid said curtly. "That was a pretty hard fall you took."

"Wasn't it, though?" he snapped, tone brittle with sarcasm. He rubbed the lump on the back of his head. "Thanks to you and Grant for catching me, by the way."

Brigid glared at him. "We didn't know you were going to faint."

"I didn't faint," he retorted defensively. "I just sort of fell down."

"You just sort of passed out, Kane...even though you were only unconscious for perhaps thirty seconds."

"It felt a lot longer than that."

They reached the end of the corridor. The multiton

vanadium security door was already folded aside accordion-fashion, and a cool breeze wafted in from the plateau. They passed the illustration of Cerberus on the wall beneath the door controls. Although the official designations of all Totality Concept-related redoubts were based on the phonetic alphabet, almost no one who had ever been stationed in the facility referred to it by its official code name of Bravo. According to Lakesh, the mixture of predark civilian scientists and military personnel simply called it Cerberus and the name stuck.

One of the enlisted men with artistic aspirations went so far as to illustrate the door next to the entrance with an image of the three-headed hound that had guarded the gateway to Hades. Rather than attempt even a vaguely realistic representation, he used indelible paints to create a slavering black hell-hound with a trio of snarling heads sprouting out of an exaggeratedly muscled neck.

A spiked collar bound the neck, and the three jaws gaped wide open, blood and fire gushing between great fangs. In case anyone didn't grasp the meaning, emblazoned beneath the image was the single word *Cerberus*, wrought in overdone, ornate Gothic script.

Kane and Brigid stepped out onto the sprawling plateau. It was broad enough for the entire population of the redoubt to assemble without getting near the rusted remains of the perimeter chain-link fence. The flat expanse of tarmac was bordered on one side by a grassy slope rising to granite outcroppings and on the

The Gold Eagle Reader Service — Here's how it works:

Accepting your 2 free books and free gift (gift valued at approximately $5.00) places you under no obligation to buy anything. You may keep the books and gift and return the shipping statement marked "cancel." If you do not cancel, about a month later we'll send you 6 additional books and bill you just $31.94* — that's a savings of 15% off the cover price of all 6 books! And there's no extra charge for shipping! You may cancel at any time, but if you choose to continue, every other month we'll send you 6 more books, which you may either purchase at the discount price or return to us and cancel your subscription.

If offer card is missing write to: Gold Eagle Reader Service, 3010 Walden Ave., P.O. Box 1867, Buffalo NY 14240-1867

NO POSTAGE
NECESSARY
IF MAILED
IN THE
UNITED STATES

BUSINESS REPLY MAIL
FIRST-CLASS MAIL   PERMIT NO. 717   BUFFALO, NY

POSTAGE WILL BE PAID BY ADDRESSEE

GOLD EAGLE READER SERVICE
3010 WALDEN AVE
PO BOX 1867
BUFFALO NY 14240-9952

Get FREE BOOKS and a FREE GIFT when you play the...

LAS VEGAS

GAME

Just scratch off the gold box with a coin. Then check below to see the gifts you get!

YES! I have scratched off the gold box. Please send me my 2 **FREE BOOKS** and **gift for which I qualify**. I understand that I am under no obligation to purchase any books as explained on the back of this card.

366 ADL ENWS

166 ADL ENX4
(GE-LV-08)

FIRST NAME	LAST NAME

ADDRESS

APT.# | CITY

STATE/PROV. | ZIP/POSTAL CODE

7	7	7	Worth TWO FREE BOOKS plus a BONUS Mystery Gift!
🍒	🍒	🍒	Worth TWO FREE BOOKS!
🔔	🔔	♣	TRY AGAIN!

Offer limited to one per household and not valid to current subscribers of Gold Eagle® books. All orders subject to approval. Please allow 4 to 6 weeks for delivery.

other by an abyss plunging straight down to the tumbling waters of the Clark Fork River nearly a thousand feet below.

The indigo sky overhead glittered with a vast panorama of stars. The night was quiet except for the chirps of insects and the faint rush of water over rocks in the riverbed far, far below.

"The unconscious mind can't accurately gauge the passage of time," Brigid continued. "Thirty or so seconds was apparently long enough for Fand to bring you up to speed on why the Priory of Awen gated the seal here—apparently through a parallax point in Cornwall."

Kane didn't respond. He removed a cigar from his shirt pocket, put it in his mouth and struck it into flame with the simple flint and lighter he always carried. He puffed on it with a single-minded intensity, trying to slow down his racing thoughts.

After regaining consciousness on the laboratory floor with the priory seal clutched between his hands and a painful throbbing in his skull, he had experienced an overwhelming urge to escape the confines of the redoubt.

To the consternation and relief of his friends, he assured them he felt fine and briefly outlined what he had glimpsed in the telepathic vision, but he withheld certain details until he could work them out himself. Lakesh demanded a full account, but Kane brushed him and the very annoyed Grant aside, telling them he needed fresh air. Despite his insistence that he wanted to be alone, Brigid accompanied him.

"Myrrdian," Brigid murmured contemplatively. "A rather significant name in Celtic legend and lore."

"Yeah," Kane drawled. "So is the name of Strong-bow."

Lines of alarm furrowed Brigid's brow. "What are you talking about?"

"Fand told me that this Myrrdian person is really Strongbow, returned from where the hell it was I threw him all those years ago."

Outright fear replaced the alarm in Brigid's eyes. He knew the kind of thoughts wheeling through her mind—like him, she recalled the incident in Strong-bow's fortress. Due to her eidetic memory, her recol-lections were probably a lot more vivid than his own.

"Tell me everything," she said.

A bit reluctantly, Kane did so, not soft-pedaling any of the details of his telepathic vision. He knew Brigid wouldn't cast aspersions on his sanity or lack thereof.

When he was done, Brigid's face locked in a grim mask. "I often wondered what happened to Karabatos. Evil that profound can't just disappear."

The man named James L. Karabatos had, like Lakesh and a select few others, survived the nukecaust by tech-nological means. Through a process of cryogenesis that created a form of suspended animation, the subjects were enclosed by an impenetrable bubble of space and time, slowing to a crawl all metabolic processes.

By the time Kane and his friends met him on a mission to the British Isles, Karabatos had proclaimed himself Lord Strongbow, a name borrowed from Richard de Clare, a twelfth-century Norman aristocrat who led the first completely successful British invasion and occupation of Ireland.

He confided to the Cerberus warriors that in the performance of his duties in the twentieth century as a liaison officer between the Totality Concept's Mission Snowbird and Project Sigma, he dealt directly with a representative of the Archons, a creature called Balam. He also revealed he knew a great deal about the Annunaki, the mythical Serpent Kings.

Strongbow showed them the physical remains of Enlil, the last of the Dragon Lords. The creature wasn't mythical at all, but part of an extraterrestrial race known in Sumeria as the Annunaki, who had arrived on Earth some three hundred thousand years before the dawn of recorded history.

Strongbow admitted to using Enlil's genetic code to mutagenically modify himself and his dragoons. Furthermore, he told how Enlil had created a hybrid mixture of three races—human, Tuatha de Danaan and Annunaki. Enlil died after impregnating a woman with Danaan blood. After which, he placed both himself and her in cryonic suspension. They had revived nearly thirty years earlier, but the woman escaped Strongbow to Ireland and gave birth to an infant having the mixed blood of all three races.

That infant was Fand.

Strongbow also created an artificial black hole by combining the working principles of the quantum interphase inducers developed for Project Cerberus with the temporal dilator capacitors of Operation Chronos.

Despite the passage of more than five years, Kane could easily recall the huge orb of absolute, impenetrable blackness floating in the center of a complex of electronic consoles, relays and snaking power cables. It was like a bubble of burnished obsidian, but its surface reflected no light whatsoever.

Although he was loath to admit it, he also remembered Brigid Baptiste's explanation of its existence, later expanded upon by Lakesh. Hyperdimensional physics depended on the directed acceleration and deceleration of subatomic particles. Powered by a small thermonuclear generator, the Singularity was the black maw of eternity, potentially the hub of a wheel to every time, place and person.

Kane knew Strongbow envisioned the Singularity as a method to wring order from chaos by channeling the energies of the quantum stream into the artificial black hole. Once that was accomplished, Strongbow believed he could impose true order on all humanity simply by willing it, as a stone thrown into a pond sends ripples to the farthest shores.

"Hell might very well *be* where he came back from," Brigid intoned bleakly.

Kane nodded, an image of his last sight of Strong-

bow flashing into his mind. Impaled by a lance, Strongbow had dropped from the bronze spearhead and som-
ersaulted into the center of the imploding Singularity.

Both Kane and Brigid remembered hearing a pop of
air rushing in to fill the sudden vacuum left in the space
the man had occupied—and then he was gone, like the
flame of a snuffed-out candle.

Hugging herself, Brigid said, "I suppose it's logical
to an extent...if the Singularity acted as an interdimensional portal, it stands to reason he would have ended
up someplace—and he could return from that place at
some point."

"But with weapons of the Danaan?" he asked. "With
the hounds of Cullan?"

"We know that the Danaan mastered interdimensional travel millennia ago," Brigid replied. "They
came here from an alternate world. They might have
been able to visit various pocket universes or dimensions."

Teeth clamped on his cigar, Kane squinted toward
her through a veil of gray smoke. "What *kind* of universes?"

Brigid smiled ruefully. "It's connected to the multiverse theory you love so much. Pocket universes are a
type of very small parallel universe. They're theorized
to be attached to a larger parent universe, making them
literally pockets of space, but this isn't a necessary
feature. The name generally just refers to their small
size. Small size can be a relative and subjective thing,

however——some pocket universes are large enough to contain entire solar systems."

Kane nodded impatiently throughout her impromptu dissertation. "So Strongbow fell into one of the pocket universes where the Danaan stored all of their old toys?"

"Maybe." Brigid shrugged. "Who knows? We're both well aware that thousands of years ago the Tuatha de Danaan had mapped all the quantum pathways, the vortex points on Earth. The Danaan bolted into the vortex points and scattered themselves, maybe among countless pocket universes. Not even Maccan, the last full-blooded Danaan, knew to where his people had fled."

Kane recalled that Morrigan, the blind priestess of the Priory of Awen, claimed the Celtic cup and ring markings, as well as the knot patterns, were one-dimensional depictions of multidimensional geometrics. The Tuatha de Danaan had isolated a technique for translating the reality of one universe into its reflection. In such a manner, they had brought their entire culture, their whole race to Earth some twenty thousand years before.

Exhaling a stream of smoke, Kane said, "The question is what we're going to do about it."

Brigid angled a questioning eyebrow at him. "Do? We'll go to the site in Cornwall, obviously. What else can we do?"

When Kane didn't reply, she regarded him gravely. "Is there another reason you're reluctant to answer Fand's summons?"

"You damned well know there is, Baptiste—it's the fact that Fand summoned me personally."

"She's done that before."

"Yes," he said bluntly. "And I didn't like it then, either. This time, she showed me another vision of my so-called past life as Cuchulainn…and his relationship with the Danaan Fand."

"I was under the impression you two had settled your past-life-regression issue the last time you were together." Brigid's tone acquired a frosty edge. "At least, that's what you told me."

"It was settled as far as I was concerned," Kane declared. "I can't speak for her."

"Regardless," Brigid said, "we can't let this pass. If Strongbow is back and is passing himself off as Myrrdian, then he's got a major agenda. He certainly didn't choose that name at random, just like he didn't pick the name Strongbow out of a hat."

Kane cocked his head at her quizzically. "How so?"

"Myrrdian Wyllt is a character from the Celtic lore of Wales and Cornwall," Brigid stated matter-of-factly. "He was also called Merlinus Caledonensis."

Kane paused in his attempt to blow a smoke ring. "Merlin? Of Camelot fame?"

Brigid nodded. "The one and same adviser to Arthur, the once and future king of Britain."

Kane didn't even bother repressing a groan. "The calm before the storm, my ass. More like we've been in the eye of the hurricane."

The corners of Brigid Baptiste's lips lifted in a challenging smile. "Like you said to Grant—you wouldn't have it any other way."

Chapter 16

Darkness and light merged into an awesome boil mixture of golden-and-black clouds. A massive lightning bolt split the clouds and impaled their minds.

For a long, terrifying moment, they felt their bodies dissolve, with no sense of gravity, of up or down or any kind of control.

There was nothing to see but a raging torrent of light, wild plumes and whorling spindrifts of violet, of yellow, of blue and green and red. At a million, a billion miles per hour, they shot through coruscating clusters of stars and followed the glowing globules of tiny planets.

Streaks of gray and dark blue became interspersed with the multicolored swirls. They were conscious of a half instant of vertigo, as if they hurtled a vast distance, as if they were projectiles launched from mile-long cannons.

Then, the sensation of an uncontrolled plunge lessened. Slowly, as if veils were being drawn away one by one, the darker colors deepened and collected ahead of them into a pool of shimmering radiance.

Brigid, Kane and Grant stepped out of the energy field and into a chill sunset.

They moved away from the interphaser as the cascade of light whirled and spun around it like a diminishing cyclone, shedding sparks and thread-thin static discharges. As quickly as it appeared, the glowing cone vanished, as if it had been sucked back into the apex of the pyramidion.

The three people looked down at the geodetic stone marker at their feet, then at the Sun as it slowly sank beneath the horizon. The air temperature was very cool. The wind sighed around the stone dolmens arranged in a loose ring around them.

"As the saying goes," Brigid remarked in a voice barely above a whisper, "this must be the place."

Grant and Kane didn't reply. They stepped down from the rock slab and visually inspected the perimeter. The stone marker at their feet was twelve feet in diameter and deeply engraved with Celtic cup-and-spiral patterns, as well as interlaced designs. The inscriptions formed a perfectly integrated geometric design, twisting, swirling and intersecting in the center upon which the interphaser rested.

The megalithic stones surrounding the area looked somewhat familiar to Kane, but he also experienced a sense of disorientation. The cut stones were so worn by time, weather and the gnawing wind that they had lost the shapes he had seen in his vision.

Brigid bent over the interphaser, removing the brick-shaped power pack from its base and storing it in the machine's carrying case. She was very careful in her movements, for which Kane felt gratitude, since a damaged interphaser could either not function at all or worse, malfunction.

When making transits to and from the Cerberus redoubt, they always used the mat-trans chamber as the origin point because it could be hermetically sealed. The interphaser's targeting computer had been programmed with the precise coordinates of the mat-trans unit as Destination Zero. A touch of a single key on the interphaser's control pad would automatically return the device to the jump chamber, but sometimes the phase harmonics needed to be fine-tuned. These adjustments were normally within Brigid's purview.

Unlike the mat-trans gateway jumps, phasing along a hyperdimensional conduit was more akin to stepping from one room into another—if the rooms were thousands of miles apart.

The possibility that the interphaser could materialize them either in a lake or an ocean or underground was a concept Kane privately feared. He knew an analogical computer was built into the interphaser to automatically select a vortex point above solid ground.

When Interphaser Version 2.0 was completed, Kane, Grant and Brigid had endured weeks of tedious training in the use of the device on short hops, selecting vortex points near the redoubt—or at least, near in the sense that if they couldn't make the return trip through a quantum channel, they could conceivably walk back to the installation.

When the interphaser was activated in conjunction with the energy produced by the mat-trans unit, a different set of control protocols were engaged.

Several years earlier, Lakesh had linked a switching station with the main gateway board to govern the temporal dilation of the experimental Omega Path program. Since the energy outputs of the vortex points and the temporal dilator were of similar frequencies, it hadn't been much of a task to put the system back into use.

As had been done during the Omega Path experiments, the mainframe computer network was reprogrammed with the logarithmic data of the Parallax Points Program. The program prolonged the quincunx effect produced by rematerialization, stretching it out in perfect balance between the phase and interphase inducers. Upon standard gateway activation, a million autoscanning elements committed to memory every feature of the jumpers' physical and mental composition even, Kane supposed, down to the very subconscious. The data filtered through the system's built-in memory banks, correlating it with a variation range field.

Once the autoscanning sequence was complete, the translation program of the quincunx effect kicked in, a process by which lower dimensional space was translated, phased into a higher dimensional space along a quantum path. The jumpers traveled this path, existing for a nanosecond as digital duplicates of themselves, in a place between a relativistic *here* and a relativistic *there*.

Brigid finished packing the interphaser into its cushioned carrying case and stepped down from the stone slab. The megaliths rose from a moor covered by knee-high grass. An eddy of wind brought the whiff of wood smoke.

"What's the plan?" Grant asked. "Stay here or explore? Not that there's a hell of a lot to see."

"I'd prefer to explore," Kane said. The stone circle felt like an evil place to him. He sensed many lives had been lost here over the centuries, most of them by violence.

"I sort of hoped the priory would have an emissary waiting for us," Brigid remarked, unconsciously lowering her voice, as if she experienced the same sense of foreboding. Her mane of red-gold hair fell down her back in a long sunset-colored braid to the base of her spine.

"We could be in enemy territory for all we know," Grant rumbled.

The moor was a grassy plain filled only with dark, flinty outcroppings. Regardless of the direction in which Kane looked, the view was identical. The only deviation was southward, where he could barely make out a dark copse of trees a quarter of a mile to the east. He glimpsed a red sputter of firelight within the woods.

"For lack of another direction," he said, saluting toward the trees, "let's go thataway and see who's burning what."

"Or the other way around," Grant commented dourly.

Kane kicked at the ground between a pair of the megaliths, scattering ashes and charcoal. "Speaking of burning, somebody had a fire here...not all that long ago, either."

Hands on her knees, Brigid bent and sniffed. "Smells like they used fish oil as a fuel or an accelerant. I'd guess the fire was part of a ritual of some sort."

Putting on dark-vision glasses, the Cerberus warriors strode through the ring of the stones and out onto the moor. Bracken and pink-tipped heather crackled underfoot. The three people were attired in one-piece black garments that fitted as tightly as doeskin gloves. The coveralls were known as shadow suits for a variety of reasons and not just because of their midnight color.

Although the shadow suits lent Kane, Brigid and Grant a sinister aspect, the garments had become important items in their arsenal over the past few years. Ever since they absconded with the suits from Redoubt Yankee on Thunder Isle, the suits had proved their worth and their superiority to the polycarbonate Magistrate armor, if for nothing else than their internal subsystems.

Manufactured with a technique known in predark days as electrospin lacing, the electrically charged polymer particles formed a dense web of formfitting fibers. Composed of a compiled weave of spider silk, Monocrys and Spectra fabrics, the garments were essentially a single-crystal metallic microfiber with a very dense molecular structure.

The outer Monocrys sheathing went opaque when exposed to radiation, and the Kevlar and Spectra layers provided protection against blunt trauma. The spider silk allowed flexibility, but it traded protection from firearms for freedom of movement.

The inner layer was lined by carbon nanotubes only a nanometer thick, rolled-up sheets of graphite with a tensile strength greater than steel. The suits were almost impossible to tear, but a high-caliber bullet could penetrate them and, unlike the Mag exoskeletons, wouldn't redistribute the kinetic shock. Still, the material was dense and elastic enough to deflect knives and arrows.

Sin Eaters were holstered to Kane's and Grant's right forearms. Long combat knives, the razor-keen blades forged of dark blue steel, hung from sheaths at their hips. Both men wore grenade-laden combat harnesses over their upper bodies.

Brigid carried a Copperhead, and her TP-9 autopistol rode in a cross-draw slide rig at her waist. A flat case containing survival stores, such as bottled water and concentrated rations, hung from her right shoulder and the interphaser case dangled from her left.

Almost all of the ordnance was supplied by the Cerberus armory, quite likely the best stocked and outfitted arsenal in postnuke America. Glass-fronted cases held racks of automatic assault rifles. There were many makes and models of subguns, as well as dozens of semiautomatic pistols and revolvers, complete with holsters and belts.

The armory also housed heavy assault weaponry: bazookas, tripod-mounted 20 mm cannons, mortars and rocket launchers. All the ordnance had been laid down in hermetically sealed Continuity of Government installations before the nukecaust. Protected from the ravages of the outside environment, nearly every piece of munitions and hardware was as pristine as the day it was first manufactured.

Lakesh himself had put the arsenal together over several decades, envisioning it as the major supply depot for a rebel army. The army never materialized—at least, not in the fashion Lakesh hoped it would. Therefore, Cerberus was blessed with a surplus of death-dealing equipment that would have turned the most militaristic overlord green with envy, or given the most pacifistic of them heart failure—if they indeed possessed hearts.

As the Sun dropped completely below the horizon, a mist rose from the ground, tendrils of it twisting around their ankles like ghostly fingers.

"Can't say much for what I've seen of Cornwall so far," Grant remarked.

Brigid forced a chuckle. "It's a bit more picturesque in the daylight I imagine…but the Penwith peninsula is primarily farmland. Still, we might come across a few more Neolithic sites."

"We're on a peninsula?" Grant asked, his tone surprised. "Nobody told me that."

"That's what you get for skipping the prejump briefings," Brigid replied. "We're on a promontory of land at the western end of Cornwall…in fact, the most westerly district on mainland England. The district's name is derived from the two Cornish-Gaelic words, *penn* meaning 'headland' and *wydh* meaning 'at the end'."

"Fascinating," Kane said dryly. "How far are we from the ocean?"

"Six or seven miles," Brigid answered. "On a really windy day, we could probably smell the sea from here."

The sky lightened with the first pale hint of moonrise. As it did, the faint murmur of voices reached their ears. Kane stopped, holding up a hand for silence. He and his friends strained their hearing. The distant sound of many voices blended in a repetitive chant floated from the direction of the dark woods. They saw the red flicker of a fire between the boles of the trees.

"Pretty good-sized fire going in there," Grant observed inanely.

Kane did not reply. The words of the chant weren't familiar, yet something about them awoke an uneasy, almost atavistic response in him. His skin crawled beneath his shadow suit.

"Baptiste, do you understand that language?" he asked.

Her brow furrowed in concentration for a long moment, then she shook her head. "Some form of Gaelic, but I can't pick out individual words. It could be a local dialect, maybe a kind of prayer song. That wouldn't be surprising. We know the old Celtic ways made a comeback in this part of the world."

Kane took a deep breath and started walking again. "Let's go and find out."

The light grew brighter as a full Moon ascended into the sky. When they reached the edge of the forest, they saw gleaming along the edges an elaborately carved stone Celtic cross, rising seven feet from the underbrush. It marked the mouth of a footpath.

"Convenient signpost," Grant grunted.

The Cerberus warriors made their way around the great trees festooned with vines and creepers. The ground underfoot, thickly padded with moss and leaf mold, muffled their footsteps. The boughs of the great trees shut out almost all of the sky, and the moonlight filtering through turned an unhealthy shade of green.

The farther they proceeded down the cathedral aisles of the gargantuan tree trunks, the aroma of wood smoke grew sharper and the chanting became louder. Along with the smoke, they smelled the sweetish stench of overcooked meat. They walked slowly, pushing aside and bending branches.

Thorns and briars caught at them, snagged their arms and legs. If not for their shadow suits, they would have been scratched bloody a score of times. The chanting rose in volume, a keening litany that held a dark, disturbing melody. Harp strings thrummed, stroked by expert fingers. The music was not beautiful, but Kane felt as if he had heard it before. He walked steadily toward the glow of the fire blazing beyond the black tree trunks.

A voice spoke from the shadows, cold and without intonation, which made it sound even more forbidding. "Who comes to defile the ritual of rebirth in the sacred grove?"

Chapter 17

The voice wafted from a wedge of shadow between two trees, backed by a thicket. Even with their night-vision glasses, Grant, Kane and Brigid could barely discern the outline of a tall figure standing there.

"We don't mean any harm," Brigid said calmly.

Kane took a step forward but came to a halt at the unmistakable rasp of metal sliding against a scabbard.

"Stop," the voice said again. "Do not approach."

"Why not?" Grant demanded. "Who the hell are you to give orders?"

"I am Lenan, a warrior of the grail. You encroach upon a sacred ritual celebrating the rebirth of our people. If you heed me not, you will suffer eternal damnation and the peace of the afterlife will be denied you forever."

"That's a pretty formidable curse," Brigid side-mouthed wryly.

"Yeah, well," Kane said impatiently, "we've heard variations of it before over the past few years. It means no more now than it has the other times."

Kane started walking again. He did not unholster

his Sin Eater, but kept his hands open and free, swinging at his sides. "Lenan, we aren't threats to you. We only want to talk."

A dark shape slid around the trunk of a tree and stood to block Kane's path. "Stop, I command you."

"Bite me," Kane snapped, not breaking stride.

"Die, then, you who spit on our wisdom!"

Kane glimpsed a flutter of robes, gray in the dim light, and then saw the glint of a golden blade arcing through the air. The weapon slashed at his head, but Kane easily sidestepped and Lenan stumbled, off balance. Kane figured he had been given training in how to threaten interlopers but not in how to deal with them directly.

Lenan whirled, dragging the sword with him, his eyes flashing fanatically within the shadows cast by a feature-concealing cowl. Kane didn't use his fists on the man, and he resisted the impulse to shoot him dead.

When the sword hacked at him again, Kane dodged, and the blade chopped deeply into the trunk of a tree. As Lenan jerked at the hilt to free it, Kane swiftly struck with a backhanded ram's-head blow where he figured his attacker's nose would be. Cartilage crunched under his fist.

The self-proclaimed warrior of the grail staggered backward, tripped over a root and fell heavily. He scrambled to his knees, put his hands to his face, then stared incredulously at the blood glistening on his fingers.

"You dare—" he began.

Kane kicked him, the toe of his boot connecting against the underside of the man's jaw and knocking him onto his back. He made no movement afterward.

Brigid knelt beside him, pulling away the cowl. Lenan's head was long jawed and closely shaved, the stubble showing black. Despite the blood smearing the lower half of his face, he appeared youthful, barely out of his teens.

"Just a kid," Kane commented.

Brigid nodded distractedly and opened the front of the dark gray robe. Lividly emblazoned on Lenan's left pectoral was the mark of a branding iron, in the shape of a goblet with what appeared to be a tree growing out of it.

"What the hell is that?" Kane asked, leaning over.

"The emblem of some sort of Druidic sect, I would imagine," she replied. She traced the configuration with a forefinger. "A cup or a grail containing an oak tree."

"Did Druids go around attacking people with golden swords?" Kane asked skeptically.

Grant worked the sword free of the tree trunk and turned it over in his big hands. "Only the hilt and grip are gold. The blade is made out of bronze. It might not have cut through your suit, but if Lenan had gotten a good whack at you, it sure as hell would have left a mark."

Kane nodded, jaw set, staring at the glow of the fire several hundred yards away. "Warrior of the grail he called himself. Does that mean anything to you, Baptiste?"

She arose, brushing off the knees of her shadow suit. "You know it does. In Celtic mythology, King Bran the Blessed had a magic cauldron given to him by—or stolen from—the Tuatha de Danaan. When the freshly dead people were put into it, the cauldron could restore them to life. Legends of the Holy Grail, the Grailstone and even the purpose of Egyptian sarcophagi are all connected to it in one way or another, depending on what part of the world you're in.

"Sometimes the grails generate a never-ending supply of food—sometimes they can heal the sick or restore youth. Sometimes they decide who the next king should be, as only the true sovereign could hold them."

She shrugged. "Your guess is as good as mine what the truth is."

Kane smiled. "I'm fresh out of guesses. Let's go get us some facts."

The Cerberus warriors moved cautiously toward the orange eye of the bonfire, Grant using the gold-and-bronze sword to push their way through a thicket. When they reached a broad glade, they crouched behind a screen of shrubbery.

The glen was bathed in both firelight and greenish moon glow. Near the roaring bonfire, a large platform had been erected, put together from rough-hewed planks. A scaffoldlike structure with an iron hook held a cage that looked disquietingly similar to the one in which Grant had been imprisoned barely seventy-two hours earlier.

The cage, although made of wicker, looked almost intact, but within the shadows of the interior, a blackened shape could be seen, curled in the fetal position that was the hallmark of death by fire. Smoke still wisped from it.

"What the hell is that thing?" Grant asked, his whispering voice edged with disgust.

"Looks like they burned something in there," Kane replied.

"No, looks like they burned *someone* in there," Brigid contradicted. "Looks like a wicker-man setup to me."

"A what?" Grant demanded.

Brigid swallowed down bile. "It was a form of human sacrifice used by ancient Druids, first reported by Julius Caesar. The Druids generally used thieves and criminals, although they sometimes sacrificed innocent men and women."

Kane felt his stomach heave as he made out more details of the shape inside. A blackened skull with sightless sockets peered down, the browned teeth exposed in a permanent rictus of agony. "Nice bunch."

There were perhaps twenty of the robed and cowled people circling the huge fire, their faces hidden in shadow. They danced wildly, arms and legs flailing. The bonfire spit and crackled, throwing grotesque shadows onto their robed bodies as they crisscrossed in front of the fire. The people passed around earthenware jugs from which they drank copiously. Every now and then one of the dancers would stop, bend over and vomit just as copiously.

"They're boozed up to the gills," Grant murmured.

"They're drinking poteen," Brigid said. "A sort of wood-grain alcohol. It's supposed to be potent stuff. I'm surprised any of them can still stand, much less dance."

"If you call that dancing," Kane remarked dourly.

A quartet of musicians stood to one side, strumming harps, beating drums and playing the pipes. Beside them on the ground lay a naked woman, and although a black hood completely concealed her head, her posture still exuded stark terror. She strained against her leather bonds, working her arms and legs.

The chanting and dancing stopped suddenly, but the music went on. Half of the dancers left the fire and went to the wicker cage, pulling it down and shaking out the crisped remains. Others went to the hooded woman, pulling her to feet while another group began piling more logs onto the pyre. A whirling column of sparks and embers corkscrewed into the sky.

"For lack of a better plan, I suggest we interfere," Kane whispered.

"Until we know what this is all about, we shouldn't step on any local religious customs," Brigid said hesitantly.

Grant raised an eyebrow and said, "You think shoving someone into a wicker cage and roasting them alive is a religious custom and not just torture?"

"It very well could be. The people of Wales and Cornwall are Celts, after all. We don't know much about the Druids or their religion, but apparently human sacrifice of this sort was an accepted part of their religious practice."

Kane straightened. "As arrogant as it sounds, it's not ours."

The two men flexed their wrists, and with the faint drone of electric motors, the Sin Eaters slid from their forearm holsters and slapped into their waiting hands. Brigid sighed, drew her TP-9 and stepped up beside them.

"I suggest we surround them," she said quietly. "Or try to give them that impression."

After a brief, whispered conference, the Cerberus warriors separated. Grant remained in position, Sin Eater in his right hand, the bronze-bladed sword in his left. Kane went to the left while Brigid crept off to the right.

Kane circled the glade, placing his feet carefully so he wouldn't trip over any roots. When he reached a point facing the musicians, he activated his Commtact and subvocalized, "Set."

"Acknowledged," came Grant's response.

"Set," Brigid said.

Kane watched the Druids haul the woman to her feet and drag her toward the cage. Distantly, he realized there was something familiar about her form, but under the circumstances he was too preoccupied to make a connection.

"They're about ready to put her in the broiler," Brigid said impatiently. "Let's make with the diversion while there's still time."

Kane aimed his Sin Eater at the apex of a pair of large logs in the bonfire. Cupping his right hand in his left, he sighted down the barrel. "One diversion coming right up. Follow my lead."

He squeezed off a triburst. The brief stutter of the autopistol was followed a fraction of a second later by Grant's own Sin Eater. Flaming fragments of wood exploded upward, like lava ejected from the mouth of a miniature volcano.

Screams erupted from the Druids as they were showered with sparks and struck by burning splinters. They lurched drunkenly into one another, dropping the woman to the ground. The report of Brigid's TP-9 sounded like the breaking a giant tree branch. The bullet punched into a log and sent it rolling out of the fire amid a storm of embers.

Although most of the Druids ran in a wild panic, a group of five detached themselves from the sidelines and spread out across the glade. They did not move as if they were inebriated. They tossed aside their robes and unlimbered compact H&K MP-5 subguns from leather harnesses.

Kane stared in astonishment. His head echoed with Grant's growl of "What the fuck?"

The Druids opened fire, the rattling of the weapons sending out waves of eardrum-compressing sound.

Steel-jacketed rounds scythed through the trees and undergrowth. Twigs, leaves and bark rained down on Kane as steady streams of autofire ripped into the foliage from three points.

Over the Commtact, Kane commanded, "Down, everybody down!"

Dropping flat, Kane heard the bullets snapping over his head, like the cracks of a whip. He figured the Druids only had the most general idea of his position and were shooting blind. He brought a cowled and robed man into target acquisition and depressed the trigger stud of the Sin Eater.

Three bullets hammered the man directly in his chest, and he staggered backward, the front of his robe bursting into dark splashes. His finger constricted convulsively on the trigger of the MP-5. A barrage of bullets continued to spew from the barrel and struck a man near him.

Clutching at himself, the Druid folded in the middle and pitched headlong into the bonfire. He flung himself backward, his robe wrapped in fire. He screamed and rolled over and over on the ground, trying to extinguish the flames.

Kane rolled himself, toward the protective bulwark of a tree trunk. He heard the crack of Brigid's TP-9 and glimpsed a Druid buckle, his limbs twisting. Clenching his teeth, he silently swore at himself for violating the hallmark rule of a dark territory probe—to always, *always* expect the unexpected.

He gripped a V-60 grenade on his combat webbing. "Baptiste, Grant—status?"

"As good as you can be when you're facedown in the dirt," Grant said breathlessly.

"So far so good with me, too," Brigid stated.

"All right, then. Listen up—I'm going to chuck a gren into the fire. That ought to break up the meeting."

"Just give me the high sign before you—" Grant replied.

Brigid's agitated voice broke in, "No, you can't!"

"Why the hell not?" Kane demanded.

"Look at the woman—the sacrifice!"

"What?"

"Look at her!"

Hitching around on his right side, Kane looked over the gnarled roots of the tree and into the glade. The naked woman on the ground had succeeded in freeing one arm from her bonds and yanked away the hood that had covered her head.

Long falls of steel-gray hair framed a fair-skinned, heart-shaped face with a snub nose and full lips. Despite the terror contorting her face, she was beautiful.

Her eyes were blue-white, with no irises or pupils.

Kane groaned in frustrated disbelief. *"Morrigan."*

Chapter 18

Wisely Morrigan remained on the ground as the Druids dashed past her. She knew she was exposed and helpless, so she did not draw attention to herself.

The men with the MP-5s continued to fire prolonged bursts into the murk around the glade as they backed away, disheartened by the casualties among their number. The subguns continued to chatter, muzzles wreathed in little halos of flame, bright brass arcing from the ejector ports.

Grant squeezed off a triburst with his Sin Eater, but he aimed at the Druids' knees. One of the men fell head-first, howling and screeching, clawing at his right leg. He frantically crawled away from the bonfire. Another man pirouetted away and fell heavily, disappearing from view into the thicket.

"Hold your fire," Kane whispered to Brigid and Grant. "Let 'em keeping hosing their ammo around until they're dry."

The former dancing Druids fled howling into the forest. The staccato hammering of autofire punctuated the yells and screams. When the armed men realized they defended only a bonfire, they stopped firing and retreated. One of them reached down to grasp Morrigan and haul her to her feet. Brigid's pistol bammed and the man staggered backward, blood squirting from the hole in his left shoulder.

Wild with pain, dazed by the shock of impact, he screamed a stream of hard-edged words in Gaelic and ran toward the woods, hand clapped over his shoulder. His comrades lost their nerve and raced after him, blundering through the underbrush.

Cautiously, Kane, Brigid and Grant emerged from their hiding places and entered the perimeter, their eyes scanning all parts of the zone to make sure it was secure. Two bodies lay leaking fluids into the soil. The Druid who had been gut shot and burned lay on the ground, curled around his belly wound, groans issuing from between blistered lips.

Raking her hair out of her face, Morrigan stared around blindly. She did not speak, but when Brigid knelt beside her and laid a hand on her shoulder, she flinched.

"Morrigan, it's Brigid Baptiste," she said soothingly. "Do you remember me?"

Morrigan stared in her direction and nodded. "Of course. Are your friends with you?"

Her soft, lilting voice was touched by an Irish brogue.

"Yes," Kane said. "So is Grant. Are you hurt?"

At the sound of Kane's voice, Morrigan exhaled in

relief. "A few bruises and a bit of battered pride, but I think I'll get better. If somebody could free me—"

Kane bent over her, drawing his combat knife. Swiftly, he slashed through the rawhide thongs wrapped around her ankles and the bindings immobilizing her right arm. She shivered, hugging herself.

Grant found a discarded robe lying on the ground and brought it over to Morrigan. "Put this on."

The woman took it, sniffed the cloth and smiled wanly. "It's mine."

As Brigid helped her slip it on, Kane demanded, "Could you tell us what the hell is going on here?"

"Pretty much what it looked like," Morrigan answered. "I was being sacrificed."

"To whom?" Brigid asked. "Or to what?"

"Myrrdian," the blind woman said. "I had incurred his wrath, y'see."

Grant gazed around at the dark forest. "Was he here?"

Morrigan shook her head. Wincing, she tried to rise. Brigid helped her to her feet, arranging the robe over her legs. "Nay, he was not. I had joined the Druidic circle of his so-called warriors of the grail, but I was found out and denounced as a spy of the Priory of Awen."

She paused and added, "Which, of course, I was."

"Of course," Kane repeated sarcastically. "For somebody who is a telepath and works undercover, you never seem to know when you're going to be denounced as a spy."

Morrigan cast him a reproachful glance but said nothing in response. He had encountered the blind, tele-pathic priestess of the Priory of Awen twice before. The last time she had tried to manipulate a madman named Quayle into loosing a holocaust that would have not only destroyed Great Britain but devastated most of Europe, as well. Quayle had discovered her true inten-tions and very nearly killed her.

"We received a summons from the priory," Brigid said.

Morrigan nodded, brushing back her hair. "Aye… Fand activated the vortex point at the Merry Maidens and sent you the message."

Kane tensed, drawing in a sharp breath. "Where is Fand?"

"I'd like to know that myself. Come with me."

"Come with you where?" Grant rumbled.

"To the village. 'Tis not far."

She started to stride out of the glade, but then when she realized no one followed her, she paused and glanced over her shoulder. "Why do you tarry?" she asked impatiently.

"We're not going anywhere with you until you tell us what's going on," Kane stated matter-of-factly.

She gestured toward the thicket and the moor beyond. "We shall talk while we walk."

Grant, Kane and Brigid exchanged quizzical glances, then joined Morrigan.

Following her instructions, they guided her out of the woods and onto the moor.

The Moon had climbed to a high point in the sky and was heading west. Its wavery, pale light illuminated the path cutting over the gorse and heather. It was narrow and made rough underfoot by stones and flints. Morrigan suffered in silence.

"Talk," Kane suggested gruffly.

"About six months ago," Morrigan said, "a group of Druids hereabouts began the working that brought the man they know as Myrrdìan out of the Skatha, the land of shadows."

Kane asked, "What do you mean, 'working'?"

"A magical working. A summoning…the Druids brought Myrrdian out of the land of shadows. The priory has known about the Druids of Penwith for quite some time—they kept a tight grip on the local politics and religion. Like the priory, they kept their faith through century upon century and passed the knowledge and spells and workings on from generation to generation."

She smiled sadly. "Even before the End of Days they were isolated here. They stayed true to their old ways, to their roots. So in a way, it's not surprising that they involved themselves in such an undertaking."

"What really happened?" Grant demanded.

Morrigan fingered a breeze-tossed lock of steel-colored hair away from her face. "We can only speculate that someone among the Druids had the ability to manipulate the energies of the natural vortex point within the Merry Maidens."

"We know Fand had the power—through simple focused thought—to dilate the matrix points in Ireland," Brigid said.

"She also could allow elements of the otherworld to seep into this one," Morrigan replied. "Someone with a similar power interacting with the vortex point here brought Myrrdian through a portal from another dimension."

"Why do you keep calling him that?" Kane inquired. "I thought he was really Strongbow."

Morrigan shrugged. "Myrrdian is an ancient name for Merlin. Legend has it that he went or was sent to another realm, or that's what some folktales say."

Brigid added, "The figure we know as Merlin is actually a composite based primarily on two figures— Myrrdian Wyllt, also called Merlinus Caledonensis, and Aurelius Ambrosius, a highly fictionalized version of the historical war leader Ambrosius Aurelianus.

"Supposedly a bard who went mad after witnessing the horrors of war, Myrrdian was said to have fled civilization to become a wild man of the woods. There's really not much about his background in either legend or history. He was reputed to be half-demon or perhaps half Danaan and is credited with building Stonehenge by dancing the stones into place with music."

"I thought he was hooked up with King Arthur," Kane said.

Brigid nodded. "In most legends he is, yes, as an adviser and even something of a father figure. Myrrdian was also reputed to be able to change his shape and he has a connection with the Holy Grail…which, judging by the insignia we saw, is still going on."

"Stories differ," Morrigan went on. "Some believe Myrrdian was entombed in a rock cairn or locked away in a crystal cave."

Kane sighed in exasperation. "But it's not Merlin or Myrrdian, is it? It's really Karabatos or Strongbow, right?"

"Not according to the people here on Penwith," Morrigan countered. "They think he really *is* Myrrdian, a powerful wizard, the chief priest of the Druids, who can travel back and forth in time and who was imprisoned in a place outside of time many centuries ago."

She paused for breath. "Those are just a few of the beliefs of the people here."

"A thousand years ago, maybe," Grant said darkly. "You'd think they would have advanced beyond those pagan beliefs, even after the nukecaust."

"The Celts knew something long ago that seems to have eluded the rest of humankind," Morrigan retorted. "There are many forms of science, of knowledge. Didn't you know early Irish Christianity was as steeped in magical ideas as ever was Druidic paganism?"

Brigid nodded in agreement. "It's obvious that the stone circles and cairns were built by a sophisticated society with an interest in tracking the Sun's movement. It's also obvious that the cairns and their enclosed passages were constructed with a specific purpose in mind. They still work well as calendars, but over time they have lost some of their usefulness, mainly due to the changes in climatic conditions and, in the case of Newgrange, a change in the obliquity of the ecliptic.

"Nevertheless, they probably still can be used to precisely define major events in the Sun's cycle. The enormous engineering feat involved in their creation, plus the precise orientation of their position to the Sun on important days in the Sun's cycle, means that this ability to understand the world around them must have been of critical importance to the society that created them five thousand years ago."

"Of course it was important for the ancient Celts to know the Sun's cycle," Morrigan said peevishly. "So they might know the proper days to pray, to plant crops, to harvest grain and make their sacrifices."

"Sacrifices like you?" Kane inquired snidely.

Morrigan did not appear to be offended. "Timing is everything."

The path bent to the left and entered an open field, bordered by a crude, waist-high wall of piled stones. They caught a whiff of salt air, and Kane guessed they were nearing the coast.

"The village isn't much farther," Morrigan said.

"What should we expect when we get there?" Kane asked.

Morrigan shrugged. "Not much. There are very few people left there now. Just a garrison of solders."

"Whose soldiers?" Grant wanted to know, suspicion edging his tone.

Morrigan started to answer, and then sighed. "I'm not sure."

They climbed a gentle slope and stood at the crest of a long ridge. Below them, an eighth of a mile away, they saw the flatlands stretch to a cliff that fell away to a mirror-calm sea, the surface shimmering with the waning moonlight.

Inland lay a little village—or the remains of one. All of the cottages had been burned to skeletal frameworks, and the cultivated fields were overgrown with weeds. Cows lumbered among the furrows, nosing through the growth, looking for graze.

Sadly, Morrigan said, "This was once a thriving little community…before Myrrdian arrived and corrupted the place."

"It looks like he did a lot more than corrupt it," Brigid murmured, gazing toward the single structure that still stood, a great house made of rough-hewed timbers.

"Aye," Morrigan agreed. "He gutted it, looted it and forced all the people here to join his army. He put the Druids in positions of ultimate power, to enforce his edicts and his whims."

Grant scowled. "You're not giving us a hell of a lot to work with."

Before Morrigan could answer, the breeze carried the baying of hounds. She stiffened and looked around, her sightless eyes wide and staring. Her lips worked as if she were trying to bottle up a scream.

"What now?" Kane demanded.

She swallowed hard. "The hounds of Cullan have been loosed. They have caught our scent and are tracking us."

Grant turned and gazed back in the direction they had come. "Dogs?"

Morrigan shook her head, tresses flying. "No, hounds…monsters from the otherworld that do the bidding of Myrrdian. Our only hope is to reach the village."

Her words evoked a sense of fear in Kane. He stared out at the moor stretching around them, and he caught flashes of movement other than that of wind-stirred heather or grass.

He took Morrigan by the hand. "Come on, priestess…we're going to run a little."

Chapter 19

Their feet churned up scraps of heather and gorse, tearing a path through the grass. To the surprise of the Cerberus warriors, Morrigan ran down the slope with a steady lightness and sureness of stride that came of complete confidence.

Kane hazarded several backward glances, but he saw no movement on the ridgeline. He wondered if the baying they heard was just that voiced by ordinary dogs, and Morrigan's superstitious nature turned the sound into something else.

When they reached the base of the hill, Kane paused long enough to look back again, and a shape shifted atop the crest. Limned by the moonlight, the shape resolved into a lean, four-legged figure. Between one eye blink and another, it was joined by two others. Although the creatures were only in his field of vision for a fraction of a second, he realized they definitely did not resemble ordinary dogs. Their eyes shone like freshly minted coins.

Dread knotted in his belly like an icy fist and he lifted his Sin Eater. Before he could squeeze off a shot, the shadow shapes disappeared. Turning, he said hoarsely, "Everybody run."

"I thought that's what we *were* doing," Grant panted, face twisted in a grimace of exertion. Moonlight glinted from the edge of the sword in his fist.

"Do it better," Kane bit out grimly. "Do it faster."

The four people raced across the open field stretching between the hill and the stone wall enclosing the outskirts of the village. Kane heard Grant gasping and wheezing, and he began favoring his left leg as they sprinted. A couple of years before the big man had suffered an injury that resulted in partial paralysis, and he occasionally experienced trouble with his left leg.

As it was, the pain of a stitch stabbed along Kane's side, and the muscles of his legs began to feel as if they were trapped between the jaws of a tightening vise. Nevertheless, he kept running, his every footfall jarring his entire body and blurring his vision. The breath seared his lungs, and his heart pounded against his ribs. His laboring legs seemed weighted with half-frozen mud.

With blood-chilling suddenness, a deep-throated howl pierced the darkness, full of malign triumph. Kane risked a glance backward and what he saw chilled him clean through.

Three of the largest dogs he had ever seen loped over the moor, racing at the Cerberus warriors with relentless speed. Kane lifted his pistol and squeezed off a shot. He wasn't sure if he missed or if the animals were in truth otherworldly in nature, since their speed did not slacken. The beasts surged over the ground, their black-rimmed lips drawn back from their fangs in a contortion of blood lust and their eyes glistening.

Kane forced himself to continue running, ignoring the pain in his legs and the fiery ache in his chest. From all around came a tremendous paralyzing roar as the hounds hailed one another with their eerie calls.

Reaching the low stone wall, he used one hand to vault over it. Before his feet touched the ground on the other side, he felt a great weight slam into his back, knocking him asprawl on his belly. He jerked his head up and around with grit in his mouth, only dimly aware of Grant and Brigid shouting.

Frantically, he elbowed himself onto his back, catching only fragmented glimpses of saliva-wet fangs and a drooling muzzle scant inches from his face. Gunshots cracked. Kane lifted his Sin Eater, but the hound closed its great jaws on Kane's upflung forearm and shook him as a terrier would a rat.

The animal's strength was enormous and for what seemed like an eternity, Kane felt as if his arm were being torn from its socket. With a contemptuous shake, the hound flung Kane to one side, rolling him over and over. Dizzy, spitting out grit, Kane fought his way to his hands and knees just in time to see one of the dogs spring in an arching leap straight for Brigid's throat.

The beast's great forepaws struck her breasts and bowled her over. Although she dropped her TP-9, she fell back with her feet braced against the hound's belly and she used its momentum to carry it over her body. It tumbled snout over rump to land gracelessly on its back. It scrambled to all fours and bounded away with eye-blurring rapidity.

Staggering erect, Kane helped Brigid up. He noted that the hound's fangs hadn't managed to penetrate the fabric of his shadow suit, but his arm still ached from wrist to shoulder. Forming a rough circle around Morrigan, the Cerberus warriors stood back to back, guns at the ready as the hounds circled them, making snarling, rushing feints. Lean, shaggy forms leaped all about them, eyes gleaming, teeth snapping.

A black bulk lunged soundlessly from the murk, and Brigid triggered her TP-9, squeezing off three rounds. The staccato cracks didn't seem to faze the creature, but it veered away with a speed that defied the eye.

Kane felt panic rising within him, a sense that the hounds were supernatural monsters that had slipped their leashes in Hell and would tear out the souls of him and his friends and gnaw on them for all eternity, like soup bones.

Kane depressed the trigger stud of his Sin Eater, and the pistol stuttered on full-auto. Divots of dirt sprang up and round struck the stone wall with the high-pitched keen of ricochets. The hounds continued to bay as if mocking the humans' attempt to slay them.

The beasts moved like wind-borne black wraiths, affording the Cerberus warriors only nightmarish glimpses. Flames wreathed the muzzle of Grant's and Kane's Sin Eaters, smearing the gloom, casting an unearthly strobing effect on the hounds snarling all around them. The night became a wild babel of howls and snarls, punctuated by the bull-fiddle roar of Sin Eaters on full-auto. Brigid's handgun snapped out steady, hand-clapping bangs.

"Your firearms will do no good!" Morrigan shrilled. "They are from the otherworld and only weapons forged there will harm them."

"Weapons like what, for example?" Grant demanded angrily.

Before she could answer, a hound sprang out of the shadows and crashed into Grant with breath-robbing impact, the fanged jaws snapping for his throat. Staggering backward, Grant fell against the wall. At the same time, he thrust blindly with the golden-hilted sword into the creature's belly.

He put all of his considerable upper-body strength into the thrust. He heard and felt the blade grate against the ribs. The giant hound twisted away with an agonized howl and went into death convulsions at his feet. Grant stabbed it through the heart in a mercy stroke.

"Weapons like that, I imagine," Kane panted.

"The sword brought it down!" Brigid exclaimed in wonder.

Morrigan sagged in relief. "Thank the goddess."

The other two hounds continued to circle, but much more cautiously, and their snarls were interspersed with quizzical whines. Suddenly both animals froze in place, their heads whipping toward the village. Then they turned and bounded away, where they were almost immediately lost in the gloom.

"Another one-percenter on the scoreboard," Kane said as he tried to regain his wind. "We still have some luck in our savings accounts."

Despite the fact her hands shook with fear, Brigid couldn't help but smile. She, Kane and Grant had been in tight situations many times before, and in more than a few of them she hadn't expected to survive. But she and her friends always did, even if they lost some blood, flesh and peace of mind in the process.

Lakesh had once suggested that the trinity they formed when they worked in tandem seemed to exert an almost supernatural influence on the scales of chance, usually tipping them in their favor. The notion had both amused and intrigued Brigid. She, like Kane, was too pragmatic to truly believe in such an esoteric concept, but she couldn't deny that she and her two friends seemed to lead exceptionally charmed lives.

Suddenly, they heard a jangle of metal and the tramp of running feet. They turned to see a contingent of armed and armored soldiers jogging toward them. They carried swords and spears, as if they were the cast of a historical movie.

The man in the lead shouted, "Morrigan?"

Gulping air, Kane trained his Sin Eater on him, but Morrigan seized his hand and pulled it down. In a trembling whisper she said, "That is Conohbar, captain of the garrison. He is an agent of the priory but you must not let on that you know. Whatever happens, you must not resist."

"Did he know the Druids were going to burn you alive?" Brigid asked.

Morrigan nodded. "Aye, but he could not intervene without betraying our plan and forfeiting more lives than just mine."

The man Morrigan called Conohbar wore a bronze helmet with the forepart inscribed with the design of a goblet with a many-boughed tree sprouting from it. The same image was worked into the boss of the round shield he carried on his left arm. In his right he gripped a six-foot-long, steel-bladed lance.

"The Druids get to carry MP-5s and professional soldiers are stuck with Bronze Age ordnance?" Kane asked softly.

"Hush," Morrigan spit. "From here on out, do not speak unless you are spoken to. Whatever I say, you must not contradict me."

"Who does she think she is?" Grant demanded in a fierce whisper. "Lakesh?"

Conohbar stopped a few feet away and gestured to the soldiers behind to halt. They eyed the outlanders apprehensively and whispered among themselves.

Apparently paying no attention to the black-clad strangers, Conohbar declared, "Morrigan, did not our Druids choose you for the rebirth ritual?"

Morrigan nodded. "They did indeed and it was a great honor…but these outlanders interfered."

In a single smooth motion, she stepped forward and stood behind Conohbar. "Take them prisoner so our lord Myrrdian will temper his displeasure with their lives."

The soldiers drew swords and leveled their pikes. Kane, Brigid and Grant raised their own weapons.

"You traitorous little—" Kane growled.

"Silence!" Morrigan cried. In a cold and haughty tone, she said, "You three must surrender yourselves to the captain here, else the dark magicks of Myrrdian will make sure you will suffer eternal damnation and the peace of the afterlife will be denied you forever."

"Heard that one before," Grant muttered. "Must be a standard curse hereabouts."

Conohbar glared at them. From a scabbard strapped to his back, he drew a broadsword identical to the one in Grant's hand. "What decision will you make, strangers?"

Kane, Brigid and Grant all exchanged quizzical glances. Brigid shrugged and handed over her pistol, butt first. "Very well."

Conohbar took the weapon, inspected it briefly, popped out the magazine and slid it into his belt. In a voice so low that it was barely above a whisper, he said, "All of you are on sufferance…the moment it is known you interfered in a holy rite of the Druids, I will be given the order to kill you at the wink of an eye. I will do what

I can to save you, because the priory has plans for you, but your life depends on me alone. If you try to resist or escape I cannot arouse suspicion by helping you. Understand?"

Kane gave him an insouciant half smile. "Sure, we do…because we have plans of our own for the priory. Understand?"

Chapter 20

For the next hour, Brigid, Kane and Grant languished in a small hut. It was a miserable affair, blackened inside by decades' worth of wood smoke and a floor of packed earth. A circular hole cut in the thatched roof provided the only ventilation.

There were no furnishings, so the outlanders sat on the bare floor with their backs to the walls. Everything had been taken from them, including the case holding the survival stores. Stars glinted frostily through the roof hole, but rather than gaze at them, Kane stood up and began to pace. He strode to the plank door and pressed an ear against it, listening to the murmur of many voices and clink of weapons.

When he could make no sense of the sounds, he undid the seal on the glove of his shadow suit and peeled back the right sleeve, examining his arm by the inadequate light peeping in through the roof aperture. Although the flesh of his forearm bore angry red streaks, the skin hadn't been broken.

Brigid rose to eye his arm with a clinical intensity. She turned it this way and that. "If you had been wearing anything else—except maybe armor plate—that dog would have taken off your arm."

"Dog?" Grant echoed. "I've never seen dogs like those hounds." He snorted derisively. "Dog, my ass."

"Any theories on what those things actually were, Baptiste?" Kane asked.

Brigid hesitated and released Kane's arm. "One theory anyway. Remember our discussion about pocket universes?"

Kane nodded, rolling down his sleeve. "I can't say I understood very much of it."

"You don't need to. Assuming there are such things in the first place—and Strongbow's reappearance as Myrrdian suggests there are—then the hounds of Cullan might have come from one of them."

Grant stared at her incredulously from beneath a furrowed brow. "You mean those hounds were supernatural? Magic?"

"Not exactly," Brigid replied. "According to Celtic lore, when Cuchulainn—Ka'in to his friends—was a child, he was given to a smith named Cullan to be his apprentice. Cullan had several giant hunting hounds reputed to be gifts from Lugh, king of the Tuatha de Danann. One day, while at play, the hounds set upon Cuchulainn and he killed one of them. When the blacksmith reprimanded him, Cuchulainn reputedly said, 'I will be your hound.'"

Grant shook his head in annoyance. "What does that moldy old myth have to do with anything?"

Accustomed to Grant's curmudgeonly attitude, Brigid only smiled. "If we theorize that the hounds were taken from one of the pocket universes visited by the Danaan and given to Cullan—"

The door rattled from outside. Kane and Brigid stepped away from it as it swung inward. Morrigan and Conohbar entered. The man carried a lamp in one hand and a lance in the other. The blind woman held a tray covered by a square of linen. "We thought you might be hungry and thirsty," she said.

Conohbar gestured meaningfully with his lance. "Mind, give us no trouble. There are guards posted right outside."

He shut the door behind him, leaned the spear against the wall, hung the lamp on a hook and pulled off his helmet. He gusted out a sigh. "That's better."

Without the helmet he was not as mature as he first appeared, although his reddish hair was touched with gray threads.

Kane took the tray from Morrigan and asked softly, "Are we real prisoners or are we just playing for the benefit of the soldiers?"

Morrigan answered, just as softly, "You're only play-acting for the nonce. Depending on other events this night, you may find the roles become real enough."

Grant pushed himself to his feet, towering menacingly over the small woman. He glowered at Conohbar. "If that's the case, the play will turn out to be pretty damned short."

"And the audience won't be real happy with the final curtain," Kane interjected grimly.

Conohbar ran a hand over his sweat-damp hair. "No need to get on the prod with me, laddie. You were summoned here as allies of the Priory of Awen to help us in our battle against Myrrdian."

"Speaking of him," Grant rumbled, "is he really Strongbow?"

Morrigan laughed. It was not a sound of amusement, but more a bitter mockery of a laugh. "Who knows at this point. But he has very nearly been death of the Priory of Awen in the six months since he fully manifested."

"Manifested?" Kane, in the process of eyeing the thick slabs of bread on the tray, squinted toward her. "What do you mean?"

"Nearly a year ago," Conohbar said, "one of the priory's sisters named Rhianna reported dreams of Myrrdian. He came into them and communicated with her. She—"

Morrigan waved her hand at him in a peremptory gesture. "Stop, Conohbar. I'll tell this part of it, since Rhianna is not just a sister of the priory, but my own by blood."

She took a deep breath. "You remember the philosophy of the Priory of Awen and our history, do you not? We are scholars, we maintain the old ways, the old beliefs of the Tuatha de Danaan and the ancient gods of the Celt…we exalt the mysteries of existence, all the knowledge and education of our forebears. We practice all the higher spiritual arts and crafts, especially that which was known as geomancy, Earth magic. I am a telepath…as is my younger sister Rhianna, though her abilities are of a slightly different order than mine."

Although Kane, Brigid and Grant were skeptics by nature, they had witnessed enough events of high strangeness to suspend their disbelief in Morrigan's tale. Brigid had toured the Priory of Awen's main citadel in Ireland some years before.

"We remember," Kane said, handing the tray to Grant. "Let's get on with it."

Morrigan's smooth brow acquired a line of irritation. "It actually started over a year ago, after Rhianna came to this village as a votary, a representative of the priory, to act as liaison between us and the Druidic sect here. Their legends were intertwined with the origins stone circle, the Merry Maidens. They believed Myrrdian had built it in the much the same way he was credited with constructing Stonehenge. According to Druidic lore, he was buried beneath it. Apparently, he was—after a fashion."

Grant frowned. "Who was buried beneath it? Myrrdian? Merlin? Or Strongbow?"

Morrigan shrugged. "I don't think it matters any longer. The legends of Myrrdian and King Arthur have been associated with Cornwall for a thousand years. The real Camelot is believed by some to be Tintagel Castle, not so very far from here."

"According to Geoffrey of Monmouth," Brigid inter-jected, "Arthur was born there, but most historians believe the castle was actually a Celtic monastery."

"Even so," Kane said, "how'd Myrrdian end up buried underneath the Merry Maidens?"

"Supposedly Myrrdian became enamored of a Danaan woman named Vivane. Apparently they were romantically involved, but after a time she grew annoyed by his unwanted attentions. Vivane sealed him alive inside of a tree, a cave or a tomb, depending on which version of the legend is followed."

"More than likely," Brigid stated, "trees or caves were just convenient synonyms for a prison in a pocket universe."

Morrigan nodded. "Aye, that's what the high council of the priory have deduced. Furthermore, we speculate that when Strongbow was flung into the heart of the Singularity he created, he ended up in one of those pocket universes explored by the Tuatha de Danaan, perhaps the same one to which Myrrdian had been banished. The nexus point portal was located within the heart of the Merry Maidens monument."

"If that's the case," Brigid asked, "why didn't he just pop out there shortly after Kane dropped him into the Singularity?"

Morrigan shrugged "Most likely the energies were dormant. Regardless, very much like Myrrdian himself, Strongbow must have found himself trapped like a fly in amber, neither living nor dying. He needed someone on this side of the world to build a bridge that he could use to cross back over. He found that someone."

"Your sister Rhianna?" Kane inquired.

"Aye," Conohbar said bleakly. "I can attest that Myrrdian's mind was powerful, his words and visions filled the child's dreams. She could get no rest until she agreed to help him. Day after day, night after night, she went to the Merry Maidens and entered into a trance, so she could communicate with him."

Grant munched on slice of bread, took a sip of water from a stoneware mug and asked blandly, "You *do* know how stupid all of this sounds?"

Conohbar directed a challenging stare at him. "Ah, you bloody arrogant Yanks…with your guns and your swagger and your attitudes about science. Has it never occurred to you that what you think are silly fairy tales are actually tales of science disguised?"

"Of course it has," Grant replied stolidly. "But this story still sounds pretty stupid."

Not bothering to repress a smile, Kane said, "Go on."

Still staring at Grant in annoyance, Conohbar said, "Over a period of time, Rhianna reported what she learned in her dreams. The Druids here, of course, thought she was channeling Myrrdian."

He paused and added quietly, "So did she. So did I. Who wouldn't?"

"Yeah," Grant drawled. "Who wouldn't. That would be my first guess, too."

"She knew nothing of Strongbow," Morrigan said defensively. "There was no reason for her not to believe that she was truly in telepathic contact with Myrrdian, especially since he was reputed to be of Danaan blood, as are most of the priests and priestesses of the Priory of Awen."

"You make it sound like Rhianna bought into the story pretty easily," Kane observed.

Morrigan's eyebrows drew down to the bridge of her nose. "Don't you understand what it's like to live here, in this ancient land, where the past has never stopped breathing? Wales, Ireland, Britain, Cornwall… all of them are known as Merlin's Isles. He is a figure of great power and renown here. The idea that a trickster might impersonate him would be as blasphemous a concept as impersonating Christ. Do you understand what I mean?"

"I think I can make a guess," Brigid said dryly, "based on what you showed me in the priory's citadel. Your lives follow a system of magical thinking. Wherever those of the Celtic heritage travel, they're likely to enter the realm of a god, a goddess or nature spirit, regardless of the objective reality. They take such things for granted."

She glanced toward Grant and Kane, adding, "It's part and parcel of paganism."

"Are you saying Rhianna has no critical faculties?" Kane asked.

"She had them, aye," Conohbar snapped. "But by the

time she began to wonder if she had truly reached Myrrdian in the other world, in Skatha or Tir Na Nog, it was a bit too late for the poor lass. The portal was unsealed, she couldn't unseal it."

"Why not?" Grant inquired.

"The Druids were all involved by now. With their help and Rhianna's mind energy augmented by the proper ceremonies performed at the Maidens, Myrrdian crossed back from the other world."

"And then what?" Brigid wanted to know.

Conohbar shrugged and sighed. "Not to put too fine a spin on it, but he took over…with the eager help of the Druids. Myrrdian was able to cross back and forth at the portal, going from one place to another. Each time he came back with more and more treasure and artifacts. He had us seeking them out, too."

"Artifacts?" Brigid repeated. "Like what?"

Conohbar seemed reluctant to continue, but he said quietly, "We did only as we were bid. We could not find everything that he had asked for, but we found enough to enable him to start his campaign."

"What artifacts?" Brigid asked again, her tone edged with impatience.

"What campaign?" Kane asked.

Conohbar shifted his feet uneasily. "Myrrdian demanded much of us here. He gave us instructions on where to find hidden vaults and storehouses of Danaan relics."

"Priory relics," Morrigan said bitterly. "They were

ours to safeguard. Myrrdian sent the people all over Cornwall, Wales and Ireland, seeking them out. They were looted of everything of worth."

"How did he know where they were?" Grant asked suspiciously.

"He gained the knowledge while he was in the other world," Morrigan answered. "That's the only explanation that makes sense."

"*None* of this makes sense," Kane argued.

Conohbar nodded miserably. "Myrrdian promised heaven and earth to the clans here, swearing to reunite all the Celtic peoples and reclaim our empire."

Grant rolled his eyes. "We've heard that dodge before."

Shamefacedly, Conohbar said, "I have to admit I was swayed by his words. So was Rhianna. We believed him…at first."

"What did he use an inducement to do all of this?" Brigid asked.

When Conohbar didn't answer, Morrigan said in a soft, rustling whisper, "Rebirth."

Kane squinted toward her. "What?"

"The Cauldron of Bran the Blessed…the Cauldron of Rebirth, the Chalice of Resurrection. A means to restore the dead to life. Myrrdian sought it out."

"That's just a legend," Kane ventured. "Right?"

Morrigan turned her sightless eyes toward him. "By no means. The Celtic clans here, in Scotland, Wales and Ireland are going to go out and fight a holy war to suit the decidedly unholy agenda of Myrrdian. They're not willing do it for a mere legend. They've been convinced that even if they're killed they'll be brought back to life. Half the world is going to be drowned in blood unless somehow we can stop it."

They heard a brief commotion at the door, a garble of frightened voices. It swung open forcefully, slamming against the wall. Hand gripping the shaft of her staff, Fand strode over the threshold and stated deliberately, "And that's why I summoned you, Kane. To help us stop it."

Chapter 21

Fand's flaxen hair flowed to midthigh, held back from her high-boned face by a silver band. Her body armor leather was dark red, molded to conform to her body. It did little to conceal the thrust of her full breasts. Around her waist was a belt of bronze links from which hung a long-bladed dagger. High-topped green boots rose to above her knees.

She wore a heavy cloak trimmed with a glossy fur, possibly sea otter. Although her pale complexion held the blue-white hue of skim milk, her eyes burned hot and bright like droplets of molten gold. They haughtily surveyed the people in the hut.

"Hello, Fand," Kane said, knowing how inane the greeting sounded under the circumstances. "It's been a while since we've met in the flesh—" He broke off and hastily amended his comment. "I mean since we last saw each other."

"There is little time for amenities, Kane," Fand said brusquely, the melodic voice he remembered as pleasing to the ear now grim and cold. "Many things have changed since you were last in this part of the world. I will be brief as I can be and I hope you and your friends will not think me rude. We go to fight Strongbow, and I wish you to join me. If you do not, you may return to America and no one will molest you."

She heeled around, the hem of her cloak nearly sweeping the floor. She marched from the hut. "All of you follow me—you in particular, Morrigan. I understand you had a narrow escape."

Conohbar and Morrigan trailed after Fand. Kane lingered in the hut for a few seconds, standing in baffled irritation.

"Not quite the reunion you expected, I guess," Brigid murmured.

Jaw muscles knotted, Kane stalked out of the hut. Grant and Brigid fell into step beside him. With surprise, they saw converging on the village a steady stream of armed men, assembling in the central square. These soldiers were dressed and equipped far differently than the sword-and-spear-wielding village garrison.

They wore red-and-green coveralls, as well as dark green berets emblazoned with three-triangle symbol of the Priory of Awen. They carried Heckler & Koch 53 assault rifles, and they appeared as if they knew how to use them.

"Who the hell are they?" Grant demanded.

Conohbar looked over his shoulder. "They're the militia of the Priory of Awen. Fand has been their commander for several years now, ever since New London fell."

"Things really *have* changed since we last here," Kane commented.

"Mainly due to the actions of you and friends," Fand stated.

Kane recalled that when he arrived last to visit to the former United Kingdom, Lord Strongbow's Imperium Brittania had fallen to an organized rebel force made up primarily of the Irish. Hundreds of the Celts had already been assimilated into Imperium society, concentrated in New London. Although they worked primarily as laborers and servants, a considerable number were attached to the military.

In the months following the disappearance of Strongbow, cracks began weakening the foundation of the Imperium, and more Celts began arriving, setting up secret bases on the Shetland Islands. Allies among the Scots helped them slip ashore in secret. Within a couple of months, the Celts were fifty thousand strong, spread out all over Britain. The overthrow of the Imperium had not been protracted, but Kane vividly recalled the carnage of New London and how hundreds of corpses were shoved into gutters and stacked against walls like cordwood.

The Cerberus warriors followed Fand and her retinue to the outskirts of the village, past soldiers setting up tents and campsites. Kane shook his head to drive away the growing disorientation. In the past three minutes, he and his friends had stepped out of the Bronze Age and into the age of refined steel and modern weaponry.

Fand came to a halt at the stone wall. Seated on it, under the watchful eyes and gun barrels of two soldiers, was a robed Druid, the cowl thrown backward. She was a young woman with her black hair falling in disarrayed strands about her face. Her dark eyes held a hard, determined glitter and her mouth was a firm, grim line. She wore peculiar headgear of somber black leather, open at the top but with squared-off flaps that extended vertically over each ear.

Morrigan stiffened, turning her head to and fro as if catching a scent. Her lips stirred. "Rhianna?"

Fand put a hand on the shoulder of the seated girl. "Here is your sister, Morrigan. Speak to her if you can."

Conohbar led the blind woman to the girl. Carefully, gently, she fingered her face, but Rhianna's expression remained impassive. After a moment, Morrigan cried angrily, "What has been done to you?"

Rhianna did not respond, but her lips curved in a mocking, defiant smile.

"She's been enchanted!" Morrigan exclaimed, taking a clumsy step back and bumping into Conohbar. "Myrrdian did this to her, the bastard!"

"Who else?" Fand asked. "As always, Strongbow misuses all Danaan knowledge that comes into his possession."

"Where did you find her?" Morrigan asked.

Fand waved her staff in the general direction of the sea. "We engaged a ship carrying supplies to Strongbow's invasion force based on Great Skellig. She was aboard it."

"Great Skellig?" Brigid repeated, her eyes widening. "Strongbow is in Ireland?"

Fand frowned in her direction. "As of two weeks ago, aye. He finally reached the objective he had set for the Imperium Britannia when he ruled it. He has occupied the priory monastery on Great Skellig Island. From there he has been making forays to the mainland, gathering his forces to lay siege to the main citadel of the Priory of Awen."

"Why?" Kane asked.

"That is where he believes he will find the Cauldron of Bran."

"Will he?" Grant demanded bluntly. "Does the cauldron actually exist?"

Fand's lips tightened. "It doesn't matter, does it? Strongbow has tricked enough clansmen into thinking he is actually Myrrdian, Merlin reborn. They will fight to possess it. My guess is that even if he takes the citadel, he'll claim the cauldron was destroyed in the battle. He'll have what he wants."

"Which is what, exactly?" Brigid wanted to know.

"To conquer Ireland," Fand retorted. "And me."

Morrigan shook Rhianna violently by the shoulders, rocking her head back and forth. Pulling off the headgear, she spoke urgently to her in Gaelic. The girl's half smirk did not falter. Her face remained as immobile as if sculpted from marble.

Turning toward Fand, Morrigan asked beseechingly, "Can you do nothing to help her?"

"I can but try," Fand answered, hefting her staff. "But I wanted your permission before I took action."

Morrigan nodded in relief and stepped back. "You have it."

Fand touched Rhianna's shoulder with the egg-shaped knob of her staff. The girl flinched, eyeing it with trepidation. In a hoarse whisper, she said, "No. Do not defile me with your witchery."

"I channel my own bioelectric energy through this, drawing upon the electromagnetic field of the Earth," Fand stated. "It is not sorcery as you would know if you were truly in your right mind."

As the knob moved toward Rhianna's forehead, she leaned fearfully away from it, cursing in Gaelic.

Fand gestured for Conohbar to come forward. "Hold her."

The man did so, pressing down with both hands on her shoulders to keep her immobile. As the girl swore, Fand pressed the end of the staff against the center of her forehead. They heard a faint crackle. Almost instantly Rhianna's body jerked, and a keening cry burst from her throat. Kane winced in sympathy, remembering all too well the painful shock Fand's staff had administered to him upon their first meeting.

Fand kept the staff's knob in place, squeezing her eyes shut in concentration. Rhianna kicked and thrashed. Her groans changed gradually to sobs, then to a peal of wild, triumphant laughter. Her eyes gleamed with a wild, deranged light and her lips peeled back from her teeth in a grin. Kane felt an inward cringing from the grin—it was as if the girl's face were but a thin mask and beneath it lay Strongbow's malicious leer.

Tendons standing out in relief on the slender column of her throat, Rhianna's mouth worked and a hoarse, labored voice rasped from between her lips: "My day has come again and all those who stood against me will perish. Fand, I thank you—all of my enemies have come at your call and you will watch them die."

Fand whipped her away her staff, inhaling sharply. A faint dew of perspiration filmed her forehead. In a grim whisper she said, "I cannot the break the geas. Whatever Strongbow has done to her mind, it has overwhelmed her identity."

Conobhar released Rhianna, who continued to grin at Kane.

"Strongbow has grown as powerful as you feared," Conohbar said uneasily.

Fand speared him with a challenging glare. "He was powerful once before, and he was defeated. We can do it again."

"If you want our help to stop him," Kane said, "then I assume you have a battle plan to share with us?"

Fand locked eyes with him, and for an instant he felt a tingling at the base of his spine. Then she wheeled around, cloak belling out behind her. "Come with me."

Trailed by a contingent of soldiers, Fand led the Cerberus warriors across an open stretch of moor, striding at an oblique angle away from the village. The salt smell of the sea hung in the air.

"It is only a matter of days before Ireland runs red with the blood of its own people," she announced. "And after that—"

Fand spoke no more. Kane matched her swift, long-legged gait so he could walk beside her. Ignoring the resentful glances of a soldier on her left, he said challengingly, "You're not telling us everything, Fand."

She smiled for the first time and chuckled briefly. "There's *much* I haven't told you. Where Strongbow has been since you dropped him into the Singularity all those years ago, how he has been able to jump from the other world to this world, the kind of weapons he has at his disposal, including the Eye of Balor."

At the mention of it, Kane repressed a shiver. "Maybe you could start bringing us up to date. I think I can speak for my friends when I tell you that none of us like putting our necks on the chopping block without knowing what we're offering up our heads for."

She did not seem to notice to edge of sarcasm in his tone. "Ask your questions, then."

"For starters, how do you propose we get to Ireland?"

The moor fell away, sloping gently to a rocky cliff. Beyond the rim glistened the moonlit sea. Bobbing at anchor on the slow swells lay a long, dark ship. Kane, Grant and Brigid instantly recognized its knife-blade configurations.

The sleek, sharp-prowed ship was painted a matte,

sinister black, its streamlined, oddly faceted contours lending it a resemblance to a gigantic sword, seen edge-on.

Placed amidships, the snouts of three 40 mm cannons jutted from behind metal deck shielding. Affixed near the bow they saw a quartet of three-foot-long hollow pipes slanting upward at forty-five-degree angles. They knew it was the Limbo antisubmarine system. A pair of tripod-mounted L7A1 heavy-caliber machine guns were bolted to the roof of the elevated bridge housing.

The ship was of the corvette class, 114 tons, and the regenerative gas turbine engines were capable of driving it at a maximum speed of fifty knots on smooth seas. Nearly one hundred yards long, the vessel was one of the first ships in the Royal British Navy to apply stealth technology, on the cutting edge of radar and sonar baffling outlines, as well as employing a form of camouflage.

"Strongbow's black ship," Kane said.

"The *Cromwell*," Grant intoned.

Fand cast him a slightly surprised glance. "No longer, Mr. Grant. We've renamed her the *Cu Sith Awwn*."

"The what?" Kane demanded.

"The *Cu Sith Awwn*," Brigid declared matter-of-factly. "Gaelic for *Cerberus*."

Chapter 22

As the Moon began to wane, thick thunderheads massed far in the distance, rising like mountains above the horizon. Lightning flared within them, and the sea below reflected the flashes with the color of old silver.

The Cerberus warriors stood within the elevated bridge housing of the black ship. The *Cu Sith Awwn* pitched and rocked slightly on the restless combers. Fand conversed quietly with the pilot in Gaelic, apparently discussing the weather and course settings. The instrument lights cast a greenish, unhealthy glow over everyone's faces. They had been brought aboard the vessel only a few minutes before by a small launch. The ship looked the same as when it had bore the name of *Cromwell*.

On the short trip from the beach to the ship, Fand had explained that the vessel was the primary means of moving men and equipment about the British Isles and usually held a crew complement of forty.

Turning away from the instrument panel, Fand undid the clasp of her cloak and slipped it from her shoulders. She handed it to a young sailor, who gazed at her with undisguised adoration.

As a deliberate counterpoint, Kane scowled at her in straightforward impatience. "We've been asking a lot of questions, and I think we've waited long enough for them to be answered."

Fand swept past him, through the open doorway and to the stairway that led to the deck below. "I agree. Ask away."

As they followed her down, the three people were impressed anew by the beveled contours of the hull and superstructures. They remembered that the corvette was designed not to merely hide from an enemy, but confuse him, too. The stealth ship possessed the capability of changing the size and shape of its radar signature by raising and lowering a set of retractable reflectors in the aft communications pyramid.

Kane knew the *Cu Sith Awwn* also had the ability to generate an artificial fog made by heating seawater in special boilers that helped to blank out enemy radar. Of course, the vessel had never been brushed by hostile radar, since ocean warfare had played no significant role in the final conflagration two centuries earlier.

As Fand ducked beneath an antiship-missile emplacement, she asked, "Morrigan told you some of the backstory, did she not?"

Grant grunted. "Just the stupid-sounding parts."

To their surprise, Fand did not react with annoyance. Reaching a starboard side rail, she leaned against it. "Placed within context, it's not stupid, but I can't deny it sounds more than a little mad to outsiders."

"More than a little," Brigid agreed. "Can you tell us where Strongbow has been for all these years?"

Fand surveyed them all, her eyes intent and glinting in the moonlight. She let the silence draw out for a long moment, listening to the smack of waves against the ship's hull. At length she said flatly, "As you probably know, the myth that gave a unified basis to the lore of the Tuatha de Danaan was that of a primordial conflict between a divine race and a demonic race, in Gaelic called the Formhoire or the Formorians."

Brigid nodded. "The Formorians had divided Ireland into five provinces, which all converged on Balor's Hill."

"Aye," Fand intoned, her gaze fixed on Kane. "Evil-eye."

Kane met her stare steadily, knowing she referred to the events of the last time he had seen Fand, when he dueled a half-blind, maimed giant of a man who might have been a reincarnation of the legendary Formorian chieftain.

"The Formorians held almost all of Eire in a tyrannical grip until the coming of the Tuatha de Danaan," Fand stated.

"We know all that, Fand," Kane broke in impatiently. "The Danaan supposedly arrived on Ireland from the sky. The four cities which they originated were Findias, Gorias, Murias and Falias. The Danaan were skilled in poetry and magic. With them they brought four great treasures, Nuada's sword, Lugh's terrible spear, the

Dagda's cauldron and the Stone of Fal, the Lia Fail or Stone of Destiny."

"Yeah," Grant rumbled. "Strongbow had stolen all of those artifacts and kept them in a vault in New London's Ministry of Defense. But I thought the artifacts were recovered after the Imperium was overthrown."

"They were," Fand answered bluntly. "And almost all of them they turned up missing again, shortly after Strongbow as Myrrdian reappeared."

Brigid arched her eyebrows in surprise. "Weren't they protected?"

Fand frowned, obviously irritated by the question. "Of course they were. They were placed in heavily guarded Priory vaults all over Ireland, separated just in case of a catastrophe. But over a period of days, all of the relics were stolen from their individual vaults—all but one."

"Let me guess," Kane said bleakly. "The Dagda's cauldron…which of course is the same thing as the Cauldron of Bran the Blessed."

"You guess correctly," Fand replied. "The Dagda was the supreme ruler, the High King of the Tuatha de Danaan and so only he was entrusted with the power of life and death imbued within the Cauldron."

"It actually functions?" Brigid asked skeptically. "It brings people back to life?"

Fand sighed. "I have no idea, really. None of the Priory does. I'm sure you're aware that the legends of the cornucopia, the Horn of Plenty as well as the Holy Grail are derived from tales of the Cauldron."

"Not to mention Egyptian sarcophagi," Brigid replied, "which were believed to have the powers of rejuvenation. By the Middle Ages, most of the myths about it were Christianized."

Fand nodded impatiently throughout Brigid's brief dissertation. "Aye, we know that to speak of the Cauldron or the Grail as a single legend is a mistake. The hard reality of the artifact was taken from New London, returned to Eire and sealed with an impregnable vault deep beneath the Priory's citadel."

"How were the other relics stolen?" Grant asked.

Fand combed her long hair with nervous fingers. "The high council of the Priory is still trying to reason that out. We have our theories."

"So do I," Brigid said.

Kane glanced toward her. "Which is?"

"We know from prior experience that both the Annunaki and the Danaan understood and to some extent had the ability to manipulate the indivisibility of space and time. The Danaan in particular discovered that matter and energy could be interchangeable—the deeper the Danaan probed into the minutiae of matter the more they found energy and complexities of energy at the bottom of everything. These realizations became not only the building blocks of their technology, but millennia later, the entire template for Project Cerberus."

"Not to mention Strongbow's Singularity," Grant pointed out.

Fand nodded. "Precisely, Mr. Grant. Our high council is of the opinion that the Singularity opened into one of the so-called bubble or pocket universes, more than likely a dimension that the Danaan were reputed to have vanished into nearly a thousand years ago as part of the pact with the Annunaki."

"What is—or where—is that dimension exactly?" Grant asked.

Fand's full lips creased in a smile. "No one, not even your science's most accomplished physicists, could answer that."

"Probably not," Kane said, matching her smile. "I'm sure our friend Lakesh would have a lot of fun trying to figure it all out. But how could Strongbow have fallen into one these bubble dimensions through the Singularity? As I recall, he used it to open shortcuts through linear space, like we do with the interphaser and parallax points."

"Possibly the Singularity was rotating," Brigid said. "And it created what's known as an Einstein-Rosen bridge."

Grant squinted at her. "A *who* bridge?"

"Way back in the 1930s, Albert Einstein and a colleague, Nathan Rosen, concluded that the general theory of relativity implied that black holes served as gateways between points in space. They calculated that such a bridge extends through the space-time continuum, and that theory led to the multiverse hypothesis."

"Great," Kane muttered in disgust. "My favorite hypothesis, in which everything that could possibly happen *does* happen—in some damned universe or another."

"More than likely," Brigid went on, "since the original purpose of Strongbow's Singularity was to open up conduits through hyperspace from one location to the other, he probably found a way to activate local wormholes, much like the interphaser does. Maybe he even found a way to pass through white holes."

Grant cocked his head at her in puzzlement. "Say again?"

"A white hole is pretty much what the name implies—the opposite of a black hole. Whereas energy and matter is sucked *into* a black hole, the same could come *out* of a white one."

"Wherever Strongbow went, into a black hole and then out of a white one," Fand declared, "he found artifacts from the Danaan that he brought through to this world."

"Like what, for example?" Kane asked.

She regarded him gravely. "Like the original device that served as the basis for legends of the evil eye of Balor, for one."

Kane's throat constricted. "What is it, really?"

"You would probably call it a death ray," Fand answered. "Knowing what I do of Danaan technology, I surmise that it projects a form of concentrated electromagnetic radiation. It most definitely has a destructive effect on matter."

"What's the power source?" Brigid asked.

Fand shook her head. "I have no idea." She paused and added sardonically, "Perhaps one of those white holes you spoke of."

Brigid's green eyes glinted with suppressed irritation. "That actually might not be too far from the truth. It's theorized that white holes exist only in another universe, one parallel to ours. Physicists postulated that they could be energy receivers transmitting the energy collected by black holes from our dimension to another. If that's the case, we're talking about zero point energy."

Kane had heard the term before when in the company of Lakesh and Philboyd, but he usually tuned out the details, dismissing them as technobabble. Now he asked with studied blandness, "Is that bad?"

"Bad enough," Brigid retorted. "A zero point energy transmitter would be capable of generating immense amounts of power by utilizing the energies that derive from subatomic wormholes opening and closing constantly in and out of hyperspace. That might explain not just the power source for the Eye of Balor, but how Strongbow travels from one dimension to another, looting the vaults of the priory at will."

Fearful comprehension flitted over Fand's alabaster features. For a long moment she seemed to struggle to come to terms with the implications, her eyes veiled. Then, in a hoarse half whisper, she said, "That must be it. Strongbow has never been seen without the helmet that supports the Eye of Balor. Aye…that *must* be it!'

Shoving herself away from the rail, she began shouting in Gaelic. Red-and-green-uniformed sailors came running across the deck from all directions, assembling in front of her. She spoke to them tersely for less than a half a minute. When she was done, they turned and raced from one part of the *Cu Sith Awwn* to another. The Cerberus warriors watched the commotion in confusion.

When Fand strode in the direction of the bridge housing, Kane reached out and grabbed her by the arm. She jerked free with surprising strength, whirling to glare at him.

"What's going on, Fand?" he demanded.

Fand smiled, but humor never touched her eyes. "We sail for Great Skellig as soon as I recall the garrison and get them aboard. Hopefully by noon tomorrow, we will finally engage Strongbow and stop him once and for all."

She paused, her hot aureate eyes searching his. "Are you with us in this battle, Ka'in?"

It was the first time she had addressed him by the diminutive of Cuchulainn, and the sound of it sent shivers of fear and expectation up and down his spine.

He could only nod in response.

Chapter 23

Kane slept poorly in the small cabin he shared with Grant. He couldn't help but remember the last time he had been belowdecks of the black ship, when he and Fand were imprisoned in the brig by the mad Captain Aubrey Quayle.

Memories of that time flittered through his mind, half dreams, half memories. Finally he was fully roused by dawn's light peeping through an open porthole and the increased throb of the diesel engines. He guessed with arrival of daybreak, the *Cu Sith Awwn* increased her speed.

He arose from the cot, careful not to awaken Grant, snoring beneath a blanket. The man slept heavily, the past few days of hardship in Manhattan finally catching up to him. Brigid had been assigned a cabin with Morrigan.

Quietly, Kane pulled on the shadow suit by opening a magnetic seal on its right side. The garment had no zippers or buttons, and he put it on in one continuous piece, from the hard-soled boots to the gloves. The fabric molded itself to his body, adhering like another layer of epidermis. He smoothed out the wrinkles and folds by running his hands over his arms and legs.

He left the cabin, walking along the gangway to the ladder that led to the deck. The air felt chilly and clammy, partly created by the patchy fog hanging low over the sea. He moved to the wet foredeck and leaned on the metal railing, drawing in deep lungfuls of air. Brine and kelp and a wet, wild wind sent shivers of excitement through him. The hull vibrated slightly as the *Cu Sith Awwn*'s turbines pushed it over the open sea.

Because of the fog, he could see only a gray emptiness of water stretching to a deeper gray of the horizon. He couldn't help but remember the first time he had stood on the prow of the black ship at dawn, five years before. Then as now, Kane put a slim cigar between his lips and, cupping his hand around the lighter, he set fire to it. Because of the damp air, it took him several strikes.

Relishing the bittersweet smoke mixed with the tang of salt, he stood and puffed on it, letting the deep rumble of the ship and the thundering strength of the ocean fill him.

At the sound of footfalls behind him, he turned quickly. Fand approached him, her tall body cloaked against the chill sea air. There was a glitter in her eyes that he had seen before, and he felt uneasy.

"Good morning, Kane," she said, stepping up beside him. She pronounced his name without the insertion of the glottal stop. "I take it you did not sleep well?"

He smiled slightly. "Certainly not for very long."

The night before, two hours had been required to recall the garrison and station them back aboard the *Cu Sith Awwn*. The ship had not set sail until after midnight, and Kane and his friends had retired barely an hour before the weather turned wild.

A violent storm closed in on the ship, and huge seas thundered over the sides. The waves seethed with white foam as they crashed against the *Cu Sith Awwn*, rocking her up and down until Brigid and Morrigan succumbed to seasickness.

Kane and Grant were luckier than their companions and did not become ill. In fact, Grant managed to sleep soundly through the worst of the storm. Kane, however, was more concerned about being tossed from his bunk and so got very little rest.

"I am sorry for that," Fand replied, even though she did not sound apologetic. "We are caught up in turbulent events that we can barely understand, much less control."

"You seem to be doing a passable job," he said, turning his head to exhale a stream of smoke. "The last time we saw each other, you told me the role of warrior queen didn't come naturally to you."

Fand smiled crookedly. "I remember. We were down below, locked in the brig. I was tending a stab wound in your right leg. How is it, by the way?"

"I only feel it in wet weather…or when I'm walking."

She looked at him with troubled eyes. "Really?"

"I'm joking. I've suffered a lot more cuts and bruises and concussions since then."

"You saved the world then, Kane."

He put the cigar in his mouth and rolled it from one side of his mouth to the other, feeling very uncomfortable. "Seems like that old thing always needs saving, doesn't it? My friends and I have done it a couple of more times." He added softly, "Besides, I couldn't have saved it that time without you."

She leaned close against him, and he felt her warmth even through the cloak and his shadow suit. "What has happened to you since that time...when we saved the world?"

"It's complicated," he said hesitantly.

"No more so than life itself. Has Brigid become your woman?"

Kane glanced at Fand in surprise. "Not exactly. Baptiste is ever her own woman. But we—"

He trailed off, groping for words.

"It's complicated?" Fand supplied helpfully with a sly smile.

Kane chuckled. "Not as complicated as it was once. In fact, it was right here, where we're standing now, that I finally began to understand about Baptiste and me."

"Aye," Fand whispered, "when you first learned you were *anam-charas*."

"Morrigan told you?"

"She did."

Kane exhaled a stream of smoke and removed the

cigar from his mouth, tapping the ash into the sea foaming below. Memory of the hallucinations he and Brigid had shared during a bad mat-trans jump to Russia flooded through his mind. The hallucinations had suggested that Brigid and Kane had known each other in past lives.

A short time after that, Morrigan—standing where Kane now stood on the deck of the black ship—had told him that his soul and Brigid's were inextricably bound.

He shifted uncomfortably and looked behind him at the elevated bridge housing. Through the tinted glass he made out the outlines of several sailors, but he saw no sign of Brigid.

"The lady is your saving grace," Fand whispered to him. "Trust the bond that belongs between you. The gift of the *anam-chara* is strong. She protects you from damnation—she is your credential."

"You've said that to me before," Kane replied. "Somewhere…at some time or another."

Fand arched an eyebrow. "Have I now? It must have been in another life. Now…share with me about this life and what you and your friends have seen and suffered through."

Slowly, drawn out by Fand's gentle encouragement and questions, Kane began to talk, slowly and reluctantly. She knew some of the tales of his past—of his and Grant's years as Magistrates in the service to Baron Cobalt and how they along with Brigid Baptiste learned they were essentially exiles on the planet of their birth.

Kane told her how the hybrid barons had simply walked away from their villes, their territories and their subjects. As they evolved into their true forms, incarnations of the ancient Annunaki overlords, their avaricious scope expanded to encompass the entire planet and every thinking creature on it.

The overlords were engaged in reclaiming their ancient ancestral kingdoms in Mesopotamia. They had yet to cast their covetous gaze back to the North American continent, but it was only a matter of time.

Fand closed her eyes and murmured, "Enlil is restored to life. My worst fears realized."

"Not exactly," Kane said reassuringly. "This latest incarnation of Enlil carries a lot of the same genetic materials and memories of the original, but it's all mixed up with human DNA and definitely his neural patterns are different. Hell, I don't even know if he or any of the Supreme Council are still alive at this point. He hasn't reared his spiny head in a couple of months. None of the overlords have."

Fand was not comforted. She leaned away from him, hugging herself. *"D'anam don diabhal."*

Kane didn't understand the Gaelic she whispered, but he guessed the meaning. The day before the nuclear holocaust, the day before doomsday as it were, Strongbow had arranged for the abduction and rape of Fand's mother, who bore the same name.

According to the terms of the original pact, struck between the Tuatha de Danaan and Enlil, the Annunaki overlord agreed to be imprisoned until Judgment Day, and the Priory of Awen acted as his warders. For nearly a thousand years, Enlil lay in a form of suspended animation within a stasis canister.

The terms of the pact were simple, although later clouded by myth and religious interpretation. On Judgment Day, when Enlil was to be set free, Saint Patrick—or his representatives, in this case priory—was to provide him with a mate, so the Annunaki's pure seed would not vanish forever. The mate was specifically selected. She was to carry the blood of the Tuatha de Danaan.

However, since the Danaan had long ago left Earth, only humans who possessed traces of their DNA remained. According even to ancient Celtic lore, the Danaan practiced their own program of genetic engineering, mixing their traits with those of humans they felt showed superior qualities. Brigid had speculated that this ancient process of hybridization gave rise to the tales of changelings, of fairy children born of human parents.

Over the course of the centuries the Danaan-human progeny were exalted in legend as mystics, seers and mighty warriors. Merlin-Myrrdian was one of the most famous examples. Saint Brigid was another.

The priory knew which of their members claimed descent from the Danaan, and by the 2001, there was only one female whose bloodline was direct and unbroken. The young woman known as Fand practiced as a holistic healer and herbalist and was something of a local celebrity because of her beauty and chastity.

That chastity was forevermore lost when a resurrected Enlil raped her before expiring, but she passed on her beauty to her daughter, Fand. And as mad it seemed, she carried the genetic material of human, Danaan and Annunaki.

Fand bowed her head. In a low, groaning voice she said, "Perhaps all is lost, then. Why contend with Strongbow when the Dragon Lords have returned to reconquer all of their former kingdoms?"

Kane hesitantly placed a hand on her shoulder, and turned her to face him. "They haven't reconquered," he said in a fierce whisper. "We've fought them, just like we'll fight Strongbow."

She lifted her face. He locked gazes with her, probing her huge golden eyes brimming with tears. She leaned toward him suddenly, eager lips seeking his.

"Land ho!" a sailor cried over the public address system. His electronically amplified voice reverberated like a ghostly echo through the pale blue dawn.

Fand and Kane pushed away and stared outward past the prow of the *Cu Sith Awwn*. Wispy scraps of fog whipped past the bow. Dead ahead the black triangle of Great Skellig reared out of the sea.

A massive spire of rock and castellated walls, it loomed hundreds of feet above the North Atlantic, a dark silhouette thrusting up and piercing the sky. Misty clouds wrapped its sharp summit. Thundering waves crashed and broke on the bare rock, foaming spray flying in all directions.

They stared for a few seconds in silence, then Fand spun away from the rail, flinging back her cloak. She strode swiftly toward the bridge, shouting, "Battle stations!"

Chapter 24

Fand stood tall on the prow of the ship, her cloak belling out behind her in the wind, a bronze helmet tucked beneath her left arm. She struck a deliberately dramatic pose, both to inspire her troops and also to let the forces of Strongbow know she was unafraid.

"Let Strongbow see me," she declared defiantly, "commanding the flagship he was so proud of for so many years."

"Simple way of giving him the finger," Kane said, staring across the roiling gray water. He flicked ashes from his cigar over the ship's railing. "Simple way of making yourself a target for a sniper, too."

Fand's lips curved in a contemptuous smile. "Unlike the Imperial Dragoons, the soldiers who follow him now aren't professionals. I doubt any of them could hit the ship at this distance, much less me."

Grant and Brigid pushed through the press of sailors. Both looked haggard, and Brigid's hair was disheveled, in dire need of a brushing. The Klaxon signaling battle stations still blared over the public address system.

"What's going on?" Grant demanded, gripping the topmost rail. "Have we been attacked?"

"Not yet," Kane said.

Brigid gazed at Great Skellig from beneath a shading hand. "I don't see anyone."

"They're hiding," Fand said confidently.

Kane studied the island, noting how a vertical stone slab projected out into a small, straight-walled inlet protected on three sides from the open ocean. A paved footpath cut into bare rock led away and up from it. The path terminated in a weather-eroded stairway, chipped out of the naked rock face by monks a thousand years before. Countless steps of differing widths rose straight up the sheer black cliff and out of sight over the uppermost ridge.

"It looks pretty deserted to me," Kane said. "I don't even know if the ship can make it through that channel."

"It can." Fand's tone rang with authority.

"Let me put it this way," Kane replied. "I don't know if it should."

Grant took his binoculars from the war bag slung over a shoulder. He scanned the barren shoreline, seeing shelves of black basalt jutting over the sea. Vegetation was too sparse to provide adequate cover for one man, much less a squad.

"No boats, no signs of people at all," he said, lowering the binoculars and casting a glance toward Fand. "What makes you so sure Strongbow has set up a base here?"

"We have spies whose reports are absolutely reliable."

"Spies on the inside?"

Fand shook her head. "Not exactly. The selkies…I'm sure you remember them."

Brigid did a poor job of repressing a shudder. The memories of the bloody battle aboard the *Cromwell* between Strongbow's dragoons and the aquatic semi-humans were still vivid, even after five years.

The Cerberus warriors easily visualized the selkies, with their streamlined, torpedo-shaped bodies, seallike pelts and bestial fanged faces. For Brigid, who was very nearly drowned by them, the memory of their huge, dark eyes alive with human intelligence and savage animal cunning still gave her occasional nightmares.

"You consider the otter people unimpeachable sources of intel?" Kane inquired, not bothering to dilute the doubt in his voice.

"Why wouldn't I?" Fand countered.

"For one thing, I recall how Strongbow turned Rhianna. Isn't it possible he could have done the same thing to the selkies?"

"No," Fand retorted, but she didn't sound completely certain.

"We have only the vaguest idea of what we're facing here," Brigid declared. "The Eye of Balor and the hounds of Cullan could be the least of the arsenal Strongbow could've brought out of a pocket dimension."

Fand snorted. "I fear not his magic."

"Good," Brigid shot back coldly, "because I'm not talking about magic. We'll be going up against the science of a race of beings far more advanced than we can understand. What you call the Grailstone and the Eye of Balor were created at a time in the past that our history doesn't remember."

Nothing the hint of uncertainty in Fand's bearing, Kane said quietly but firmly, "Until we have a better idea of what's waiting for us on Great Skellig, let's minimize potential losses. We should send in a landing party."

Fand nibbled at her underlip for a long moment, her eyes clouded with worry. Then she turned, gesturing for a sailor to step forward. "Drop anchor. Go fetch Morrigan and prepare the launch for immediate departure."

GULLS DRIFTED alongside the *Cu Sith Awwn*, watching sailors raise a hatch cover amidships. A hydraulic hoist and winch system rose from beneath. Cables and grapnels connected it to the gunwales of the skiff. The small craft was barely eight feet long, the contours much like those of a high-sided bathtub. An outboard motor was clamped to its squared-off stern.

The hoist lowered the boat over the side of the *Cu Sith Awwn*. When it floated there, still attached to the cables, Fand, Grant, Kane, Brigid and Morrigan scaled a rope ladder to the launch. Morrigan wore one of the red-and-green uniforms, but without the beret.

The boat rocked slightly on the swells. A number of

sailors watched quietly from the rail. After they were seated, Kane started the outboard with a single yank of the pull cord. The grapnel hooks snapped automatically open, and he gunned the engine, the prow riding on a rush of foam.

The wind was raw and biting. Clouds scudded across the sun, and a few drops of icy rain fell. As the launch made for the inlet, the water churned and bubbled up around the boat.

"Something is below us," Brigid said in a strained whisper. "*Big* something."

"Selkies," Fand announced. "Watching over us."

Kane did not feel comforted by their presence and, judging by the expressions on the faces of his friends, neither did they.

Speaking loudly to be heard over the roar of the motor, he asked Fand, "What do you think the Grailstone is exactly?"

She glanced at him, her lips creased in a bemused smile. "Exactly? I don't know if anyone could answer that question. It may exist mainly as an idea, a spiritual concept."

"If that's the case," Grant asked impatiently, "then what the hell makes it so important?"

"The ancient Celts were primarily concerned with finding natural harmonies," Brigid announced, "or more precisely the relationship between Man and the divine. The Tuatha de Danaan either played on this part of the Celtic mentality or were responsible for it."

"Almost all the tales of the Holy Grail are derived from the Celtic lore," Fand said a little defensively. "Oral and written traditions go back at least four thousand years. The grail figured very prominently in their belief systems."

Brigid nodded. "Regardless, the Grailstone had to have been some sort of technology. A few years ago we came across a device very much like it—a manna machine, it was called. It created food, what was known among the ancient Hebrews as shewbread. The machine itself was apparently Annunaki manufacture."

"Annunaki?" Fand echoed. Her brow acquired a line of consternation. "How could that be?"

"We've found evidence there was a give-and-take relationship between the Danaan and the Annunaki… what eventually became known as the Grailstone was probably what we would call a replicator."

"What is that?"

"It's a machine and a process that replicates organic material down to the cellular level…food, for example. Perhaps, if a human body was not too seriously injured, the damaged parts could be replicated, and thus the legends of the machine returning the dead to life. Not too long ago, we saw a device in the possession of the overlords that healed injuries."

"And judging by the manna machine, they could also use it as a fairly inexpensive way of synthesizing rations," Kane commented.

"Over the centuries," Brigid continued, "the Grailstone or different versions of it were scattered across the world. They formed the basis of the legends about Bran's Cauldron of Rebirth, the fountain of ever-lasting youth, the cornucopia and even the Holy Chalice, the cup from which Christ drank at the Last Supper and in which Joseph of Arimathaea caught a few drops of his blood at his Crucifixion. The grail legend grew from its original Celtic sources and then influenced the entire world, but in markedly different ways."

"The question," Grant rumbled, "is whether Strong-bow actually has the damned thing or is just giving the impression he does."

"Aye." Morrigan spoke for the first time, her iron-gray hair streaming out behind her in the wind. "Either way, he cannot be allowed to continue."

Kane piloted the launch over the roaring breakers at the mouth of the inlet. The boat rose and fell and rose again. He pretended not to notice how pale Brigid became. Waves lapped over the sides, the salt spray stinging their eyes. Kane kept the small craft on course, knowing how easily a swell could pile them up against a boulder.

The violent buffeting ebbed somewhat. Shafts of early-morning sunshine broke through the cloud cover, glinting on the rippling waves of the little bay. Gulls and cormorants wheeled and squawked overhead.

Kane steered the skiff slowly to the concrete jetty. Turning the rudder, he ran alongside it, so close that the hull scraped against the edge. He tried not to look at the forbidding dark ramparts towering high overhead.

As the craft bobbed on the shallows, Fand and Grant climbed out and secured it to the dock with a hawser, snugging it fast. Kane handed their provisions and weapons up to Grant, and Fand helped Morrigan step out. When all of them stood on the quay, they looked at the black bulk of Great Skellig looming over them. It seemed to cast a palpable aura of menace. To Kane, it looked like a fortress, all harsh angles and outthrust cliffs. There was an aura of the alien about the giant rock formation, something he could not explain. He guessed the summit stood more than three hundred feet above quayside.

Fand stared at the mist-shrouded pinnacle with a grim intensity. She intoned softly, "This is the place where I was conceived…by the forced union of Enlil and my mother."

Rather than respond to the remark, Grant checked the action of his Sin Eater and asked, "Do you know the way around?"

Brushing damp strands of hair away from her face, Fand said, "I have never been here before. But I do know Great Skellig is honeycombed with tunnels, chambers and vaults. Until the last day of the twentieth century, it served as the main house of the Priory of Awen. That all ended when Karabatos—Strongbow— came here."

Kane repressed a shiver that the woman's words caused to creep up his spine. Striving for a tone of nonchalance, he said, "I don't know about the rest of you, but the longer we stand out here thinking about climbing up the damned thing, the less eager I am do it."

Fand regarded him gravely, then strode toward the base of the staircase. "Let us tarry no longer, then."

The five people began their climb up the face of Great Skellig, trudging up the damp steps. Fand took the lead, moving gracefully between the crags of upright stone that had been carved by the elements into bizarre shapes.

They scaled the time-pitted risers, picking their way carefully. In some places the steps were deeply cracked and slippery with lichens and sea campions. Some stretches of the narrow stairway were steeper than others, treacherous with loose slabs of rock underfoot. In spite of the occasional close call and one near fall by Grant, their progress was steady. Even Morrigan required little help.

"What's a Skellig anyhow?" Grant wanted to know, voice tight with exertion.

"The true name is Sceilig Mhichíl," Morrigan said. "It means 'Michael's Rock' in Gaelic. For more than six hundred years it was a secret monastery of the Priory of Awen. The Catholic monks were basically a cover story. Even though it was supposedly abandoned in the twelfth century, priests and priestesses of the priory still lived here in the caverns and chambers within."

"Who made the chambers inside the place?" Kane asked, wincing as a step cracked loudly beneath his foot.

"Who else?" Fand asked from above him. "The Tuatha de Danaan."

"Yeah," Kane muttered beneath his breath. "Who else?"

When less than a hundred feet separated them from the summit, they reached a section of the stairway that was completely buried under rock that had collapsed from above. Much of the stone was loose shale, and the way the larger rocks were positioned made climbing over it an exceptionally risky venture.

Brigid, after visually examining the rockfall, said, "I believe I can climb over it and anchor a rope so the rest of you can make your way. Other than Morrigan, I guess I weigh the least of us all."

She cast Fand an apologetic smile. "No offense."

"None taken," Fand replied stolidly, running her hands over her body armor. "You're quite correct."

Brigid took a coil of nylon rope from the war bag carried by Grant and looped it over her shoulders, knotting one end beneath her arms. Forming a stirrup with his hands, Kane heaved her up atop an outcropping, saying, "You be damned careful, Baptiste—if you fall from here, it'll take a hell of a lot of iodine to put you back on your feet again."

"So noted," she replied diffidently.

There were plenty of handholds in the loose rock, and Brigid guessed that a reasonably agile child could have easily climbed over the pile. But she reminded herself ruefully that despite weighing considerably less than Grant, Kane or even Fand, she still weighed a good deal more than a child.

Yard by yard, Brigid climbed upward. The higher she ascended, the more she felt a faint, irregular vibration within the stones. Small pebbles jiggled in rhythm to it. Placing her hands flat on the rocks, she felt a faint thumping, as of an enormous drum being tapped over and over, far in the distance.

The last few yards were very tricky. Every movement stirred up miniature avalanches in the loose rock beneath her feet and hands. She called warnings to her companions below and heard Grant cursing.

She inched and wriggled her way over the last boulder. Through the tangle of her hair she glimpsed a flat surface, like a metallic gray tabletop spread out beyond the arch of a retaining wall. Swiftly, but with an economy of motion, she took one end of the rope and wrapped it twice around the base of a pumpkin-sized rock.

As she triple-knotted it, she heard a melodic thrumming as of harp strings. Startled, she craned her neck, looking for the source of the sound. Agony seared her nerve endings, seeming to erupt outward. Dazzling light filled her eyes.

Crying out, Brigid clapped her hands over her face. She fell backward into space down the side of the cliff.

Chapter 25

For a moment sky, earth, rock and the sea spun about her in a crazy pinwheel. Her plummet halted with twin stabs of fiery pain in her armpits, driving through her shoulder sockets into the base of her neck. Anchored by the rock above, her body swung like a pendulum at the end of a rope. She crashed into the steep slope of the cliff, then bounced into space again.

She slammed back against the rocks and darkness swept over her. She fought back to consciousness, aware that she dangled limply from the rope, her face up to the sky. Agony jabbed and pulsed through her arms. Her face felt numb. She stared up at the reeling clouds, blinking away the last blurred specks of the flash that had blinded her.

When the sound of the blood pounding in her ears faded, Brigid heard Kane shouting urgently from below, "Brigid? Are you all right? Brigid!"

Absently, she realized Kane called her by her first name. Slowly, she twisted around, gripping the rope at the point where the loop encircled her upper body. Planting a foot against the cliff to stabilize herself, she looked down. Kane, Grant, Fand and Morrigan all stared upward, their faces registering various degrees of consternation. She hung less than six feet above them.

"I think I'm okay," she rasped.

"Did you fall or what?" Kane demanded.

"Not exactly." She paused, replaying the last few seconds in her memory. "I think I was zapped by a harp."

"A harp?" Morrigan and Fand echoed simultaneously, their voices rich with incredulity.

Using both arms, Brigid pulled herself up so the rope didn't cut so painfully into her armpits. If not for the material of the shadow suit, she knew her flesh would have been abraded and bloody. After a couple of parallel kicks, she managed to rest most of her weight on a jutting finger of stone.

"An infrasound harp to be precise," Brigid said grimly. "I didn't see it but—"

With tentative fingers, she touched her forehead and winced. Sensation had returned and her face felt tender to the touch, as if she had been struck by a club. "I'm guessing the range was fairly long—otherwise my head would have exploded."

"What?" Fand asked, eyes slitting in confusion.

"We've seen it happen before," Grant said bleakly.

The Cerberus warriors retained vivid memories of the harplike devices the transadapts of the Cydonia One colony had found in the pyramid on Mars, which had built by the Tuatha de Danaan. The weapons of the

Danaan operated on the principles of sound manipulation, producing sonic radiation forms with balanced gaps between the upper and lower frequencies. If the radiation within particular frequencies fell on the atoms of living matter, they were stimulated the same way a gong vibrated when its note was struck on a piano.

Taking in a deep breath, Brigid looked toward the rock-ringed summit of Great Skellig, then began climbing up the cliff face, hand over hand, foot over foot.

"What the hell are you doing?" Kane asked in disbelief.

"Going back up," she replied, voice strained with exertion and pain. "There's no other choice unless we want to turn around and leave, and just write off this mission."

If Kane replied, Brigid did not hear him. She struggled up the cliff, hoping the pain in her shoulders did not get worse. The wind buffeted her, pushing her first against the rocks and then away from them.

Gasping, her lungs on fire, her heart pounding, she reached an outthrust shelf of rock beside the stone-clogged stairwell and heaved herself atop it. She lay for a few seconds, breathing hard. She heard nothing but the keening of the wind and a very faint thudding rhythm. The silence from the summit was ominous. There should have been an alarm.

Unholstering her TP-9, Brigid thumbed the safety to the off position and crawled over the tumble of the rocks to the base of the retaining wall. Carefully, she raised her head to peer over the boulder—and suddenly her right cheek stung as fiercely as if bitten by an insect. Dust clouded her vision as tiny fragments of stone exploded directly in front of her. The eerie whine of harp strings reached her ears an instant later.

Brigid rolled to the right, glimpsing a giant black flapping shadow launch itself toward her position through the archway. She squeezed off three rounds as she rolled, the cracking reports coming so fast they sounded like a single, prolonged bam. She heard a brief cry of pain and a series of running footfalls.

"Brigid!" Kane yelled from below.

She lifted her head and saw no sign of movement in the arch. Slowly, she rose to her knees, making sure several large rocks lay between her and the retaining wall, just in case her attacker had fallen out of her field vision.

"I'm all right," she shouted over her shoulder.

"What the hell were you shooting at?" Kane bellowed.

"I don't know—get ready to come up."

She wriggled out of the lasso and tossed the rope over the rockfall blocking the stairwell. "One at a time," she said. "I'll cover you."

"Cover us from what?" Morrigan asked pensively.

"Just do it," Brigid snapped, tension and pain shortening her temper. "I have a feeling we don't have much time to get this done."

The process of throwing down the rope and the four people making the climb required more time than Brigid had assessed. She stood by, gun in hand and flexed her arms and legs. It dawned on her that she was extremely thirsty. When Kane reached the top, he handed her a water bottle and she drank deeply, washing down an analgesic taken from the medical kit. Fand and Morrigan came up after him.

Kane eyed her face and said, "You're a little bruised up, Baptiste."

Her hand automatically went to the sore spots on her cheek and forehead. "I don't doubt it—a shot of infrasound has that effect, you might recall."

"Are you sure that's what it was?"

Brigid nodded. "It certainly sounded like one of the harps the transadapts used on Mars."

Puffing and grunting, Grant pulled himself to the summit. "You didn't see anybody?"

"I saw someone," Brigid answered. "I think it was a man…dressed in a druidic type of robe. That's who I shot at."

"You did not hit him?" Fand asked.

"I don't know," Brigid replied. "I might've winged him."

Fand turned to Morrigan. "Do you sense anything, Morrigan?"

The blind woman's long tresses stirred, as if touched by wind, but her hair slid around her neck and shoulders against the direction of the breeze. The Cerberus warriors had seen the phenomenon before when Morrigan cast her telepathic senses wide.

After a long moment, she sighed. "Nay, I detect nothing. But that doesn't mean there isn't danger."

Brigid smiled ruefully and rubbed her forehead. "That's a certain thing."

Sin Eater sliding into his hand, Kane said, "As long as we went to all the trouble to get here, let's make sure."

He led the way through the tunnel beneath the retaining wall and they made their way up a steep slant, boots slipping and sliding on the wet stones. A flagstone path widened into a miniature walled plaza, lined by leaning tombstones topped by Celtic crosses. Their inscriptions and carved gryphons had long ago been smeared into illegibility by the harsh wind and the merciless hand of centuries.

On the stones glistened spattered speckles of crimson. Grant nodded to them. "Looks like you winged somebody."

Brigid forced a smile. "Good…I'd hate to be accused of wasting ammunition again."

The path wound among a cluster of little beehive-shaped stone huts, constructed of flat, interlocking rocks. Fand touched one of them, saying, "These are the *clochans*, where the monks lived. Their lives were very Spartan by our standards."

"By any standards, looks like," Kane murmured.

The monastery atop Great Skellig might at one time have been an impressive, even awe-inspiring place, but now the settlement looked depressing and forlorn, a place fit only for the ghosts of the long dead. There was a round tower, two stories high, and a cracked terrace with a series of crumbling monoliths, pocked and worn, that completely encircled it.

"This seems to be a damned inaccessible place for a secret holy order to make their headquarters," Grant commented.

Fand said, "The priests and priestesses of the Priory of Awen were the last representatives of the first-century faith of Jesus and his disciples. Although I disagree with many of their policies, I have no doubt that their actions kept the various dragon cults springing up around the Annunaki and Enlil from gaining dominance during the Middle Ages."

"We've been helping a little bit in that area ourselves over the past couple of years," Kane said softly.

Fand gave him a fond smile, but did not respond.

The five people passed through the plaza and stopped in a clearing among the stones. No lichen, grass or moss grew on the earth. In the center of the bare patch rose a stele, an eight-foot-tall stone column with a crosspiece of two blunted knobs. The weathered carvings formed swirling geometric abstractions.

"There's no place your attacker could hide up here," Grant said quietly to Brigid, eyes and gun barrel questing for threats.

Kane glanced toward Fand. "There has to be a way inside."

She nodded. "According to my mother, yes."

She said nothing more, only scanned the plateau with narrowed eyes. The silence atop Great Skellig was unbroken except for the wail of the chill wind and distant crash of the surf.

After a few moments, Kane was finally nettled sufficiently to demand, "And?"

"And," she said, "if the citadel within is inhabited, then our presence is already known."

"That was settled already," Brigid said peevishly. She touched the bruise on her cheek. "Remember?"

Fand pointed to the stele. "Very well. Look."

Barely visible on the left side the stone surface were two red smears, the imprint of bloody fingers. Brigid stepped forward, her hand hovering above the bloodstains. "Looks like he pushed here. Any reason why I shouldn't do it?"

"Millions," Kane said, deadpan. "But go ahead."

Brigid pressed her hand against the stele. The mechanical throbbing she had detected earlier increased in volume. The carved column of rock suddenly quivered, and a circular crack split the naked ground around it in a symmetrical pattern, forming a perfect square. Slowly, smoothly, the stele began to rise, like a single finger at the end of a fist.

A cube of brooding black metal pushed its way from below. The air seemed to pulse about it. Dimly came the sound of buried machinery, gears, chains and the prolonged hissing squeak of hydraulics.

Kane, Brigid and Grant all aimed their weapons at it, automatically shifting position to place it at the apex of a triangulated cross fire.

The cube's slow ascent came to a clanking halt. A flat slab of metal slid aside.

The interior of the cube was as blank and featureless as the exterior, except for two buttons protruding from one wall.

After a long, expectant moment of silence, Fand declared, "It appears we've been invited inside."

Eyeing the open elevator with apprehension, Kane said, "I don't know if I'd make that assumption. This seems more like a baited hook."

Grant grunted. "I don't think we have much choice but to bite."

The Cerberus warriors hesitated, looked at one another, then with a fatalistic shrug, Kane stepped inside. "We may have to take the bait, but we can make it tough for Strongbow to land us."

Fand, Morrigan, Grant and Brigid joined him inside. With the barrel of the Sin Eater, Kane depressed a button. With a hiss, the cube sealed and began to drop, slowly and without a lurch.

Chapter 26

Kane felt his stomach muscles flutter in reaction to the adrenaline coursing through his system, but his tone was calm and flat. "Any idea of what we'll find when we stop?"

Morrigan turned her head in his direction. "Are you asking me?"

"You're the one with the telepathic powers," Grant reminded her gruffly. "Not that they've been too useful so far."

The blind woman frowned, then faced the door panel. She gazed at it intently, as if she hoped that through sheer force of will she could see what lay on the other side. After a long moment, she released her breath in a frustrated sigh. "I'm sorry...I'm not receiving any impressions at all. It's as if there are no living minds here."

"That's impossible," Fand said sharply.

Brigid fingered her discolored cheek. "We know there's at least one mind here—whether it's still alive or not remains to be seen."

The cube sighed to a stop. Kane lifted his Sin Eater

and put his back against the right-hand wall. The steel doors hissed back into a groove, opening to reveal a large low-ceilinged room. It was filled with computer terminals and electronic communications equipment, most of it dating back to the twentieth century.

Kane sidled around the edge of the lift car and stepped into the room. Following a procedure that had become ingrained habit, Grant and Brigid fanned out behind him, taking positions on his left and right.

Cool air brushed Kane's face, blown from a distant, unseen ventilation system.

Brigid eyed the computer stations and said, "The power is on."

Console and panel lights flashed and blinked purposefully. A bank of closed-circuit monitor screens ran the length of the far wall. They showed images of the rough Atlantic seas and the *Cu Sith Awwn* riding at anchor.

"Somebody turned it on," Grant observed. With the barrel of his Sin Eater he pointed at several drops of blood gleaming on a keyboard.

Fand and Morrigan stepped out of the elevator. The blind woman held Fand's left arm, her face paper-pale. In a whisper she said, "The Priory of Awen had no more use for this place, as far as I know."

"It looks like it has been maintained, nevertheless," Fand said matter-of-factly.

Kane crossed the room and pushed open a door. Beyond stretched a cold gray corridor lit by fluorescent strips glowing on the ceiling. It looked as if it had been carved out of the naked rock. An overpowering sense of overlapping layers of history was sunk deep into the stonework of the floor and walls.

He moved down it, moving heel-to-toe as he always did in a potential killzone. Grant and Brigid followed him in the standard deployment of personnel and fire-power. Fand and Morrigan brought up the rear. All of them became aware of a distant, rhythmic sound like the pulse of some great piece of machinery. Kane sensed other presences, as if eyes, cold and remote, watched them from the shadows. The feeling ate at his nerve endings like acid.

The corridor opened up after a few yards, and at its end stood an immense carved stone door with serpen-tine, spiraling designs incised across it. A body lay on the floor before it. With narrowed eyes, Kane studied the black-robed figure, looking for any sign of life or movement.

"Cover me," Kane whispered to his friends and moved forward, pistol trained on the fallen figure.

On the floor beneath the man's outsplayed right hand lay a duplicate of the harplike device used by the trans-adapts on Mars. He nudged the lopsided wedge made of a glassy substance away from the man's fingers.

Kneeling beside the body, he pulled back the face-concealing cowl. For a few seconds, he wasn't sure if he looked at a man or a woman, the features were so regular and androgynous. The pale flesh had a waxy sheen that Kane had never seen except on the skin of a corpse. He wore ear-flapped headgear of the same leathery type and color as Rhianna.

Kane didn't detect a pulse. He found a bullet hole low on the left side of his chest, but blood did not dampen the fabric of the robe. "I think he's dead," he announced.

"You think?" Grant asked suspiciously.

"Best I can do. Come and take a look."

Grant and Brigid approached cautiously. "What about the harp?" she asked.

He picked it up and handed it to her. "Right here. You were lucky he didn't get in a clean shot."

Brigid turned the harp over in her hands, examining the double-banked strings. "You're telling me."

"Who is he?" Fand asked.

"How should I know?"

Brigid loosened the cassock, and light glinted from a silver chain around the man's neck. From it hung a small charm, a talisman fashioned in the shape of three circle-topped triangles.

"A priest of the priory," Brigid said in surprise. She shot a glance toward Fand and Morrigan. "I thought you said the priory abandoned this place."

The two women came forward. Fand glanced into the waxen face of the corpse and shook her head. "I do not recognize him. The priesthood of Awen isn't large. If he truly is one of the order, I ought to know him."

Morrigan knelt and touched the man's face. She

jerked her fingers back as if scalded. "He's as cold as if he's been dead for days!"

"That's impossible," Brigid snapped. "I'm sure this is the same man who attacked me."

Grant lifted the man's right hand. The fingers were painted with streaks of wet scarlet. "You're right."

Impatiently, Kane pulled open the cassock, heedless of the clasps along the front seam. Under the robe, the man wore a reinforced garment covering torso and groin, like an armored vest. Nestled within a little depression over the left pectoral was a flattened bullet. A raw red scrape showed lividly on his right shoulder. Blood had seeped from the graze down his arm.

"You nailed him good, Baptiste," Kane said. "If not for the body armor, you would've dropped his ass dead outside."

"Then the question begs to be asked," Brigid said tersely. "Why is he dead now? His armor stopped one bullet, and he hasn't lost enough blood from that scratch to kill him."

Grant knuckled his chin thoughtfully. "Damned good question. Another damned good one is where he came from."

Fand eyed the heavy door. "Through there, I imagine."

Kane straightened. "Let's find out. Morrigan, Fand, do either of you know how to open it?"

Morrigan's tongue touched her dry lips. She stepped to the door, her small hands pushing at the stone molding in several places, pressing certain points in certain ways. Then, very slowly, the great carved slab of stone began to tilt inward at the top. It was precisely balanced on oiled pivots. The aperture beyond was black with a darkness that was almost solid. A musty odor poured forth like invisible smoke. At the same time, the muffled mechanical sound ceased, as if a volume knob had been turned down.

The five people stood and stared at the doorway for a long moment, then Kane stepped into the blackness. The others followed him. The light from the corridor barely penetrated into the murk. They walked slowly along the passage past half a dozen openings, doors that were sealed with cross-braced timbers.

With the amber beam of Kane's Nighthawk light illuminating the way, they saw that the walls were covered with straight-line inscriptions in Ogham, the ancient Celtic form of writing. Faded banners depicting incidents in the lives of various saints and warriors hung from pegs.

With Grant treading almost on his heels, Kane turned a hairpin corner and descended irregular stairs hewed out of rock. Ahead and below glowed a dim light. At the foot of the stairs spread a gallery, a natural, bowl-shaped cavern. The light shone from a dozen copper braziers placed in a circle around the curving rock walls. Globes of luminous, fluorescent green glowed from within the bowls.

Painted on the cavern floor in greens and reds was a

large cup and ring glyph, a semicircular interlace spiral design that confused the eye with its complexity.

"That was laid there to entrap and destroy malignant entities," Fand said softly.

With a crooked grin, Kane said, "I'll be careful not to step in it, then."

They descended the stairs, walking along the edges of the intricate labyrinth of lines. Shapes loomed in the shadows, objects and artifacts concealed by linen coverings.

In a shallow recess sat two life-size images crafted out of stone. The right-hand statue squatted cross-legged in an attitude of meditation. It wore a cassock much like the one on the corpse above.

Eyeing the stone effigy, Fand murmured, "Saint Patrick, founder of the Priory of Awen."

The left-hand statue was a brawny, half-naked man, wearing a diadem of miniature grinning human skulls above a grim, clean-shaved face. The right hand gripped a sword, but the point of the blade branched into the stylized image of three triangles. A pair of huge hounds crouched between his wide-spread legs, stone lips curled in vicious, fanged snarls.

"Cuchulainn, the most fierce, yet mystical warrior in Celtic legend," Fand said with a smile, her eyes fixed on Kane's face.

Brigid glanced from one to the other, then over at Kane. "Patrick and Cuchulainn. Peace and war. Yin and yang."

Kane felt uncomfortable standing there with the two women staring at him, so he stepped between the statues to examine the oblong pedestal rising between the effigies.

Four small pyramids crafted from pale golden alloy were placed at equidistant points around it. Resting on their points was a smooth, crystalline ovoid, about eight feet long. Behind it bulked the cylindrical outlines of two cryostasis units.

The Cerberus warriors had seen similar machines before, from Mongolia to the Moon. They knew the one shaped like an ovoid did not operate on conventional cryogenic principles, but rather employed an advanced technology that froze a subject within an impenetrable bubble of space and time, slowing to a stop all metabolic processes. Such stasis devices had been used by both the Tuatha de Danaan, the Annunaki and the custodial race known as the Archons, but they preferred to think of themselves as the First Folk.

"What is this place, anyway?" Grant asked, his voice hushed.

"You might call it a museum," Fand answered. "Or a memory box…of the Danaan and the old times when my people loved them as parents yet feared them as demons."

Morrigan moved tentatively to one of the linen-draped shapes. She fingered the cloth and pulled it away. A great face balanced on a pointed chin stared outward with blind eyes bulging out on either side of the bridge of the nose. The forehead slanted back to the wall. It was at least eight feet tall.

Brigid grimaced at the sight of the grotesque visage, with its mouth only a downturned slash, partly open to reveal the tip of a tongue, like the flattened head of a serpent. A sculpted raven with wings outspread was perched, frozen in midflight, atop cranium. Its beak gaped wide as if voicing a warning squawk.

"Lovely," she muttered.

Morrigan touched the surface of the face with tentative fingers. It did not look as if it were made of stone, but rather a gun-metal gray gleaming with a dull sheen. She whispered, "The head of Bran the Blessed."

Kane turned around to look and repressed a shudder. "A handsome son of a bitch, wasn't he?"

Fand laughed, but it sounded forced. "According to Danaan lore, King Bran was mortally wounded in a battle and asked his followers to cut off his head and place it in his Cauldron of Rebirth. For centuries afterward, the head continued to speak and offer counsel to his brethren who live in exile in Cornwall. After eighty years, the head of Bran asked that they take his head to London and bury it beneath the Gwynfryn, the White Hill, believed to be the site where the Tower of London was later built. According to legend, as long as his head remained there, Britain would be safe from invasion.

"Allegedly, King Arthur dug up the head, declaring that the country would be safeguarded by his strength and that of his knights. He kept the head in Camelot and often consulted it in regards to tactics."

Kane eyed the sculpture skeptically. "That thing isn't really Bran's head, is it?"

Fand chuckled. "I seriously doubt it, even though Bran was reputed to be a giant."

"More than likely," Brigid said, "the legend of Bran's immortal head derived from the ancient Celtic practice of head-hunting. The clansmen believed that the skull was the home of the soul."

"What's with the bird on it?" Grant asked.

"'Bran' means 'raven' in Gaelic," Fand answered. "Which is why the Tower of London also served as a rookery. The traditional belief is that as long as ravens remained at the tower, Britain would never fall."

Grant and Kane snorted at the same time.

Suddenly, Morrigan staggered back from the sculpted face and breathed in stark disbelief, *"It lives!"*

Grant whirled toward her. "Are you crazy or what?"

Even as he snarled out the words, the face changed. The sheen faded from the bulging eyes. The mechanical throbbing they had heard above suddenly returned, swiftly increasing in volume and tempo.

Crying out in Gaelic, Fand reached for Morrigan. The air crackled and blurred around the eyes, and then a halo of white fire surrounded Fand's headband in a flashing corona. She uttered a choked scream, took a drunken reeling step, dropped her staff and pitched as limp as a corpse into Kane's arms.

Chapter 27

Fear and shock froze Kane's mind and reflexes. He could only stand and stare, uncomprehending, as he lowered Fand to the floor.

The mouth in Bran's face opened wide and the gray tongue lashed forth, a tendril that snaked out and closed around Morrigan's neck. Crying out, she clawed wildly at the tongue as it pulled her toward the gaping maw and gleaming eyes.

Grant sprang forward to grab the woman, but another tentacle whipped out from the open mouth and seized him around the right forearm, coiling and constricting, covering his Sin Eater. With his free hand he snatched his combat dagger from its sheath and slashed at the metallic limb. The blade bounced away without leaving so much as a scratch.

Kane bounded to Morrigan, dragging her backward against the pull of the alloy-coated tongue. The eyes flashed with white fiery bolts, licking at his head. He threw himself to the right, and the discharge of energy struck the statue of Cuchulainn. For an instant it shed a shower of golden sparks.

The tongue sprouted another cable. It arched out and wrapped itself around Kane's ankle. Another whipped out of the maw and fastened itself around his right wrist. He struggled as it began to pull at him, dragging him directly in front of the glowing eyes.

Brigid lunged forward, brandishing the harp, aiming it like a rifle. She shouted, "Watch yourselves!" and stroked the strings frantically.

The sound exploding out of the instrument bore no resemblance a melody, but the directed vibrations struck the bulging orb. The metallic surface acquired a dent, then a pattern of jagged cracks bisected it. The right eye exploded in a blinding fireball, and then the other vanished in a flaring explosion.

The concussion was so overwhelmingly loud their ears couldn't completely register it. A wrecking ball seemed to smash into their bodies, and compressed air drove the oxygen back into their lungs. Brigid staggered backward but managed to retain her grip on the harp. She caught only a glimpse of the tongue and its connected tentacles retracting.

Grant, Kane and Morrigan stirred on the floor, panting and coughing. Knuckling the amoeba-shaped floaters from his eyes, Kane staggered to his feet. He moved swiftly away from the head of Bran.

"What the fuck is that thing?" he demanded, dismayed by how hoarse his voice sounded.

Brigid shook her head, still aiming the elongated neck of the harp at the face, now locked in a permanent expression of astonishment with the mouth gaping wide. Throat-abrading smoke curled from the empty eye sockets. "I couldn't say with any degree of certainty. My guess is that's some sort of ancient alarm system, maybe designed for a Danaan treasure vault. Electrical pulses are directed toward metal objects…I really don't know."

As she spoke, Kane went to Fand, who feebly tried to push herself into a sitting position. Her eyes blinked repeatedly and her respiration sounded labored and harsh.

"Are you all right?" he asked, propping her up.

She touched her headband and winced. "I think so…but my head hurts considerably."

"I don't doubt it," he said dryly. "It's a wonder you're not dead."

Grant cautiously approached the head of Bran, eyeing the gaping mouth. No mechanical noises emanated from it, but cool air smelling of the under-earth wafted out.

"Hey, there's a chute back here," he announced.

Kane helped Fand to her feet. "Back where?"

"At the back of the throat."

Brigid and Kane joined him, very conscious of putting their heads into the open maw. They saw a sleek and shiny metal shaft plunging into the darkness at a forty-five-degree angle, like an artificial gullet.

Picking up her staff, Fand walked on unsteady legs over to them. "It must go to the lower levels."

"Obviously," Brigid said, sarcasm edging her tone. "But what's down there?"

Fand's face tightened into a tense mask. "More secrets of the Danaan, mayhaps...and those of Strongbow, as well."

Uneasily, Kane looked at the yawning aperture and felt the back of his neck flush cold. "There's got to be another way down there."

Morrigan sidled close. "I doubt there would be. More than likely, what is down there was meant to stay down there."

Fand inhaled deeply. "I agree. But I also would like to have some notion of what might await us."

Morrigan's tresses stirred. She stared intently at the face of Bran. Softly, in a voice barely above a rustling whisper, she intoned, "I sense presences below...they are what drew me here to the head to begin with."

Grant uttered a scoffing snort. "*Now* your mind powers work?"

Brigid frowned. "That's very convenient."

Eyes narrowed, Fand demanded, "What are you implying?"

"I'm only making an observation about the timing," Grant rumbled. "You can figure out the rest for yourself."

Morrigan did not seem to be offended or to even have heard the exchange. Deliberately, she strode over to the sculpted face, secured a two-handed grip on the upper lip and levered her body inward, feetfirst.

"Hey!" Alarmed, Kane snatched at her.

Morrigan's body disappeared down the throatlike chute. Jaw muscles bunched, Grant snapped, "Has she gone crazy or what?"

Fand stared into the open mouth for a long silent moment, then her lips curved in a mirthless smile. She gathered her cloak about her and leaped feetfirst into the maw of Bran. She landed on her rump and slid out of sight, her arms crossed over her breasts, her staff held between them.

Kane rolled his eyes. "Oh, for the love of—"

Grant gusted out a sigh. "Now what?"

"We don't have many options," Brigid said.

"That doesn't mean we shouldn't explore them—" Kane began.

Brigid leaped lightly into the chute. As she disappeared, she called out, "Slide feetfirst and keep your arms in."

Very softly, but with a great deal of feeling, Grant said, "Ah, *shit*."

KANE WASN'T TOO SURPRISED to find out the chute was a spiral, but by the time he had whipped around the third corkscrewing twist of the helix, he became dizzy. He lay on his back, arms crossed over his chest as his body plunged down the slick tube. Since it was completely dark within the shaft, he could see nothing by which he could gauge his speed. He could have been traveling at three miles per hour or three hundred.

He understood that the spiral design of the chute was most likely not chosen at random but was connected to the ancient cup-and-spiral symbolism of the Tuatha de Danaan and to and extent, even the Annunaki.

As the incline of the tube grew progressively steeper, Kane felt his back heating up due to the friction. Sweat pebbled his face. He slapped at the sides of the chute, spreading his legs, pushing with his feet to slow himself, but the braking effect was marginal.

The wild downward slide continued, and he refused to allow his mind to fixate on what might lie below. He couldn't help but toy with images of landing in a cartoon version of Hell, with baby red devils wearing diapers menacing him with miniature pitchforks. Since Grant was somewhere ahead of him, he assumed his partner would take out the first wave of the little demons.

The chute continued to corkscrew into darkness, twisting him down into the very bowels of the Earth. Then he felt a series of small blows against the soles of his feet. Semirigid flaps caught at his body, giving way as he slid past, but slowing his momentum. At the same time, the spiral straightened and the angle decreased in sharpness. His speed dwindled.

As he made one final turn, he glimpsed red lights flickering in the blackness beyond his feet. Then he shot through an opening and landed onto overlapping thick-padded plastic mats.

Despite how weak he felt, Kane struggled to his feet.

For a long moment, all he could see was a ring of globes, shining with a bloodred luminescence. He squinted around, panting for breath, trying to force his vision to adjust to the gloom. As he stepped off the mats, a shadow shifted to his left and heeled around, Sin Eater sliding into his hand.

"It's me, goddammit," Grant's voice snapped, his deep voice echoing in the vast, dome-roofed chamber.

Kane lowered his pistol, but he did not relax. "Where's Baptiste?"

"Here," she called from the darkness. "I'm with Fand and Morrigan."

Kane saw the three women standing between two of the pedestals supporting the red spheres. Inscribed on the floor in highly polished silver was an intricate, symmetrical pattern of looping, interlaced and interlinking curves. Kane and Grant had seen the design before and knew it was called a Celtic wheel or knot. The various loops and links were arranged in accordance with the compass points and represented the facets and pathways of life.

He and Grant walked across the Celtic wheel to join the women. Brigid grasped one of the lights by a three-foot-long handle, pulling it free from the pedestal. Her green eyes sparkled as if she were enthralled. Fand, however, regarded him gravely, her full lips compressed in a frown.

"Where the hell are we?" Kane asked.

Morrigan shrugged. "It is of no use to explain it. You will not understand."

Kane glared at her, realizing in the glow of the orbs she looked much younger, barely more than a child. "Try us."

Morrigan shook her head. "I don't know where to begin."

"I do," Brigid said curtly.

Addressing Kane and Grant, she declared, "According to Fand and Morrigan, we're in an old-school Celtic labyrinth. A thousand years or so ago, it was used to test the mettle of Priory of Awen initiates. If they couldn't find their way out of here, they'd die."

Kane stared at her for a long moment, then remarked blandly, "I have the distinct feeling the same rule applies to us."

Chapter 28

In the half-light of the artificial torches, the opening to the tunnel looked like the maw of some gigantic devourer. "We've got to go through there?" Kane asked.

Brigid nodded. "The old Celtic labyrinths are believed to have served either as traps for malevolent spirits or as defined paths for rituals. They were expressions of sacred geometry. We've come across examples of it before, like at Angor and in Iraq, remember?"

"I don't have a photographic memory like some people I can mention," Kane responded dryly, "but I'm not likely to forget either of those places."

"During medieval times, the labyrinth symbolized a hard path to God," Brigid stated, "with a clearly defined center that symbolized God, and one entrance that symbolized birth."

"You should think of labyrinths as symbolic forms of pilgrimage," Morrigan interposed. "People can walk the path, ascending toward salvation or enlightenment. In the old days, many people could not afford to travel to holy sites and lands, so labyrinths and prayer were substituted to meet that need. Later, the religious significance of labyrinths faded, and they were used primarily for entertainment, although their spiritual aspect was never completely forgotten."

Grant grunted in disinterest. "So we just go in there and wander around until we find the center?"

Fand chuckled, but it sounded forced. "It's a bit more complicated than that, Mr. Grant. Sacred geometry is basically the architecture of the universe itself...worlds within worlds spin because of it. Energy patterns are basically geometric forms. Both the Annunaki and the Tuatha de Danaan knew this."

Grant glanced behind him at the chute and said doubtfully, "Maybe we ought to try to climb back up."

Fand regarded the big man with a look that was almost pitying. "I'm positive the tube was designed for one-way travel only. We would be wasting precious time that we could spend navigating the labyrinth."

Kane ran an impatient hand through his hair. "That's what we're afraid of...we could waste *all* of our time wandering around in there and never find a way out."

The corner of Brigid's mouth quirked in a smile. "That's the risk all seekers of enlightenment must accept."

"I'm not looking for enlightenment," Grant growled.

"Me either," Kane said. "Only a way out, and if that's the only possible exit—"

"It is," Morrigan declared.

"Remember we're inside a rock," Brigid commented. "The labyrinth couldn't be all *that* extensive."

"Are you sure about that?" Kane asked.

"Hardly…but we never let a little thing like uncertainty stop us before, have we?"

Taking a breath, Kane faced the square opening and stepped forward over the threshold. His eardrums popped, his vision smeared and his belly turned over sickeningly. He was conscious of a half instant of whirling vertigo as if he hurtled a vast distance at blinding speed.

Then he staggered across a solid, slick floor, falling headlong to his hands and knees. He was only dimly aware of Brigid, Fand, Morrigan and Grant falling in a tangle of limbs around him. He heard the clatter of guns, torches and the cries of surprised outrage.

Heart jerking painfully inside his chest, Kane quickly got to his feet. He absently noted that the floor beneath him was a solid slab of white, featureless material closely resembling plastic. Although the wall curved away to the right, overhead arched a great dome. Vast translucent panels shed a pallid white light. Kane couldn't help but be reminded of an immense amphitheater. Spinning on his heel, he looked behind him at a blank expanse of wall. He saw no door.

Grant climbed to his feet and glared around, lips peeling back from his teeth in a grimace of anger and fear. "What the fuck is this place?" he snarled. "What the fuck happened?"

Brigid stared around in awe as she stood up, as did Fand. Morrigan leaned against the wall as if she was too weak to stand unaided. In a hoarse whisper, Brigid husked out, "The labyrinth isn't inside Great Skellig at all."

"Then where the hell is it?" Kane demanded.

When Brigid didn't immediately answer, Kane fixed his gaze on Fand. "You know, don't you?"

The woman's face had turned to the color of parchment. "I can only guess."

"Guess what?" Brigid challenged, a hint of accusation underscoring her tone.

"We're in an other world."

"Another world?" Grant repeated skeptically.

"No…an *other* world," Fand corrected. "I should have suspected it."

Kane clenched his fists. "Explain."

Fand ran a slightly trembling hand over her face. "We passed through a dimensional portal."

Brigid gusted out a sigh. "Into a pocket universe?"

Fand nodded. "If that's the term you prefer, then aye."

Both Grant and Kane glowered at the two women. "How can that happen?" Grant demanded angrily.

Brigid lifted a shoulder in a shrug. "Most likely we stepped through something like an Annunaki threshold."

"What is that?" Fand asked.

"A means of point-to-point instantaneous transportation," Brigid replied. "Thresholds were used by the Annunaki during their first occupation of Earth. It's possible the devices served as the templates for the mat-trans units of Project Cerberus."

She gestured around her and toward the blank wall at their backs. "In this case, we passed through interdimensional space. Remember what Strongbow said to us when we first met him?"

"The son of a bitch said a lot of things," Grant snapped. "Most of them self-serving bullshit."

Brigid smiled wanly. "He claimed that Ireland was a seat of hyperdimensional gateways, quantum exit and entrance points to back alleys of space-time. Think of Ireland as the hub of a wheel in our physical universe, with a multitude of invisible spokes extending into higher dimensional space. He believed that was one reason so many wars were fought for possession of it in prehistoric and historic times, why its people continued to cling to a rich tradition of magic long after the rest of the Western world had forgotten such things."

Fand nodded thoughtfully. "And it also would tend to explain why the cup-and-spiral design is so associated with ancient Ireland. They were like road maps to the other worlds."

"Assuming that's the case," Kane said darkly, "what other world are we in?"

Morrigan spoke up. "Does it really matter? We must go forward. We still have to navigate the labyrinth to find our way out of here."

"Do we?" Grant asked, turning to face the blank wall.

Deliberately, he strode toward it, one hand outstretched. He hesitated only for a second before slapping his palm flat against it. He pushed experimentally, then kicked the wall in several places.

"Solid?" Kane ventured.

Turning, Grant dry-scrubbed his scalp in frustration. "Morrigan's right."

The blind woman smiled slightly. "Was there ever any doubt?"

Kane and Grant started off, leading the way across the smooth floor. After a couple of minutes, they began to grasp the immensity of their surroundings. The dome over them was at least five hundred feet high and could conceivably cover an area of several square miles.

"This doesn't seem much like one of the other worlds of Celtic legend…certainly nothing like Tir Na Nog," Brigid said quietly.

"Nay, it does not," Fand admitted.

"However," Brigid continued, "it could fit the place to where Myrrdian was exiled, which was a cave or a hollow within something else, according to the tales."

Fand's eyes widened in surprise. "That is very possible."

Kane only half listened to the exchange, but the word "exile" had unpleasant connotations for him—for all of them, actually. In many ways, he reflected, he, Brigid and Grant had spent most of their exile trying to accept and come to terms with new knowledge and perspectives.

As they walked, the milky illumination peeping in from above dimmed gradually but quickly. They were forced to rely on the globe-tipped torches to light their way. Although the passageway curved, it didn't twist and turn as they had feared it would.

"If I'd known we'd be dimension jumping, I would've insisted we bring the interphaser," Grant muttered.

"I don't know if would have done any good," Brigid said. "In fact, activating it inside Great Skellig could have made things worse."

"That's hard to believe," Grant argued.

"Something awaits us in the dark," Morrigan said suddenly in an aspirated whisper.

Kane and Grant came to immediate halts. Kane glanced over his shoulder and saw that the blind woman was pressed against the wall, her hair coiling tight at the base of her neck. "What awaits us?" he asked.

"Hounds, I think," she said.

"Hounds?" Kane strained his ears but heard nothing. Fand drew in her breath sharply. "I see them."

Kane gazed down the dark passageway. Grant waved his torch ahead. A half dozen eyes winked red-yellow out of the gloom, and they heard the stealthy click of claws on the floor and then a faint, throaty growl.

"Bad doggies," he murmured under his breath.

Chapter 29

The eyes crept closer. Kane, Grant and Brigid hefted their pistols. Grant commented with studied indifference, "I shouldn't have left that sword behind."

Fand pushed between them, her staff held out before her like a spear. Confidently, she announced, "I believe I can drive them off."

"Why do you say that?" Kane asked.

"The so-called hounds of Cullan are the Gwyllgi of old myth," Fand said. "Giant dogs that were used during the wild hunts to sniff out the souls of the dying."

Sweat formed at Kane's hairline. He didn't examine Fand's calmly spoken declaration too closely for fear that his courage would fail. As it was, he longed to order a retreat, but he dared not.

Fand strode forward aggressively, shouting in Gaelic.

As the bestial growls increased in volume, the egg-shaped knob at the end of her staff burst forth with a dazzling white light, almost blinding in the gloom. With a click of claws and leathery rasp of padded feet, the glittering eyes vanished. But one pair remained. They moved closer, baleful and terrifying.

Fand swept her staff in a left-to-right arc, shouting again in Gaelic. The shimmering knob inscribed tracers in the dark air. Kane lifted his pistol and moved up beside her, unnerved by the eyes that seemed dead, yet still seemed to radiate hatred. He caught a whiff of a charnel house odor and heard a slobbering, growling sound that sent needles of fear up and down his spine.

He received an impression of a rushing body and he fired, depressing the trigger stud of the Sin Eater. The autopistol stuttered in a prolonged drumroll. Ricochets keened wildly throughout the passageway. Morrigan cried out in fear as a bouncing slug showered her with plastic splinters.

The hound of Cullan reared out of the dark, slapping at Fand's staff with huge talon-tipped paws. She fell back, voicing an alarmed, wordless cry, her flailing arm knocking Kane's pistol awry. The beast's jaws snapped shut barely an inch from her throat. She fended it off with the haft of her staff.

Kane struck at the hound with the Sin Eater and the frame slapped against its skull with a sound like two blocks of wood colliding. It dropped to all fours, snarled and bounded at him. The weight of the giant dog bore him to the floor, nearly driving all the wind from his lungs.

He twisted as he fell, slamming his open hand against the monster's lower jaw, forcing its head back. The jaws closed around his forearm, but the fangs did not penetrate the fabric of his shadow suit. Still, pain ripped up and down his arm.

Kane struggled against the predator's weight as both Grant and Brigid yelled and kicked at the hound, trying to drive it off him. He shoved the barrel of his Sin Eater between the foam-flecked jaws, hearing the fangs grating on steel.

He fired. Although it bayed in agony, the hound did not die quickly or quietly. Releasing him, twisting in on itself, the creature thrashed across the floor, spewing gouts of black, foul-smelling blood.

Breathing rapidly in big gasps, Kane elbowed aside the hound's body. It wasn't easy. His gun hand, arm and shoulder were covered in thick, viscous fluid. Suppressing the urge to vomit, he backed away, watching the death throes of the monster. After a few moments, it gave a final convulsive shudder and lay still. He climbed quickly to his feet, keeping his pistol trained on the hound's head.

When it no longer moved, Kane and his friends moved closer, very cautiously. The creature was no bigger than a wolfhound, but leaner and far more muscular. The canine teeth were at least four inches long.

"At least this time bullets killed it…but what the hell kind of animal is it really?" Grant said hoarsely.

Fand shook her head. "The basis of all the legends of hellhounds."

"Quite possibly they were Terran animals genetically altered by the Danaan," Brigid said quietly. "When they departed Earth a thousand years ago, they brought them here to this pocket universe and let them run free. They're not really supernatural. They can die."

Kane started at the loathsome creature and realized with a twinge of shame he was still afraid of it, dead or not. He edged around the widening pools of blood, saying, "Let's keep moving before worse things show up to eat it."

The five people wended their way along the curving passage as it twisted to the left, then sharply to the right and back to the left again. Grant took out his combat knife and made identifying scratches on the walls.

"I hope we don't have to come back this way," Kane remarked. "We can't leave by the same way we came in, right?"

"Right," Brigid confirmed.

"This is just crazy," Grant snapped. "Pocket universes used as pounds for nasty-ass hellhounds. How does that make any goddamned sense at all?"

"'Tis not up to us to make sense of the universe, Mr. Grant," Morrigan said.

"Maybe not," he grunted. "But that doesn't mean we shouldn't ask questions. If we're in another universe or dimension or whatever, then we're actually inside a big enclosed dome, right? So what's outside of it? It could be like our own world, as far as we know."

"Or," Brigid said, "it could be a lot worse. Remember what Maccan said about the homeworld of the Danaan? That they came from a Mars in a parallel universe?"

"What?" Fand asked, perplexed.

Briefly, Brigid explained about the origins of the Tuatha de Danaan they had learned from Maccan, the last full-blooded member of the race. According to him, she related, the Danaan had four million years of accumulated history to look back upon. They came from a mirror universe by means of a gigantic device and vehicle that became known as the Great Pyramid of Mars. For thousands of years, it permitted the translation from one universe into another. They brought their entire culture to Mars. The structure operated as a giant interphaser or contiguity that was originally built to pass backward, forward and sideways through the two universes.

The machine was built at the height of the Tuatha de Danaan's grand civilization and glory. The scientific and technological powers of their race expanded so much that they were able to spread out and colonize the worlds of many stars of their own universe. But when the inexorable laws of entropy took effect and as the suns of the universe burned out, they had no choice but to migrate, to retreat. Eventually they realized there was no place to retreat to and save their civilization.

As Brigid spoke, Kane mentally reviewed what they had all learned about the Danaan and their science. Obviously they deeply understood the indivisibility of space and time and of matter and energy. They knew all of them were interchangeable, one turned into the other and vice versa, according to the application.

The deeper the Danaan scientists probed into the

very composition of matter—the building blocks of material objects—the more they found energy and complexities of energy at the bottom of everything. He knew that the Danaan had earned the right to take pride in their accomplishments. Nor was it completely their fault that primitive Terrans regarded them as gods from the stars.

But almost all of the Tuatha de Danaan had left Earth around 453 A.D., after the Irish clanspeople had become Christianized. Their science was condemned as sorcery and they were characterized as demons, the fallen angels.

"There is far more to the legend and lore promulgated by the Danaan," Morrigan commented, "than dimensional travel. Actual tales of journeys through these pocket universes could have been transmitted as myths."

Brigid's eyebrows rose. "Actually, I'd been thinking along those same lines. The source of all the tales of heroes searching for fabulous treasures like the Holy Grail could be misunderstood reports of traversing an interdimensional labyrinth like this one."

Kane scowled. "What do you mean?"

Brigid gestured to the shadow-shrouded roof far above them and the curving walls of the passageway. "Think about it—in Celtic lore, the heroes like Cuchulainn and Fionn Mac Cumhaill ventured forth from their own ordinary reality and entered a world of supernatural wonder where strange forces were encountered."

"Hell," Grant muttered sourly, "that sounds like one of our average days."

"Their journey penetrated the heart of some mystic power," Brigid stated, "and eventually they won a decisive victory over great odds, returning from their magical journey transformed spiritually and possessing the power to bestow boons on those left behind. This heroic cycle appears in sacred writings all around the world."

"Are you suggesting we'll find the Holy Grail here?" Morrigan inquired, a note of distrust in her tone.

"Not at all. But if the genesis of the grail legends lies with the Cauldron of Bran and that was a technological object created by the Danaan, then it's possible this place is where all the Danaan relics were stored for safekeeping."

Fand chuckled. "The warehouse of the gods."

Thoughtfully Grant said, "That actually makes a little more sense to me. The Danaan were intelligent, and they were also more responsible than the Annunaki. We know the Supreme Council hid a lot of their own tech in vaults on Earth. The Danaan could have hidden their own stuff in a pocket dimension, which only a very select few could ever visit."

"A motif common in Celtic legends is that of the hero out hunting in the countryside," Brigid said, "where he finds himself in an otherworldly place. He engages in many adventures and even love affairs. Often, he sets out on a quest to recover great treasure from a hidden trove."

The passage curved to the right and then opened up

in a central rotunda where at least six labyrinth mouths intersected. A hundred yards ahead, round, ominous and helmet shaped, a dark structure protruded from the flat floor. It bluish surface appeared unbroken except for a rectangular slit in the side facing them.

"A trove sort of like that?" Grant whispered.

Kane tilted his head back to look upward. "I have the distinct feeling we've found the center of the maze. Easier than I thought."

Fand strode fearlessly toward the structure, staff in one hand, red-orbed torch in the other. Kane, Brigid, Grant and Morrigan fell into step behind her, the blind woman clutching at Grant's arm.

The rectangle was actually a narrow door, three feet wide by seven tall. They examined it, looking for any glyphs or writing on the wall around it. The light in Brigid's hand cast shadows on words embossed right above the entrance: *Magus Merlinus Caledonensis Absconditus En Somnio*. Inscribed below the words was the *crux ansata*, the ankh, the symbol of eternal life.

Kane read it aloud, stumbling a bit over the Latin pronunciation. "Does that mean what I think it does?"

Chapter 30

Brigid cast Kane an amused, slightly mocking glance. "That magical Merlin of Caledonia is hidden in dreams?"

"Yeah, that's pretty much what I thought it said," Kane stated deadpan.

Brigid shook her head in good-natured exasperation and ran her fingers over the frame of the door slit. "There don't appear to be any locks."

"Why would there be?" Fand inquired, stepping through the entrance.

Assuming the question to be rhetorical, Brigid followed her.

Kane looked over at Grant, who muttered, "This smells like a trap."

Then he, Kane and Morrigan sidled inside the structure. The interior was cramped. With the aid of the torches they could see sufficiently. The place was sparsely furnished, which wasn't surprising, but the consoles covering the walls came as a distinct shock.

There were enough readout screens, toggles and gauges to remind the Cerberus warriors of the main ops center at the redoubt.

Brigid ran her fingers lightly over a console, then pressed a key. Nothing happened. "Whatever powered this place is evidently long-dead."

"I do not understand," Morrigan said softly.

"There are machines here, Morrigan," Fand stated flatly.

"Machines of the Danaan?"

"Apparently."

Holding her torch high, Fand stepped through another narrow doorway. Beyond it a rack of stairs spiraled down into the dark. The light of the torches did not penetrate far.

"Now what?" Grant asked.

Without a word, Fand started down the stairway. It corkscrewed so tightly that each riser was matter of concentration. The flight ended in a chamber as abundantly appointed as the room above was sparse. The walls were hung with tapestries that showed men and beasts and knights in battle against a background of spired castles and forests.

A rug on the floor was the pelt of a creature none of them had ever even dreamed of before, like a huge tawny cat with a shaggy mane and great polished fangs. An array of panels made of rich, enameled wood occupied one wall. Swords and shields and maces were mounted on them. Reverently mounted on square display podiums were suits of medieval armor, halberds, poleaxes.

"Any of this stuff look familiar, Baptiste?" Kane asked.

"As a point of fact, yes," Brigid replied. "But it's what *doesn't* seem familiar that piques my curiosity."

"I don't get you."

"This is all of Terran manufacture, made during recorded historical periods. You'd think there would be artifacts created by the Danaan."

"You didn't think we'd find the Grailstone in here, did you?" Fand asked.

Brigid shrugged. "You never know."

On the opposite side of the room yawned a doorway. Inscribed above it, chased with silver, was a small *crux ansata*. Fand strode across the gallery toward it and entered a short corridor.

It was not long and it ended in a vault-walled chamber not much larger than the bridge of the *Cu Sith Awwn*. She jerked to a sudden halt and quickly tried to suppress a gasp. Kane pushed up beside her, squinting through a veil of light, and felt his nape hairs tingle.

Placed upon a broad, elevated platform towered an elaborate, high-backed throne. Sitting slumped in the throne was a figure that caused Kane's throat to constrict and what little moisture remained in his mouth to dry to a dusty film.

Wrapped in glowing, translucent mist, an old man sat there, silent and brooding. In his hands, thick knuckled and gnarled like old tree roots, rested the haft of a slender metal staff, barely four feet long. A golden sphere tipped it.

His entire frame was covered in a shimmering robe

of sky-blue. A snow-white beard fell halfway to his waist. Hair of the same bleached-out hue tumbled loose around his shoulders. Beneath grizzled eyebrows, his eyes were tightly closed. He wore headgear identical to that of the man they had found dead in Great Skellig. The man exuded a palpable aura of great age, mystery and power.

The back and arms of the throne were shaped like a massive *crux ansata*. As Kane stared, the legends whispered through his mind, of Merlin and King Arthur and the Lady of the Lake.

"Merlinus," Fand whispered in awe. "The real Myrrdian."

No one spoke for long, stretched out tick of time.

Grant broke the silence. "Is he dead…or in stasis?"

Fand shook her head, as if rousing from a sleep, and reached out tentatively with her staff. An inch or so away from the man's beringed right hand, the mist surrounding it seemed to congeal and thicken. A spark popped loudly against the staff's knob.

Fand jerked away, crying out in pain.

"What happened?" Kane demanded.

"A shock," Fand retorted peevishly. "He's protected by a force field or a shield."

"Which means there has to be a form of power generation going on," Brigid said calmly.

"Mayhaps," Morrigan whispered. "Mayhaps we are dealing with true sorcery here. He is the source of all the power in this place and if he awakens—"

She trailed off, but Brigid swiveled her head toward her, eyes bright with jade glints. "You might have something there. The Latin inscription made it seem as if Merlinus is dreaming, right?"

Kane eyed the figure on the throne, looking for any sign of life through the milky light curved around him. "If you say so."

"It's possible this place is like a giant suspended-animation canister," Brigid stated. "This is where Merlinus was banished to. It's not programmed to do much of anything except sustain him unless he's awake. Maybe it keeps him asleep, in stasis by monitoring his brainwave activity."

Fand nibbled at her full underlip. "Even if that is so, we would be overstepping ourselves to rouse him, would we not? After all, he was exiled here by decree of the Danaan."

"If you believe the legend, it was only one Danaan...a woman, the Lady of the Lake, who got tired of him or who tricked him into revealing the source of his magical powers. Who really knows the truth? I'm guessing all sorts of Danaan tech was put here with him, either to keep him alive or keep him imprisoned."

"It's pretty obvious Strongbow has been here," Grant argued. "Why didn't he wake him up?"

Coldly, Fand replied, "Strongbow came here as a thief. He also assumed the identity of Myrrdian. It would not have been to his advantage to awaken him, even if that is possible."

Grant glanced around the bare-walled chamber. "Any suggestions on how we do it?"

"Do what?" Kane asked.

"Wake him up. I mean, if we can't touch him—"

"Fand couldn't touch him," Brigid said. "Maybe there's a reason for that."

"Such as?" the tall blond woman demanded.

"Such as that the field around Merlinus functions as a sensor web, too. It can detect the Danaan genetic marker in your DNA."

"You'd think that would make it easier for me to reach him," Fand objected. "Merlinus was reputed to be part Danaan…a halfling, actually."

Brigid's eyes narrowed in concentration. "Except that one faction of the Danaan banished him here, and so the shield was programmed to prevent other Danaan from reviving him."

"What about the priests and priestesses of the Priory of Awen?" Grant asked. "Didn't they have to walk the labyrinth and reach this point themselves?"

"You forget that all of the priory clergy were selected because they carried the Danaan bloodline."

Brigid gestured triumphantly. "There you have it."

"Have what?" Kane snapped irritably. "Even if your theory holds water, why wake up the old guy? If he's not dead, he might be in a major foul mood. I know I would be if I found out I'd overslept by a thousand years or so."

"What's your point?" Brigid asked curtly.

"The point is that we don't know *anything* about this guy except from old legends and movies. For all we know, he could have been banished here because he went crazy and started turning people into newts and that sort of thing."

Grant cleared his throat and said blandly, "Well, when you put it like that…"

"I believe it is worth the risk," Fand declared. "We must take action. If he is really Merlinus, the one true Myrrdian, then he can help us against Strongbow."

"Or help Strongbow against us," Kane pointed out.

Brigid exhaled in a long sigh and stared at the figure in the chair intently. "Ordinarily, I'd just go ahead and test my hypothesis, but Kane's concerns are legitimate. There's something else bothering me, too."

"Other than being trapped in an extradimensional labyrinth?" Kane inquired sarcastically. "Ah, go on."

Brigid didn't respond to his comment. "Hasn't it occurred to anyone that sleeping Merlinus here is a dead ringer for all the traditional images of a Middle Ages wizard? The white beard, the robe, the magic wand?"

Grant hesitated, then said, "Well, yeah. But I assumed that he'd look like he was supposed to—"

He broke off, his brow furrowing. "I see what you're getting at. It's a little too convenient, right?"

Brigid nodded. "Right. All the legends, all the folklore, all the image patterns—from the *Sword in the Stone* to *The Once and Future King*, this guy looks like he stepped out of a road-show production of *Camelot*."

Kane wasn't sure to what she referred so he inquired, "And that's a bad thing?"

"I don't know if it is or not," Brigid said frankly. "That's the problem."

Fand uttered a short laugh. "'Tis a strange time to start questioning reality."

Brigid smiled. "Agreed. But it's never too late or too early for that, is it? Maybe Merlinus served as the archetype for all wizards and magicians, but I can't help but wonder if there's something else at work here. And the symbol of the ankh over the door into this place makes me suspicious about its true nature."

"What are we going to do?" Kane demanded. "Just turn around and leave and try to find another way out of this labyrinth before we starve to death—or are eaten by the hounds of Cullan?"

After a thoughtful moment, Brigid shook her head. "No. We don't have any choice but to put my theory to the test."

Before anyone else spoke, she stretched out her right arm. She paused for a second when her fingertips touched the mist, then she plunged her hand through it. Gingerly, she touched, then clasped the right hand of Merlinus.

The glowing mist vanished. As it disappeared, so did the figure of the old man. In his place slept a young man, not much more than a boy, his skin as white as milk. His hair, thick and long and black with indigo highlights, swept halfway down his back. He looked no more than fifteen years old, perhaps younger, his slender frame swallowed by the blue robe.

He slumbered peacefully, his lips curved in a faint smile. Then the lashes of his eyes fluttered, stirring like the wings of a butterfly. A shadow suddenly seemed to flit across his face, something not really seen, but everyone sensed it. He was rousing. Brigid released his hand and stepped back.

Slowly, the boy's eyes opened. His expression did not alter even as his eyes came to focus on the faces before him. A cold stillness breathed from somewhere within him.

The irises of his eyes were molten gold and they were old eyes, old with pain and suffering. His pale lips stirred and in a faint whisper, he asked, *"Dè an là a tha ann?"*

Then the lights came on.

Chapter 31

Kane gazed at the wavery lights shining down from fixtures overhead. "What did he say?"

"He spoke in Gaelic," Morrigan said.

"I know...what did he say?"

"He asked what day it was," Fand said quietly.

Kane struggled against the wave of unreality that threatened to engulf his mind. "How the hell is that important?"

"Apparently it means something to him." Fand turned to the boy. *"Di-ceudain."*

The boy stared at her uncomprehendingly.

"What did you tell him?" Kane asked.

"I told him it was Wednesday."

"I don't think he understands," Morrigan said quietly.

"He's not the only one," Grant whispered from the corner of his mouth. "Does anybody want to offer an opinion on what the hell is happening here?"

Her voice pitched very low, Brigid said, "Merlinus is trying to orient himself...to process."

"I gathered that much," Grant growled. "What's with

him changing from Methuselah to boy-toy in the space of five seconds?"

"Holography," Brigid stated positively. "The energy field around him also projected the image of an old wizard."

"Why?" Kane demanded.

"Protective camouflage, maybe," Fand said.

Merlinus shifted on the throne, holding out his hands, staring first at the palms, then the backs. He touched his throat, the flesh beneath his chin, then fingered his cheeks and his long hair.

"What's he doing now?" Grant asked. "Taking inventory?"

"Merlin was reputed to age backward," Brigid said, raising her voice a trifle. "So it could be that he—"

"Silence," Morrigan snapped. "Be respectful in his presence."

"We're not aiming weapons at him," Grant countered. "That's respectful enough under the circumstances."

The lips of Merlinus moved as if he was reciting something under his breath. Then a whisper issued from between them. Fand leaned close, inquiring politely, *"Duilich?"*

Merlinus coughed and said in a slightly louder voice, "Awake? I am alive and awake?"

He spoke English with a broad accent, but his words were perfectly understandable.

Fand ducked her head reverentially. "Aye, you are."

The boy's eyes suddenly flashed with amazement, then with golden fury. "Who sent you?"

Fand stepped back as if she had received a blow. "No one sent us."

"Then who awakened me?"

Brigid declared, "I did, Merlinus—if that is truly your name."

The boy's eyes fixed on Brigid's face, then flicked up and down her lissome form, encased tightly within the shadow suit. He smiled in fleeting appreciation. "Who are you, lass?"

"My name is Brigid Baptiste. These are my companions—Grant, Kane, Fand and Morrigan. We came through the labyrinth and found you here."

Merlinus bent forward, hands upon his knees. He sniffed in Fand's direction. "I smell the blood of the Danaan in you." His gaze flicked to Morrigan. "And you, as well, but the odor is not as pronounced."

"The smell is on you, as well," Brigid pointed out. "If you are really Merlinus."

The golden eyes stared in Brigid's direction again. "So you know who I am?"

"Merlinus, also known as Myrrdian."

He waved a dismissive hand through the air. "I was born in Carmarthen, which means Myrrdian Town, and I took that name in my youth, when I traveled about incognito. What else do you know about me?"

"Not much," Brigid admitted. "It's said you were the child of a human mother and an incubus, or demon. As such, he had no father in the traditional sense. This condition came in useful when King Vortigern was having trouble building a tower on Dinas Emrys. The king's seers told him to sacrifice a boy who had no father, so you were produced. But instead of being killed, you offered your own prophecies.

"You correctly predicted that the tower was built on an underground pool and that underneath the pool were two dragons fighting—one red and one white. This was to symbolize the red dragon of the Pendragon—Uther and Arthur—and the white dragon of the Saxons…your prophecies said that the red dragon would drive out the white dragon.

"Vortigern died soon after, whether by poison or by flame, and Ambrosius came to power. After a particularly bloody battle, Ambrosius asked you how the dead should be remembered, and you replied that the Giants' Ring should be built in Salisbury.

"These stones were, of course, in Ireland, but the Uther-led invasion force brought them home, with a little help from you. Finally, you were instrumental in the begetting of Arthur, making Uther appear as Gorlois so Queen Igraine would consent to having him in her bed.

"After arriving safely in Britain, you changed your name to Merlinus and established Druid worship at Stonehenge. Sometime later, Uther Pendragon killed Gorlois and took Igraine as his queen, who later gave birth to Uther's son, who grew up to become the legendary King Arthur of Camelot…if the legends are right."

Brigid paused, took a breath and added, "After that, records of your movements are unreliable and sporadic...maybe you can fill in some gaps."

Merlinus sat completely still through Brigid's straight-forward dissertation. "If the legends are right," he repeated in a taunting murmur. "And what if they are not?"

"Then you can go back to sleep and to your dreams," Brigid replied flatly.

"I am not quite convinced that you aren't a dream within a dream." Merlinus touched his face again and closed his eyes. "It is a conundrum."

"What is?" Kane asked impatiently.

"These matters of reality." For moment, he looked painfully, pitifully young and confused.

"Who put you in this place?" Grant inquired.

The eyes of Merlinus opened. "I put myself here. I was dying, I think. Perhaps I was already dead. Vivane wished to hide me until I recovered. She feared I would die before she could return. I remember that much."

"Where did she go?" Fand asked quietly.

"She called it Avalon." Merlinus shook his head. "Vivane did not send you to fetch me to her? You are not her emissaries?"

"No," Kane answered. "So you weren't imprisoned against your will?"

"Of course not." Merlinus glared at him. "If Vivane did not dispatch you, then why did you awaken me?"

Quickly, Fand spoke to him about the nukecuast,

about the darkness that swept over the world, about Strongbow, the Singularity and his return to the world, materializing within the Merry Maidens.

The last caught Merlinus's attention. He stood up slowly, as shaky and awkward as a newborn foal. "Near to a thousand years I have slept, you say?"

"That's what we estimate," Brigid said. "It could be even longer."

Merlinus frowned. "How did you find me?"

Fand explained to him, without elaboration. Merlinus nodded as if he not only expected the answer, but found the tale of traveling to a pocket universe completely reasonable.

"The Priory of Awen agreed to safeguard me and the treasures of the Danaan," he said. "Including the Grail-stone, the Cauldron of Bran. They feared the secret of immortality would destroy the world. But then, unlike me, they did not glimpse the future."

"But you could?" Kane challenged.

Merlinus nodded. "Bits and pieces, scraps and tatters…the complete tapestry was never made clear to me. All I knew was that the old world, my world, the world of magic was gone. After the death of Arthur, I knew I could no longer live among humans because I am not completely human. I perceived that their world was doomed, anyway. You have confirmed my vision."

"Now another doom threatens the world," Brigid declared, "and it is done in your name. The people who follow the impostor Strongbow believe they are following you."

Merlinus snorted. "Because he offers them immortality."

"Aye," Fand said sadly. "He has the Eye of Balor, and perhaps the Grailstone by now. Victory could be within his grasp even as we speak."

Merlinus gazed at her, surprised and even a little baffled. "You do not know, child of man and Danaan? You *truly* do not know?"

"Know what?" she asked, lines of confusion appearing on her brow.

Merlinus gestured around him, to the chair and even the entire building. "*This* is what you call the Cauldron of Bran, what you call the Grailstone. We stand within it."

Chapter 32

The domed roof arched nearly out of sight. The assembly of lights attached to the supporting ribs of the dome shone down steadily.

"So we guessed right," Brigid said as she stared overhead, shading her eyes with a hand. "Once you were revived, this whole place was reactivated."

Merlinus blinked around, touching the slick exterior wall of the helmet-shaped structure that they had just exited. He didn't reply.

"That's correct, right?" Brigid persisted.

Merlinus turned toward her, his expression reproving. "You ask a great many questions, lass."

"That's because you haven't exactly been forthcoming about too much," Kane interjected. "Like for example and in no particular order, how are you able to speak English, why are you here, what's the purpose of here and just where in the hell *is* here?"

"You're a very impatient young man," Merlinus replied.

Kane did not comment on the incongruity of a teenage boy referring to him as a young man. "Actually," he said. "I'm very patient, but I have my limits and I've reached them. I expect some answers."

Merlinus regarded him with amused eyes, twirling the staff between the fingers of his right hand like a baton. "What makes you think I can supply them?"

"Because," Kane intoned grimly, "you're the only one who can…that is if you're not another phony like Strongbow, pretending to be someone you're not."

"Have a care, Kane," Fand warned.

Merlinus turned on his heel and began walking swiftly toward the open mouth of a passageway. "Follow me and I will tell you what I can and what must be done."

As the six people marched into a long corridor that curved to the left, Merlinus declared matter-of-factly, "I speak your language because I learned it…through this."

He touched his headgear. "It permits a degree of mental interaction with your minds. If I cared to expend the effort—and if I had the inclination—I could influence your behavior to a degree."

Grant rumbled menacingly, "That explains why Strongbow exerts control over his followers. Did the Danaan make those mind-control things?"

"Aye, they did, but they were designed for teaching, for education, not mind control."

"Perhaps those are basis of the legends of the Metis," Brigid murmured. "The helm of wisdom worn by Athena."

"Perhaps," Merlinus replied brusquely. "As for why I am here—"

He trailed off as the corridor turned to the right. He paused for a few seconds, then began walking again. "Suffice it to say, I was hiding here."

"I thought you said you were dying," Fand said.

"I was. I was old and worn out, my heart was broken. I was despised by the Britons, who had once admired me and held my counsel in great esteem. My Danaan heritage was viewed as demonic.

"At the same time, the Danaan despised me because of my human blood, a halfling bastard, born of a Danaan prince and a human woman. I had no world to call my own. I had resigned myself to wandering and eventually dying, unknown and unmourned. Then Vivane found me and brought me here."

"Vivane," Morrigan commented. "She was your student in the magical arts, was she not?"

Merlinus barked out a laugh. "Quite the contrary. What could I have taught a Danaan princess, the Lady of the Lake? No, she had been my teacher, my lover. She protected me from the other resentful Danaan who wanted to punish me for allying myself with the humans of Arthur's court."

Thoughtfully, Brigid said, "So Vivane programmed the Grailstone's healing field so no one of Danaan blood could reach you and harm you?"

Merlinus nodded unhappily. "It worked apparently—worked too well. A thousand years here. The plan was to restore me to health, not turn me back into a stripling. Something must have happened to Vivane. She would not have left me here in this place for so long."

"All right, I'll buy that," Kane said. "Now where is this place exactly?"

Merlinus shook his head as if he found Kane's query utterly foolish. "There is no answer for that question. You might as well ask where a sneeze goes or where a dream comes from. The best way I can describe this place so you can conceptualize it is to picture the universe as made up of countless tiny bubbles, all floating through the ether. We're inside one of those bubbles."

"What?" Grant demanded harshly.

"We're not quite as backward as you may think, Merlinus," Brigid said, eyes flashing in annoyance. "You're probably referring to a quantum leakage of energy that forms stable pockets of matter and energy, not much different than an asteroid."

"Perhaps," the boy replied diffidently. "From what you have told me, I speculate that the man you call Strongbow fell into this bubble when he was thrown into the—what did you call it?"

"The Singularity," Brigid replied. "I speculate that it, like a neutron star, reached a point of critical mass and dropped out of the universe entirely."

Merlinus nodded. "And dropped Strongbow, where he has been ever since."

"That happened over five years ago," Grant objected. "Why didn't he starve to death, get eaten by the hounds of Cullan?"

"Possibly this bubble or pocket universe is so dense that the slowing of time becomes infinite," Brigid said. "It's called the Schwarzchild radius. If the Singularity was rotating, then the relativistic passage of time at the event horizon breaks down, perhaps halts completely."

"Another question," Kane interposed hastily before Brigid could continue. "Where are we going?"

"If the impostor is here," Merlinus said flatly, "there can be only one place where he found the artifacts left behind by the Tuatha de Danaan…and the one place where we can exit this bubble and enter it."

It was a circuitous route Merlinus walked, leading through a maze of tunnels. Kane was tempted to refuse to follow the boy, fearing that he would cause them to wander forever until they died. As they made their way through passage after passage, his fear that a madman led them to their death grew.

Merlinus turned a corner, and an opaline glow suffused the darkness beyond. They came out in the hollow core of the labyrinth, a vast space beneath the domed roof. He stopped and the others stopped behind him. Merlinus pointed upward with his wand.

Kane felt his lungs seize and his heart begin to race.

The entire air over their heads seemed laced and twined with crystal—clusters, rods, even cross-hatched screens of it. A glittering helix spiraled straight up overhead. Within it, pulsing along the curves and twists streamed a white-blue light.

It was like no light any of them had ever seen before. It looked as if it would be incandescently hot, yet they felt no heat. Parts of the crystalline structures looked as if they been sculpted from ice and filled with pure glacial meltwater. The shimmering light stretched out like a web of energy, caressing and stimulating their nerve endings. The entire structure rotated slowly, exuding an echoing, musical note as of a faraway harpstring.

"What the hell is this?" Grant husked out.

"The power behind the Grailstone," Merlinus said quietly.

Sounding enthralled, Brigid said, just as quietly, "According to medieval writers like Wolfram von Eschenbach, who wrote *Parzival*, the grail was a stone fallen out of the sky, called *lapis exillas*, the Stone of Exile. The essence of the *lapis exillas* was so pure that it was able to nourish a person who stood before its presence, as well as sustaining a mortally wounded person for at least a week and slowing the age processes."

She turned toward Merlinus. "So the legends are true? Is this the *lapis exillas?*"

He laughed shortly. "That is hard to say. But this is the source of most Danaan power. It cuts through the universes, the bubbles, the dimensions and can be tapped if only you know how."

"A zero point transmitter," Kane stated. "Just like you said, Baptiste."

"Now that we know," Fand said, "we can stop Strongbow."

"Stop him from doing what exactly?" Merlinus asked.

"Building an empire on the blood of the Celts using the ancient relics of the Tuatha de Danaan." Fand frowned at the boy. "I thought I explained that."

"Everything but why I should care."

"Why wouldn't you?" Morrigan demanded. "These are your people who he is exploiting and killing because they think he is *you!*"

Merlinus's lips compressed and his eyes glistened with tears. "The same people who said I was a blasphemy, begotten by a demon? The same people whose priests spoke against me, who forced me to run away, to roam the world, carrying my tainted blood, beset by visions of the future."

"Strongbow's evil will live," Brigid said grimly. "He will spend the blood of the Celts for power. Is that the legacy you want for your name?"

Merlinus turned his face toward Morrigan, then toward Fand. "So tell me. Why should I care for your world or people? How could I help you even if I wanted to?"

"There is still power left in you," Morrigan said urgently.

Merlinus laughed fatalistically and gestured toward the crystals. "The one you call Strongbow draws power from the force of this place and broadcasts it the same way. That is a greater power than I possess."

"You can come back with us," Morrigan said. "You can live anew among people who will revere you."

Despite the light shining upon them, Merlinus's face was shadowed. "I do not want another life, I who have had so many. I came here because I wearied of fighting for something I did not want. I am but a thing woven as if by thread."

"So," Fand whispered, "you are giving us a choice of a quick death or lingering one. We can die free, on our own feet, or we can die as slaves."

Her voice rose to a fury-filled shout. "You're no wizard, no sorcerer, you're a bitter, self-pitying ass!"

Merlinus stared at Fand with blank eyes. Then, to everyone's surprise, he chuckled. "Perhaps I am. But if anyone has any suggestions on what I can do to help, I'm willing to listen."

Morrigan stepped forward, taking the boy's hand. "I have been thinking that—"

A faint pulsing pattern, like a ripple spreading out on the surface of a pond, surrounded Morrigan, then expanded into a wavering aura. The aura carved her open diagonally from right shoulder to left hip amid a bright shower of blood.

With a moist, slithery sound, her body fell in two pieces to the floor, Merlinus still clutching her hand.

Chapter 33

Merlinus released Morrigan's hand.

A stream of white energy smoked past Kane as he dived in low, dragging Brigid and Fand down to the floor with him. The woman cried out in anger and fear. He felt the sear of heat even through his shadow suit. The bolt of light struck the wall behind them, punching a deep crater in the facade.

Shouting in wordless fury, Grant raised his Sin Eater, casting about for a target. Directly beneath the *lapis exillas* stood a shadowy figure. Grant trained his pistol on it.

"No." Merlinus laid a hand flat against Grant's chest and with surprising strength pushed him back a pace. "You must not risk the Grailstone. It has power enough to build a world or destroy it."

Kane got to his feet, his own Sin Eater in hand. He avoided looking at Morrigan's dead face, her expression stamped in a mask of eternal surprise. "Then what's the damned plan?"

"I don't know yet," Merlinus said flatly. "I don't know if there is one. I don't know if one would do any good."

He strode quickly to a point directly under the crystalline structure. Kane, Grant, Brigid and Fand watched him, listening to the crystals as they hummed of life and sang of death across the universes.

"That is Strongbow," Fand hissed, her voice made guttural by hatred. "It can be no other."

Despite the distance and the steady white shimmer, the Cerberus warriors knew she spoke the truth. Strongbow's long, lean body was encased in a gleaming silver armor from throat and heel. The light falling from above glittered on the metal as if it were dusted with a patina of diamonds.

The breastplate was decorated all over with wafers of gold, each one embossed with a different glyph and intricately interlaced designs. A long, burgundy cloak fastened to his shoulders with golden torques belled out behind him like the wings of some great bird.

The arrogance and fanaticism Grant, Kane and Brigid had all seen in Strongbow's seamed face was still there—as well as deep, abiding ruthlessness. His eyes were pits of shadow swirling with a malign energy. He wore a helmet wrought of dark gray metal. From the crest sprang out a curve, tipped by a glowing sphere.

Although he had never seen it before, Kane recognized it instantly and his belly turned a slow, cold flip-flop of nausea. "The Eye of Balor," he intoned.

"It doesn't seem in character for Strongbow not to have backup," Brigid commented. "When we first met him, he never went anywhere without those dragoons of his."

As if on cue, ten figures emerged the shadows behind Strongbow, all of them clad in black cassocklike garments. The hoods were thrown back and the Cerberus warriors saw they wore the same leathery, ear-flapped headgear as Merlinus. They carried MP-5 subguns.

"I understand now," Fand said grimly. "Strongbow used the learning helms to control the priests here."

"And he found them blasters someplace, too," Grant observed. "We'd better give the kid a show of support."

Kane, Brigid, Grant and Fand strode across the floor, toward the floating, crystalline cluster. They spread out as they walked, providing Merlinus with a protective flank. There was no discussion of strategy or tactics from Kane or Grant. There was no need—both men realized the conflict could end in only one of two ways.

As Magistrates Grant and Kane had served together for a dozen years and as Cerberus warriors they had fought shoulder to shoulder in battles around half the planet, and even off the planet. Through it all, Grant had been covering Kane's back, patching up his wounds and on more than one occasion literally carrying him out of hellzones. At one time, both men enjoyed the lure of danger, of risk, courting death to deal death. But now it was no longer enough for them to wish for a glorious death as a payoff for all their struggles. They had finally accepted a fact they had known for years but never admitted to themselves—when death came, it was usually unexpected and almost never glorious.

Merlinus stopped at a distance of three yards from Strongbow. Tonelessly, he said, "You are trespassing, and you killed a blind woman who was my guest. How will you make restitution for that crime?"

Strongbow's face creased in a cold smile. "I owed Morrigan a debt for her treachery. Now I have put paid to it, and I can turn my attention to the rest of my enemies—who have all conveniently gathered in one place to await my attention. It has worked out perfectly."

"Aye," Merlinus agreed. "For me it has indeed. I don't have to hunt you down." A burning light suddenly crackled across the staff in his hand.

Strongbow's eyes flicked toward him in annoyance, then confusion. "Who are you, boy? You're not of the Danaan, but—"

"But I have their aspect, do I not? Something about the eyes?" The light began to shimmer from the tip of the staff.

Strongbow stared at Merlinus contemptuously. "Yes," he said. "You have it. Who are you?"

"I am who *you* claim to be."

Strongbow's face twisted first in disbelief, then scorn. "I am Myrrdian. You are no doubt a noviate from the Priory of Awen, drafted to oppose me."

"You know that is not true," Merlinus declared. "What happened is that you found yourself trapped here, and you pilfered the relics of the Tuatha de Danaan. And you also learned how to manipulate the energies of the Grailstone to open portals between the dimensions. In this fashion, you went back and forth, finding followers and weapons in your gambit to control the Grailstone."

Strongbow's thin lips drew back from his discolored teeth in a silent snarl. "Even if you are who you say you are, the power in this place belongs to me now."

The Eye of Balor shone with an opalescent light, but Strongbow's eyes did not reflect so much as a spark. Shadowed by the overhang the helmet, his eyes were as limitless as evil itself.

Strongbow gestured sharply with both hands. Without hesitation, robed priests pulled the triggers of his subguns. Instantly, Merlinus struck out with his staff and a blur of force rippled from its tip, streaking out to touch the Grailstone, then bouncing back to form a shimmering dome over him and Strongbow.

The stream of subsonic rounds struck the energy barrier surrounding Merlinus with a sound like several sledgehammers banging repeatedly against an anvil.

"Kill him! Kill them all!" Strongbow shrieked.

The robed men began a surging charge across the floor, firing their weapons in a wild frenzy as they did so. The dome of wavering light stretched out to form a barricade between the guns and their targets. Bullets crashed and ricocheted with wild keenings.

Kane and Grant raised their Sin Eaters, depressing the trigger studs and unleashing 3-round bursts. Brigid stood shoulder to between the two men, firing with her TP-9. The blistering cannonade hammered into the front line of running priests, knocking them off their feet, sending them staggering. They aimed for the torsos of the priests, assuming they wore the same kind of body armor as the man they had encountered in the monastery.

Strongbow grappled with Merlinus, but he managed to fling him aside. From the tip of his staff spewed a whirlpool of golden sparks. At the same time, a bass humming note filled everyone's heads, like a prolonged roll of distant thunder.

The veil of light curved out and expanded, sweeping around Brigid, Kane and Fand. Strongbow lunged away from them, struck the barrier headlong and bounced back, right into Kane's spinning crescent kick. Strongbow grunted and staggered sideways, trying to stay on his feet.

Fand lashed out with her staff as if it were a saber. Strongbow parried the blow with a forearm, and the Eye of Balor spit sparks. The staff flew from her hands, spinning end over end. The wave of energy bowled Kane and Grant off their feet.

Strongbow's face was creased by a cold grin as he regained his balance and advanced on Fand. Brigid lifted the harp, pointed the long neck at Strongbow and strummed the strings.

His breastplate acquired a dent, then split open in a flare of flame. Screaming in agony, Strongbow doubled over and fell to his knees, clutching at himself.

Fand snatched up her staff and hit him on the point

of his chin with the knob, rocking his head back so violently everyone heard the crunch of cartilage. The wavering halo of energy surrounding the Eye of Balor solidified and plunged upward toward the *lapis exillas,* then rebounded back to its source, like an arrow made of seething light. The helmet and Strongbow's head exploded in a slurry of bone and a clutter of bloody flesh.

As Strongbow's headless body settled to the floor, Kane and Grant climbed to their feet. The veil of light tightened and rippled around them, enclosing them within a narrowing funnel.

"What the hell is going on?" Grant demanded.

Merlinus turned to face them. Sweat glistened on his pale cheeks. His blue-black hair showed streaks of silver, and his eyes were surrounded by a network of lines and wrinkles.

"Those who seek to control the fires and furies of this place find their life essences drained," he said in a hoarse croak. "Dreams live here, but Strongbow's dreams were evil and they would have eventually destroyed him."

"What about you?" Brigid asked.

"I can channel the power of the grail through me because we have developed an affinity over the centuries, but I am not its master."

"What will happen?" Fand asked urgently.

"I can open a portal to send you back to your own world, but to do so means I must remain here as the anchor for the energies."

"There's got to be another way," Kane said. "You could be a great help to Fand's people."

"They love you still," Fand declared.

Merlinus shook his head, one corner of his mouth lifting in a sad smile. "Although I have yet to pass beyond memory in your world, I have no choice but to stay here and wait."

"Wait for what?" Fand demanded. "For Vivane to return? The Danaan are long gone! All of them!"

"Then I will return to my chair and dream of them." He paused and added in a whisper, "I am but a thing woven as if by thread."

Merlinus swept his staff upward, and the Grailstone filled their eyes with a blaze of glory, like a star going nova, stabbing its white fury into the darkness of the universe.

Epilogue

Two days afterward, Kane, Brigid, Grant and Fand stood within the stony embrace of the Merry Maidens. A contingent of red-and-green-garbed soldiers stood quietly and respectfully under the afternoon sun.

Merlinus had returned them to the interior of Great Skellig. Within hours, the *Cu Sith Awwn* ferried them back to Cornwall and they had arrived back at the village that morning. They found the Druidic sect who had sworn loyalty to Myrrdian had either scattered or come back, seeking contrition. Now, as the Cerberus exiles stood at the rim of the geodetic marker stone, Kane was conscious of a sense of déjà vu as he prepared to bid farewell to Fand once again.

"The quest is done," Fand said quietly. "Strongbow is dead. Never can the Grailstone be used by another power-mad schemer. And most importantly to the people of this land, the legend of Merlinus remains intact."

"Legends are pretty unreliable things to lean on," Kane said.

Fand gazed at him steadily, the cool wind blowing her blond hair straight out behind her. "Aye, as you should know."

He stiffened. "What's that supposed to mean?"

Fand smiled at him fondly and stroked his cheek in a quick caress. Grant and Brigid discreetly moved away from them. Although the interphaser had already been set up on the geodetic marker and the destination coordinates programmed into it, the two people pretended to run a last-minute check on the systems.

"I have asked you to stay with me before," Fand said softly. "I owe you my life once again."

Kane shook his head. "You owe me nothing, Fand. You and I work together to build a new world that isn't crushed beneath the heel of old gods and old ways."

"You will not reconsider?" she murmured. Her eyes searched his.

"I'm afraid not."

She sighed. "I suppose it is for the best…so we can work toward building that new world and not be distracted by anything else." Her tone held an undercurrent of bitterness.

Kane struggled to tamp down a surge of sadness as Fand held out both hands to him. He took them and drew her to him for a moment, staring into her eyes.

"Goodbye…my Ka'in," she whispered.

Then Fand pulled her hands away, turned and strode across the field of stones, her cloak billowing out from her shoulders. She looked proud and regal and inexpressibly lovely.

Watching her go, Kane felt the fleeting sensation of having lost something of great and irreplaceable value, but then he told himself that he was simply tired.

TAKE 'EM FREE
2 action-packed novels plus a mystery bonus
NO RISK
NO OBLIGATION TO BUY

LOOK FOR

ACT OF WAR
by Don Pendleton

Technology capable of exploding cached nuclear
arsenals around the globe have fallen into the hands
of a group of unidentified terrorists. Facing an untenable
decision on whether to disarm or stand and fight, the
Oval Office can only watch and wait as Stony Man
tracks the enemy, where fifteen families of organized
crime will be masters of the universe—or blow it
out of existence.

STONY®
MAN

*Available April
wherever you buy books.*

ROOM 59

A research facility in China has built
the ultimate biological weapon. Alex's job:
infiltrate and destroy. His wife works at the
biotech company's stateside lab, and Alex
fears danger is poised to hit home. But when
Alex is captured, his personal and professional
worlds collide in a last, desperate gamble to
stop ruthless masterminds from unleashing
virulent, unstoppable death.

Look for

out of time
by
cliff RYDER

GOLD EAGLE ®

*Available April
wherever you buy books.*

GRM592